UN Real Paine – Book two of the Paine Saga.

The plague that destroyed billions of people is over, but a more insidious plot is hatched, one that threatens the privacy of everyone on the planet. Unaware of the new threat, Michael Paine Martin joins the United Nations Military Force and is sent on a mission to stop a potential war between Serbian guerrillas and the rest of Europe. Then things begin to go wrong. Steven Corvis, founder and CEO of the Corvis Foundation, attempts to set up control over the world. He enlists the aid of the sinister and vengeful General Josh Martin, Paine's father. Josh works with Corvis to discredit the United Nations and destroy the recently established government of New York. Personal and political intrigue abounds in this fight between two conflicting ideas of the future of Earth – and who will ultimately rule.

Books by J. B. Durbin
Paine Time of Anarchy (2013)
UN Real Paine (2014)
Legacy of Paine (2015)
Threshold of Paine (coming in 2016)

UN Real Paine
Book Two of the Paine Saga

Published by J. B. Durbin

Copyright 2014 by John Brian Durbin

Author photograph © Debra Durbin

Book cover by Tyler David Gillis

ISBN – 13: 978-1495384363

ISBN: - 10: 1495384365

DEDICATION

I want to say a special thank you to my wife, Debra, for reading and editing the book and supporting my writing efforts over the past few years. She is still my anchor and I could not have done this without her help and love.

This book is dedicated to the memory of George Kaniwec, my father-in-law. All the proceeds will go to support wounded warriors as would be his wish.

Acknowledgements

I want to thank Tyler Gillis, the Southington High School student who designed the cover.

I also want to thank Jen Paul, the literacy specialist at Southington High School, for helping me edit and encouraging me to continue writing.

UN Real Paine

Chapter 1 - Corvis

The Corvis Foundation monopolized the computer market and indirectly controlled most of the governments of the world. When the plague struck in 2020, the bacteria that caused it mutated and destroyed the chlorophyll-producing plants it infected. Grain crops were the hardest hit. Animals died from starvation. As the plague spread it attacked plants worldwide, causing governments to collapse and billions to die.

Steven Corvis, CEO of the Corvis Foundation, came up with a prototype plasma engine. The engine was simple in design, had a high lift capability, was easy to assemble and operated on liquid hydrogen. The foundation offered its design to the New United States Government, which put it into production and launched space platforms as orbital farms to replace the foods supplies destroyed by the plague.

Steven Corvis had already set up assembly lines in Northern California and Oregon and controlled the market. He also kept all the patents to the software needed to operate the engines, asked for and received protection courtesy of the New US Army and all the food and electricity he needed to run his operations. He became the most powerful man in the world overnight, expanding his far-reaching empire. Although his sense of entitlement and imperviousness yielded him great power, it also contributed to his belief that he possessed immunity from rules because of wealth and position.

Sitting back in the chair at the head of the conference table, Steven Corvis looked at his grandson, Danny. Unlike himself,

Danny was over six feet in height. Steven was short in stature, and it bothered him. To even the playing field, he always sat in a custom-made chair which dwarfed the others around the table, making him appear to be much larger. As he tapped his foot on the rest built into his chair, he looked at Danny and chuckled as the taller man had to sit up straight just to reach the tabletop.

Steven looked at the data scrolling across the screen embedded in the table-top and asked, "Are you sure it works?"

Danny smiled and pointed to the microphone embedded in the table top. "Go ahead and ask it."

Steve thought for a moment and said, "Jillian Corvis, eighty nine."

Two seconds later, the screen showed a map of Paris, France. A small dot was moving down the Champs d' Elysees.

"Damn that woman, she is always shopping!" He asked, "How do I know you didn't get the computer to track her?"

Danny sounded hurt when he said, "Try someone else, someone important. You'll see it works."

Steven glared at his grandson. "I will make it simple. You said it was for famous or powerful people. Computer, find Adelmo Garcia, the United Nations ambassador from Argentina."

It took the computer four seconds to locate Garcia. The map showed he was over the Caribbean Sea and moving fast.

"Computer, what is the ambassador's destination?" Danny asked.

"He is heading for the United Nations to attend a special meeting called by Secretary General Baum. Would you like me to inform you when he has arrived?" the electronic voice asked.

Steven interjected, "No. The meeting is not our affair. Cancel the request." He turned to his grandson, "Danny, how did you get the computer to do this?"

"It's quite simple." Danny got that look Steven hated, the superior one he always used when talking down to people he considered mentally deficient, like his grandfather. "I coded it to identify our nanoprobes. The billions we've produced in the past six months are fitted with a tiny transmitter designed to obtain and imprint the genetic code of whoever undergoes meditube treatment. Many rich and famous people are using the technology to reverse the aging process. I mean, look at yourself, Gramps."

"I hate it when you call me that!" Steven stood up, almost reaching out to slap his grandson, but stilled the impulse. He sat back down in his chair, glaring at Danny. "Use that term again, and you will no longer be working for me," Steven vowed.

"Sorry, Grandfather. I will not, I promise." Danny did not sound at all contrite as he continued. "That code is sent to the mainframe here at the labs and stored for future use. We can now track the most important people in the world by accessing their medical records."

Danny paused for effect, which made Steven impatient. "Not only that, but the nanoprobes record conversations and store them in our mainframe computer for analysis. The whole system is simple, yet brilliant." Danny smiled as he leaned toward his grandfather and whispered, "And the best part is, no one knows what we are doing or how we are doing it."

"How can you keep this a secret?" Steven realized if this got out, his organization would be in serious trouble. "Who else has access to the technology? You didn't do this on your own. You are not that smart."

Danny looked down at his feet for a moment and raised defiant eyes to his grandfather's.

"The six programmers and two doctors who worked on the project did so in complete secrecy. They were allowed no outside contact until the project was complete, they were given a going-away present: a trip to a tropical island." He paused. "Unfortunately, the lifter carrying them to their destination had a major malfunction and went down over the Pacific Ocean. We sent out search parties, but they found no wreckage. The lifter was swallowed sea." Danny looked down at his feet, "I did what I thought needed to be done."

Steven leaned back in his chair and put his hands behind his head. "No. You did what you had to do. If word of this leaks out, we are in deep trouble. I don't want our technology becoming public knowledge, ever. Do you understand?"

Danny nodded. "Of course I do. It would all be blamed on me."

"We wouldn't want anything to fall back on you, so forget everything you ever learned about this project." Steven said. "Now let's get on to other work."

The meeting ended three hours later, and Danny left the office, his head swimming with the strategies that his grandfather planned to put into place. As he was walking down the hall to the elevator, he thought about how late he was for his date. His new secretary had a lot of very nice features and Danny was beginning to enjoy them; he hoped that she was still waiting at his favorite downtown bar.

In the penthouse office, Danny's grandfather typed a command into his computer console. He reread the transcript of his grandson telling a woman he was trying to impress that he had developed the technology that would allow him to listen in on anyone at any time. Steven knew Danny was a borderline alcoholic, and that the secret he had would not stay undisclosed for long. Hesitating a moment, he typed a new command into the computer. Steven whispered, "I did what needed to be done." Thirty seconds later, the building shook as the elevator carrying his grandson crashed into the basement.

He looked at the screen for a moment and said, "Danny Corvis, thirty seven." Ten seconds later, the computer showed him a blank screen with the words SUBJECT NOT FOUND scrolling across the screen.

Chapter 2 – Power Play

The Secretary General's personal assistant brushed her blond hair back and checked her makeup in a hand mirror. She made sure she looked perfect, tugged at her skirt and then knocked at Allan Baum's office door.

"Mister Secretary, I have a call from Mister Corvis," she announced.

"Thank you, Monica. That will be all for now." Alan Baum turned on the scrambler and activated the screen. "Good day to you, Steven. What can I do for you?"

Steven Corvis smiled at the UN Secretary General. "Allan, you can execute the plans we made, beginning tomorrow morning. Send a message out that there will be a major policy announcement concerning the United Nations and New York. Are all the ambassadors scheduled to be in New York by then?"

"The ambassadors from Ukraine and South Africa are not here. Their delegations are present, and I am sure they will vote as we want." Baum leaned back in his chair and rubbed his temples with his fingertips. "Are you sure you want to do this now? I think we have the votes we need to make this happen. But what if they vote 'no'?"

"I will take that chance." Steven said. "The people of the world need to be under one government, and you can make that work for me," Steven paused as Baum shot him a sharp glance, "I mean us. You will have a free hand to do whatever you want to as far as governing the world, and I will maintain control of the computer systems that will aid you in your efforts."

"Very well," Baum replied. "You have been more than generous in your support of my plans to unite the world. I hope the time is right." Baum sat up straight in his chair and ran his fingers through his hair, then straightened his tie. "General Martin is ready to do what needs to be done. With his soldiers in positions of authority within the UN military, and with the modern weapons you have provided him, we should be able to secure New York and keep the United Nations under our control. As far as the ambassadors to the UN, we have that under control thanks to the nanotechnology you provided me. They will do as you ask, and I hope it works out well for us all." Baum paused for a moment and continued, "If not, then a few of my colleagues may have to die."

Steven snorted, "That didn't bother you last month. Is President Sanford going to be a problem?"

"We have that covered. He will either help us or he will join poor President Brown." Baum sighed. "For a country to lose two presidents in one month will be devastating, but it may make the NUS transition to being a part of a new world government easier, don't you think?"

"Just let none of the details get out to the public, or you will have to deal with me!" Steven cut the communication so abruptly that Baum jerked back from the blue screen.

Baum pushed the button that summoned Monica to his office.

"Yes, Mister Secretary?" she asked.

"Put out the press release we've been working on today. The meeting will begin tomorrow at ten o'clock," Allan said. As Monica turned to go he added, "And thank you for all your hard work, Monica. Perhaps we can take a short break from work and just enjoy some well-deserved vacation time."

Baum turned back to his work and did not notice the look of anticipation in Monica's eyes as she walked out the door, closing it behind her.

Monica had been hiding her infatuation with Allan for many years. She a slight shiver went through her body as she replayed his last words in her head, imagining them enjoying themselves in several ways. She looked up to the heavens as she leaned against the door. "God, I hope he will spend time with me." Then she went to her desk, opened the communications console and sent out the prepared message to the press corps.

Chapter 3 – Discovery

Four days later, Steven Corvis looked at the screen in disbelief. All his careful planning was coming apart. UN Secretary Allan Baum was the perfect person to head up the new World Government because Steven had complete control over him. Then General Martin had gone rogue on him. Damn that idiot! At least he'd killed Allan Baum. Baum knew where all the bodies were buried and could no longer tie this fiasco back to the Corvis Foundation, and to Steven himself.

General Martin's decision to nuke himself and the United Nations Building rather than be captured was a blessing in disguise. It made sure nothing could be recovered from the destroyed computer console in Baum's office. Planning on blowing it up was ingenious; it got rid of all correspondence between Steven and Baum, but Steven knew that a good computer forensics expert might get information out of the wreckage. No information existed anymore; it was all radioactive particles.

The news of the destruction of the UN building was on every channel, and drone cameras floating above the carnage recorded the efforts to rescue someone trapped in the basement bunker. One camera followed the rescue team as they cut their way into the basement level. Steven kept a close eye on the progress and informed his computer to let him know when the recovery efforts ended.

A soft chime announced that the computer was receiving the video feed showing the final stages of the rescue. Steven watched as the footage rolled. He saw two people meet at the door and a gurney wheel out with a body bag on it. The news story ended, and the announcer babbled about nuclear explosion at the UN building. Steven was troubled by what he saw.

As the stretcher was rolling out of the bunker beneath the UN building, he noticed the body bag strapped down and locked in place. That did not seem to be right. Why lock up a dead man? He moved his hands on the screen to magnify the bag.

"Computer, freeze frame at two minutes, ten seconds. Copy. Freeze frame at two minutes, fifteen seconds. Continue to copy every five seconds until the bag is out of camera range." The screen filled with fourteen stills. Steven leaned closer.

"Computer, compare the height of the bag in each frame."

The soft contralto voice he had programmed for his own personal computer purred out of the speaker. "There is a three millimeter difference between frame one and two, four millimeters between two and three…"

Steven cut the voice short. "Analyze all frames and tell me what it means."

There was a pause and then the computer's voice rang out. "The subject on the gurney appears to be breathing."

Steven ran his hand across the screen to back up the film. Ashley Miller walked up to the door after the radiation-suited workmen cut through the wall. Steven could just make out her face through her helmet visor as she spun the wheel, opened the door and her son Paine Martin stepped out. Paine leaned in and whispered something to her, but Steven could not read Paine's lips.

"Computer, do we the conversation that just took place?"

There was a long pause as the computer searched the trillions of gigabytes of information it had stored from that day alone.

"No record of anything from Ashley Miller or Michael Paine Martin. Neither one of them had any of the advanced nanoprobes in their systems on the day in question."

"What about now?" Steven asked.

"Ashley Miller has no new nanoprobes. Michael Paine Martin has none of the new nanoprobes but now has five point two million older models. Would you like his current location and status?"

"No. I have another subject for you." He paused for a moment, and then said, "Joshua Martin."

The computer searched the archives for what seemed like an eternity to Steven and then reported. "Joshua Martin received four point six thousand new nanoprobes at 0700 Greenwich time this morning. He was moved to a lifter platform and flown out of New York. It's possible he is dead, or he has left the range of our tracking system. Based on his medical status at the time we lost contact, I estimate he is out of reach of our sensors. Would you like me to continue scanning?"

"Find him as soon as possible," Corvis commanded. As long as Martin was alive, Steven Corvis was in danger of being discovered as the architect to the entire United Nations fiasco.

Chapter 4 - Katrina's Revenge

Marcus was cautious as he entered the sleeping chamber. He knew better than to disturb Katrina while she was sleeping. He almost didn't stop the blow Katrina swung at the sound of his footsteps.

Katrina recognized his scarred face, testimony of the many wounds and punishments that he endured as a slave in The Independent Young Nation. Marcus refused to get the scars removed, saying, "They are a part of my life."

Katrina shook her head to clear the cobwebs, causing her waist-length, naturally streaked hair to fly about her body. "Marcus, what the hell are you doing here? I thought you were still working on getting Paine out of the bunker at the UN compound."

"I'm glad to see you, too, my sweet," Marcus said. "Paine is fine; they should get to him any moment now. I was just in the way over there, so I thought I would come see you."

Katrina jumped into his arms. She put her arms around his bull neck and gave him a sloppy kiss. "There, is that a better welcome?"

Marcus looked into her eyes. "Do you remember my promise?" he asked.

Marcus saw a hunger for revenge come into those beautiful almond-shaped eyes. "You brought me a gift, didn't you? Where is that bastard?"

Marcus set Katrina down and stepped out into the hall. He returned, dragging the whimpering Doctor Engle, the man behind the deaths of thousands of New Yorkers, into the room. He gave Katrina a hug and left the room, closing the door behind him.

For three days, Katrina kept Engle securely tied in the corner of her room, but fed him and took him to the bathroom whenever he wanted to go. He had tried to engage her in conversation, but she would just stare at him with those slanted green eyes and say nothing. When he talked, she would stand up, staring at him until he stopped speaking. Engle thought that her hair grew into a mane; standing out from her head and making her appear to grow larger.

Katrina could still see him standing in front of her brother, in his stiffly starched white coat, with longish hair slightly graying at the temples, chiseled features, penetrating blue eyes and a charming smile. She could still see him injecting Carl; it was too much for her. Katrina stood up and moved to the disheveled and unshaven Engle.

Katrina walked over to Engle and picked him up off the floor. He felt her iron grip on his arm and recognized that escape was not possible.

The woman scared him. She put a hood over his head, then took the now thoroughly confused Engle out of the room and led him to the stairway exit.

Katrina half-dragged him down the steps until they reached the basement level. Katrina loaded him into the storage compartment of a lifter and then pulled off the hood. He could read nothing in her cold green eyes as she slammed shut the cargo door.

Katrina drove to the spot where, a few weeks before, the United Nations soldiers had swept her and her brother up and readied them for inoculation against the plague. She stopped the vehicle in the exact center of the holding pen where so many died because of 'Doctor' Engle and opened the cargo compartment. Careful not to damage Engle too much, she reached in and lifted him out of the compartment with one hand, dropping him onto the broken concrete roadway.

She reached into the leather pouch on her belt and pulled out a folding knife.

"What are you going to do with that?" Engle asked as he lay on the ground.

Katrina opened the knife and tested the edge with her thumb. Engle's eyes grew wide as she advanced on him and flipped him over on his back. He braced for the thrust and it surprised him when she cut his bonds. Katrina then walked a few feet away, and sat, cross-legged, on the ground. Her eyes never left him.

Engle sat like a deer caught in oncoming headlights for at least five minutes. He finally stood up, shaking as he took a few steps away from Katrina. When she did not move, he turned and ran for the nearest building.

Katrina let him get twenty feet away before she stood up, stretched, and caught him before he got to the sidewalk. She grabbed him by the back of the neck and dragged him, kicking and screaming, back to the spot he had just vacated. She plopped him on the cement and sat down on the curb.

"What are you doing?" Engle cried. "Who are you and why are you torturing me?"

Katrina just sat, motionless, and stared at him.

Engle looked around the street, trying to figure out a way to escape this madwoman, and then he realized where he was. "This is where the inoculations took place. Is that why you brought me here?" Katrina stared, stone-faced at the quivering man. "I know this place; I remember watching those people die...." Engle's voice trailed off as he realized what he had just said. He gulped and babbled, "I mean, I was here, and I saw people die but I feel terrible about that." When Katrina did not respond, he screamed at her, "Can't you explain why do you have me here?"

Katrina opened her mouth to speak and then thought better of it. She took the knife out of her pouch again and opened it up, rose to her feet and moved closer to Engle. As Engle flinched, waiting for the blow, Katrina set it on the ground in front of him, then moved away and returned to her spot on the curb.

Engle did not know what to do. He could not defeat the woman in a fight; as small as she was, she'd already proven to be stronger than anyone he had ever met. He looked at the knife and realized it would not help him get away. Katrina's eyes were boring into his soul as he contemplated what to do.

Fifteen minutes later, Engle looked at Katrina and noticed her eyes closed; he thought Katrina was asleep. Engle leapt to his feet. He ran for the building once again. He was running for his life and thought he would make it when Katrina jumped in front of him, spun around and crouched, waiting for his attack. Engle slid to a halt, then turned in the opposite direction and walked back to his spot, falling to the ground. He sobbed, crying, "Why don't you help me or let me go?"

He heard something hit the pavement and opened his eyes to see the knife, lying on the asphalt in front of his face. As he wiped away tears, he could see green eyes of his tormentor staring at him from ten feet away. He reached out and grabbed the knife, then put it to his own throat.

Katrina sprang at him as he cut and knocked the knife out of his hand. A small trickle of blood stained Engle's shirt collar. She stood there, waiting.

As Engle picked up the knife again, Katrina spoke. "I've thought about this for the last three days. I wanted to kill you myself, but that would have been too easy. You killed my brother with your injections, and you would have killed me, too, if it hadn't been for Carl's plan to escape." She paused and took a deep breath. "That was his name, Carl." Her eyes hardened once again as she continued. "I will make you suffer, but I won't kill you. You will do it to yourself, just like you killed all of those innocent people. I won't let you finish the job until I'm satisfied that you have suffered enough."

Engle's hand moved, the knife flashing toward his body.

Katrina bared her teeth and her hair stood out from her head as she stopped him from plunging the knife into his own chest. He managed to just break the skin and was bleeding from the cut. "And that could take a long time."

The next morning, two soldiers found a corpse lying in the middle of the street in a pool of blood. "Another homeless one for the morgue." One flipped the body over, shocked at the number of wounds. "Jeeze, would you look at this?"

His battle buddy came up to him and turned away. "Man, whoever did this must be a sicko. This guy has to have at least a hundred cuts on him, and none of them look fatal. Whoever did this must have wanted to hurt him real bad."

Marcus was in his office at battalion headquarters when the door opened and Katrina entered. He stopped rubbing the "R" branded into his forehead that marked him as a runaway slave and looked up from the mound of personnel files he was reading.

Katrina came over to the desk and slumped into the chair reserved for visitors.

"Well?" Marcus asked.

"It's done. I'm not satisfied. He bled out after a few hours." Katrina curled herself into a small ball, her head in her hands. Her voice caught in her throat as she croaked out, "He didn't suffer nearly enough for what he did to Carl."

Marcus stood up and walked around the desk. He reached down and picked up Katrina, cradling her in his arms as she broke down and cried for her dead brother.

Chapter 5 - Josh's Story

Josh had the same recurring dream every night. It was his childhood...

The entire family lived on a farm. Josh's grandparents lived in a big old farmhouse; his father built a house for the family a quarter of a mile away and his uncle built next to them. The grown-ups all worked on the farm and worked in the nearby factory. Josh grew up around guns, homegrown food and a distrust of government.

Josh had a miserable childhood. His parents insisted on home-schooling, which should have made Josh happy as he didn't like other children. Academic classes, supplemented with survival and weapons training took up every waking hour. When he wasn't being educated, he was working in the fields or chopping wood for the winter.

His earliest memories were of his father yelling at his mother and beating his brother. Josh may have been young, but he knew enough to stay out of his father's way. He couldn't escape the wrath of his father, or that of his older brother who often took out his anger on Josh after their father beat him. When Josh overheard his mother saying that the children should be left alone, his father replied, "It will make them tougher. Mark my words, this world is going to hell in a handbasket and they need to be ready to face anything."

One day Josh did not get to go to the county fair with the rest of the family as punishment for talking back. He stayed home with his aunt and uncle. Josh noticed his uncle standing by the door to his room.

"Josh, your momma and daddy..." Tears welled up in Al Martin's eyes as he looked down at eleven-year old Josh. He took a deep breath to ease the painful lump in his throat and continued, "Josh, your parents are gone to heaven."

The little boy looked up at his uncle. His only reaction was to ask, "Will they be back?"

"They won't be coming back, Josh. They are gone forever. But don't worry; you will see them again someday." Al reached down and took the boy into his arms. He engulfed Josh's small frame, but it was like hugging a rag doll. Josh did not cry. He did nothing at all.

Mary Ann, Al's wife, was standing behind her husband. She didn't like Josh; in fact, she was a little afraid of him. Once, she heard Josh playing in the yard, shooting at things with his pellet rifle. Josh had taken a peanut butter sandwich and put it on a fence post. He waited for anything to come to eat it and then he would shoot it in the eye with his rifle. He systematically built a pyramid of three squirrels, a chipmunk, two sparrows and a large rat before his parents called him to supper. She watched him sweep the corpses off the rock he'd piled them on, pushing them into a hole he'd dug and then put the rock on top of the makeshift grave.

Josh noticed her watching through the window and walked away. Mary Ann remembered calling him back and asking him why he did it; Josh didn't respond, he looked at her with his cold eyes. Mary Ann phoned her brother-in-law to tell him what Josh had done. She watched in anticipation as Josh returned with a bucket fifteen minutes later. Josh set the bucket down and lifted the rock off the grave. He pulled out the three dead squirrels and the rat, took out a pocket knife and skinned and gutted them, then cutting them into quarters. He washed the carcasses off in the bucket of water. Then he put the entrails and skins back into the hole, dumped the water into it and replaced the rock. Mary Ann had come out to watch as Josh was finishing.

Josh looked up at his aunt. "Don't tell them about the rat. They all look the same when they are dead," Josh said, with the knife still in his hand, "just like people do."

Mary Ann noticed the bruise on Josh's cheek. She wouldn't say anything about it because she feared her brother-in-law almost as much as she feared Josh. She nodded. Josh turned and walked away.

Josh's mother made squirrel stew for supper the next night.

One day, while preparing for a family picnic, Mary Ann watched Josh peeling potatoes with a knife instead of a potato peeler. She told Josh three times that if he did not put the knife down, he would hurt himself.

She reached out her hand to take the knife away as she said, "Josh, I told you to put that down, you will cut yourself!"

Josh pulled his hand back and glared at his aunt. He dropped the potato he was peeling into the bowl and opened his left hand up, spreading his fingers as wide as he could. With his right hand, he drew the knife against his taut skin, neatly slicing it open. As the blood welled out, he closed his hand into a fist, and, with blood dripping from between his fingers, walked out of the kitchen and into the bathroom to get plastiskin to seal the wound. When he returned, he looked at her and said, "Satisfied?" Then he picked up the potato and got back to work.

Mary Ann wondered what else he might be capable of doing.

Al had gotten a call from the Kentucky State Police, notifying him that there had been a terrible accident on I-65, and that James and Sarah Martin were deceased. James Junior was in the emergency room, not expected to live.

Al stopped hugging the unresponsive Josh and held him out at arm's length. "Do you understand what has happened?" he asked.

Josh nodded. His voice, always devoid of emotion, came out flatter than usual, "They are dead. What happens next?"

Fear washed over Mary Ann when Al turned and gave her that look. He turned back to the boy, but before he could speak, Mary Ann's fingers dug into Al's arm with so much force he gasped. "I need to talk to you, now." She dragged Al off to the side and leaned in close to whisper, "Al Martin, don't you even think about taking that boy into our house. The boy is fine by himself! He has been nothing but trouble his whole life, and I for one will not have him in my home." She squeezed his arm even harder and added, "Do you understand me?"

"Honey, he's just lost his parents, my brother and his wife! He needs to be with family right now. We're not sure if Junior will live or not, and Josh can't take care of himself, now can he?" He pulled his arm loose and rubbed the bruise that was already forming. "The boy is not that bad..."

Josh had walked out of his room and was standing, arms crossed, two feet from the feuding couple. "I will go into a home, somewhere else. I don't like you that much, anyway. Just take me to see my brother before I go."

Al moved toward the boy, but stopped as he looked into Josh's darkening eyes. He took a deep breath and said, "Fine, you can go to the county home after the funeral. It should be no later than

Tuesday." He turned and walked to the door, calling out to Josh, "Let's go see Junior now."

Josh was silent all the way to the hospital. He stared out the window of the moving car, watching the scenery roll past. As they pulled up to the emergency room entrance, Josh got out of the still-moving car and walked up to the automatic doors. They swung open wide, and he went up to the desk. Mary Ann looked at Al and said, "Don't even get out of the car. That boy knows where to find us."

The nurse looked up as a small boy with a shaved head walked into the emergency room and asked, "Where is my brother? His name is Junior Martin, and he was brought in a few hours ago." Josh stood in front of the counter, head up, shoulders back, with a look of determination on his face.

The nurse leaned over the counter and said, "He is in room three, but I am afraid you cannot go in there," she yelled at Josh as he turned on his heel and move to the examination room.

Junior was lying on a gurney, tubes running out of his body and oxygen pumping into his system. He was groaning in agony, and in a semi-conscious state, whispered, "Josh, is that you?"

Josh stepped up to the bed, placing his hand on his older brother's shoulder. Junior winced as pain shot down his arm.

"They told me I'll never walk again, my spinal cord is cut and I have nothing, no sensation at all, from the waist down." Junior grabbed his brother's hand. "Josh, I can't take this."

"Remember when we found that deer that had been hit by a car?" Josh nodded. "It was you that finished it off so it wouldn't suffer. You put your hands around its neck until it quit breathing. You didn't even shed a tear. I know how you can do this for me." Junior pleaded with Josh. "Please help me. I can't live like this."

The thought of Junior suffering for years appealed to Josh, but the look in Junior's eyes convinced Josh of what he needed to do. He reached out and put his hand over Junior's mouth, pinching his nose so that no air could get through. Junior's eyes locked on Josh's. He thanked Josh as he waited for the end. As Junior's eyes glazed over, alarms sounded. The emergency room doctor found Josh holding his brother's cold hand.

In a voice devoid of any emotion, Josh said, "He is gone; there is nothing more you can do for him." He released his dead brother's hand, turned, and walked away.

Fifteen-year-old Josh Martin stood in front of the headmaster's desk. He was large and well-built for his age. Josh spent a lot of time in the gymnasium and on the track because the other children avoided him. He was a loner who scared people. Even the headmaster was a little afraid of the man-child standing in front of him.

The headmaster looked up from the report on his desk. "Academically, you are number one in your class. You have the highest score on the physical fitness scale, but you won't play any sports. Not a single person calls you their friend. Every teacher is afraid of you, yet you do nothing that causes any trouble. I can't figure out what to do with you." He looked at Josh and suppressed an involuntary shudder. "Can't you at least try to make some friends?" His voice came out in a pleading tone.

Josh looked at him and said, "No."

"Then what do you suggest we do?" The headmaster asked.

Josh took the gamble he had been thinking about. To intimidate the headmaster into doing what he proposed, he leaned in and placed his hands on the frightened man's desk.

"Change my birth certificate to say I am eighteen. Give me my high school diploma. I will leave today if you do what I am asking if not…" Josh took his hands off the desk and folded his arms. As the headmaster mulled over the proposal, Josh cocked his head to one side and squinted his eyes. "Well?"

"What do I tell the other staff members? How can I explain this?" Sweat was forming on the headmaster's forehead.

"They do not have to know. Let's make it our secret, one I am sure you will keep, won't you?" Josh smiled, and fear coursed through the headmaster's entire body. It was that smile that scared most people; as though Josh was radiating something evil, even though nothing bad ever happened. What could happen made people nervous.

Two weeks later, Josh was sitting in an Army recruiting office as the sergeant slid a six-year enlistment contract over the desk. The contract offered Josh a slot in Airborne School and an assignment to the Ranger Regiment after his initial training. The sergeant had been more than impressed with Josh's physical fitness test results and he had scored off the scale on the aptitude test. He knew from experience that Josh would read every word to make sure he had gotten exactly what he wanted, so he picked up the newspaper and continued where he had left off. Something caught his eye, and he spoke to Josh.

"You went to the Paul Home for Children, didn't you? Over in Allen County?" Josh nodded. "Hum, seems the headmaster got killed in an accident last night. Says here he lost control of his car and hit a bridge abutment. Did you know him well?"

He stopped and looked up from his reading. The headmaster's car had swerved to avoid him when Josh jumped in front of it. When it slammed into the bridge, the headmaster died instantly, saving Josh the trouble of finishing him.

"Gee, that's too bad. Yeah, he and I were friends. He was a good guy. He helped me out a lot. I am sorry he is gone." Josh turned back to the contract and continued to read.

The chime roused him from his dream, and Josh awoke to another boring day in space. He really disliked this confinement. He went to work, capturing another piece of the junk endangering space traffic and changed its orbit so it would be captured by Earth's gravitational field and burn up in the atmosphere.

Chapter 6 – New York Beginnings

New York City President Ashley Miller looked around Radio City Music Hall and marveled at how big it was. She set up a meeting with the leader of the Neo Luddites and the Technos, to work out an agreement on governing the newly recognized country of New York.

The original plan was to conduct the meeting at Battery Park, but the Technos refused to go that far from their base on the Lower East Side. The Neo Luddites refused to meet anywhere except RCMH, and Ashley did not have a headquarters building set up yet. After the delicate negotiations about allowing technology into Radio City Music Hall, they agreed on a time and date.

Ashley walked into the center of the building, now devoid of seats, accompanied by her chief of staff and her new military commander.

"I have a bad feeling about this," Ryan Flagehty, now a brigadier general in command of New York military forces, said. "No weapons, limited communications' equipment and no backup. If anyone wants to start something, we are in a world of hurt." Ryan ran his hand over his close cropped hair. At a quarter of an inch, it was getting a little long for his liking. He planned to shave his head again once he got back to his quarters.

Ashley touched his arm. "These people all remember the Times Square Fiasco."

"As I recall, the meeting was for all the factions in New York." Ryan said, looking for enemies lurking in the shadows. "Once they arrived, they all were shot dead."

Ashley replied, "We are safe here, I believe that. None of us want anything like the massacre happening again!"

"Amen to that!" said Carley Squires, chief of staff to President Miller. Carley, an attractive older woman, had been the deputy of Police Chief Juan Carter and had firsthand knowledge of the disaster. She also had a lot of angst about meeting with the Technos who had kept her captive for five years after the incident. "I hope everyone else is on as good a behavior as we are."

Ashley mused for a moment and said, "I agree. I think that after recent events, all of us will work together or we will die together."

"I also agree." The voice startled all three of them. Ryan relaxed his fighting stance as he saw the leader of the Neo Luddites walking toward them, leaning on a cane.

Miley Pickers had been the head of the Neo Luddites for only a few years, but she appeared to be a middle-aged woman. Grey hair, wrinkles and missing teeth were not usual among the leaders and wealthy in New York due to meditube technology. Because of her access to the fashion industry's meditubes, Ashley, hair still black and cut to shoulder-length, looked like she was twenty years younger than Miley.

Ashley was ten years younger than Miley. An accidental fall two years ago left her partially crippled with torn knee ligaments, but Miley refused advanced medical treatment and relied on locally grown herbs for pain relief. She limped up to Ashley and held up her hand in friendship.

"Welcome to my home. I have been dreading this meeting, because I fear we cannot agree on anything," Miley said. "Your lives are much more complicated than ours, and we haven't even talked with the Technos yet."

"I have arrived." Keenan Revis, leader of the Technos, walked up to the group. Another beneficiary of meditube technology, Keenan looked like a male model. Six feet one inch of groomed perfection, his skin, hair, clothes and nails were perfect. He seemed to glide across the floor and the faint smell of cologne wafted up to the assembled group. Miley sniffed in his general direction.

Keegan brushed a stray strand of hair out of his eyes and said, "I'm rather like a newborn child without all my gadgets and gear, but thank you for allowing me a vidcorder and one communications device so my staff can hear the discussions. I brought no one else with me; my people suffer withdrawal symptoms if they cannot stay connected."

He looked at Carly and said, "It has been a long time since I've seen you, Miss Squires. I hope you will forgive me, but I thought you were the architect of the disaster that killed so many of our people. We were not aware that you tried to stop that dreadful man Juan Carver until several years later. Please accept my apology." He extended his manicured hand to Carley.

Carley hesitated for a second and then reached out to shake his hand. The grip was soft and warm, surprising Carley. She released his hand and said, "I understand. I am sure I would have done the same thing if I were in your position."

"Now that the reunion is over, let me introduce the commander of my military forces, General Ryan Flagehty, late of the 82d Airborne Division of the NUS." Ashley waved toward Ryan. "He is concerned about my safety and wonders if we can go someplace not so open."

Keenan agreed, "Let's move to a conference room where we can all sit. I am used to modern transportation and walking three blocks to get here wore me out."

"We agreed that no one brings technology into the area we control!" Miley was angry, but kept her voice calm. "Every faction represented here approved that arrangement, the one we made after Times Square Massacre."

"Oh, come on, Miley. I am just whining. I still agree with prohibiting technology in your area. That agreement has kept peace between us since the massacre." Keenan tilted his head for a moment, and then said, "My staff informs me that my Technos have conducted a perimeter sweep of your territory through this," he held up the communications' apparatus, "and find no long-range listening devices anywhere. However, they are picking up signals from within this building they can't identify." He cocked his head once more, listening to the message coming in over his imbedded hearing implant. "It seems the signals are coming from our location, but as agreed, we only brought in two devices, mine and General Flagehty's."

"Follow me, now!" Miley shuffled, favoring her bad leg, toward an open door near the old stage area. The others had to move quickly to keep up. As they entered the room, they had to walk around a metal block that ran floor to ceiling. Once he turned the corner, Keenan stopped and shook his head several times.

"I am getting nothing, my God, I am getting nothing!" He tugged at his ears as a look of panic came over his face. "I'm deaf!"

Ashley laid her hand on his left arm as Miley limped back to him and grabbed his right. Both of them dragged him farther into the room. Keenan kept his eyes closed as they sat him on the couch in the center of the room.

Ashley motioned everyone back as she knelt in front of Keenan. She took his hand and said, "Keenan, please open your eyes and look at me."

Keenan kept his eyes tightly shut as he fought the silence that was overwhelming his senses. Deprived of all of his inputs and the constant flow of information his mind did not function. It was terrifying. He shook as Ashley's voice tried to reach him through the silence.

"Keenan, please listen to us," Ashley said as she motioned everyone in the group to talk at once. The noise penetrated the blackness that engulfed Keenan. Ashley lifted both hands skyward to have the sounds increase, and finally, with everyone screaming, Keenan opened his eyes. Ashley looked at him for a moment and then shook him by the shoulders as the noise increased.

"Keenan, it's OK!" Ashley screamed in his face.

"I will be all right; just give me a minute to adjust." Keenan croaked out. He took a deep breath and fluttered his hands feebly in front of him, signally the noise to decrease. Everyone talked in normal voices as Keenan struggled to his feet. He shook off Ashley's hand as she tried to steady him. "I am all right now; it was just so frightening to be cut off from the world."

Miley walked up and handed him a cup of steaming liquid. "Chamomile tea. It will help you become calm."

Keenan nodded his thanks and took a sip, then sat back down, cradling the cup. "What is this place?" he asked.

"It's our haven, where we hold all our meetings. We didn't trust you enough to believe you wouldn't try to listen in on our conversations, so our 'low-tech' people, as you would call them, built a chamber lined with metals that block transmissions."

"How did you figure out how to do that, since you don't use technology?" Ryan asked.

"My mother came up with the idea. Most of the libraries in New York were untouched because they contained no food. We read everything we could find without relying on the technology in the main part of the libraries, the computers and e-book readers.

Our people went into the basements, to the storage areas to get real paper books stored in boxes. The technical manuals we found provided us with information on how to block transmission of signals, without using technology." Miley sighed. "We melted whatever metals we could find, using old tires for fuel, and built a false wall on the other side of this one." she reached out to touch the plaster surface, "Then we poured the molten metal into the spaces between the walls. It was in theory only, and unconfirmed until now that it worked. Before today, we were operating on faith in our ability to block the signals." She leaned over and poured more tea for Keenan. "I guess I can thank you for proving it works."

"It may work, but how can you explain the signals coming from here?" Ryan asked.

Keenan shook his head as if to clear his mind. "It could be that we ourselves are carrying communication devices, buried within us."

Miley took a step back from the others and made an X with her arms. "Please stay where you are, do not pollute me with whatever you have inside you!" She recalled that many of her people were infected and killed by the plague-carrying nanoprobes.

Ashley sat down on the couch beside the still befuddled Keenan and tapped him on the shoulder. When Keenan looked in her direction, she asked him, "The plague was caused by nanoprobes. If someone could do that, could they also build the nanoprobes to act as transmitters?"

"In theory, yes, but the technology required to do that would have to be phenomenally advanced." Keenan paused for a minute and thought. "My people do not have the ability to do that."

Ryan said, "But you have the technology to remove nanoprobes from the body. Would it be possible to do that for us so we can't be heard?"

"If I may have meditubes brought here, I could do that in less than a minute for each one of us. We use a simple filtration process that removes all non-organic materials from the body." Keenan winced. "I am not sure what the effects would be on those of us who rely on the nanoprobes to keep us young and healthy, but I for one would take that risk until I could get my people to build our own nanoprobes and develop probes that will keep unwanted devices from our bodies."

Miley set down her cup and leaned back in her chair. "I can't allow it. Our laws are specific. No technology is allowed into our lands. I had to beg to make an exception for you and General Flagehty to bring in your communications devices, and that permission runs out after today's meeting."

"Then we will all have to be very careful once we leave this haven." Ashley said. "Miley, I will respect your laws. No devices will enter your areas again without your permission. I will make sure the first law introduced to the legislature will be to guarantee your freedom from technology." She turned to Keenan. "And for you, I would guarantee you can use whatever technology you wish, as long as it does not intrude upon the rights to privacy that every citizen of New York enjoys."

Keenan nodded and sipped more of the hot tea. He was feeling better. "And I promise to get these transmitting nanoprobes out of our systems."

"You see, we just met and are already getting agreements!" Ashley stood up and walked to the conference table in the center of the room. She sat down and motioned the others to join her. "Let's begin discussing other concerns before our time together runs out."

Four hours later, they came to several important agreements.

"OK, let's review, shall we?" Ashley brushed back her long, dark hair and continued. "Neo Luddite territory will include everything north of Times Square on Manhattan, and you will be able to expand your territory, without technology, north and east into the former state of Connecticut."

Miley nodded her head in agreement as Ashley continued.

"The Technos have agreed to put four antenna arrays, like the one destroyed on the UN building during the battle for New York, in undisclosed locations around the perimeter of Neo Luddite territory. They will be put in place by Walter Biddle, who discovered and destroyed the UN array. The Technos will have the territory south of Times Square to Battery Park and will have the responsibility for running the space port which will be located on and around Governors Island, Liberty Island and Ellis Island. They also have the choice of expanding their territory into what had been New Jersey, at least to the borders of the New South, and can move people into Long Island."

"That is what we agreed to," Keenan said.

Ashley looked down at her notes for a moment and then said, "The rest of the burrows of New York will be a free enterprise zone, under control of the city government, headed by me. We also claim the up-state New York area to the border of New Ireland as part of our nation. We also agreed, albeit reluctantly, to call ourselves the Sovereign United New York or SUNY for short."

Keenan snorted in disgust, he hated the acronym. Miley grinned at him in delight as it had been her idea and Ashley sided with her. Miley hated the name, too; but voted for acceptance because it irritated Keenan.

Ashley's smile left her face as she continued. "All of us agree to block attempts by the cartels to sell, manufacture, or distribute drugs anywhere in our respective territories." Many of the drug addicts had been the first to be inoculated with the plague nanoprobes, and the drug trade had shifted southward toward the still lawless area once known as New Jersey.

Ashley finished reading her notes, "Trade will be unrestricted between the states, except for the aforementioned technological constraints." She paused and asked, "Is everyone in agreement?"

Both Keenan and Miley agreed.

"Then this meeting is at an end. I look forward to our continued friendship and wish you both well."

As Keenan stood up to leave, Ashley looked at him and asked, "Are you sure you can get these things out of our systems?"

"I promise to try. And if I can't do that, I have a great Techno who can block the signals." Keenan said and then shook his head as if to clear his mind. "You already mentioned him, Walter Biddle. I plan to have Walter dampen myself and my top scientists for a meeting, and then get to work on developing a cure, if you will pardon the term, for the new plague that infects us. It makes my skin crawl to think that I can be eavesdropped on no matter where I am." He shuddered. "And not having a constant stream of information has been relaxing, almost like being on vacation." Keenan turned to Miley and said, "Thank you for showing the way you live. I can understand the allure."

"My pleasure. And take no offense, but I hope you never show me how you live." Miley smiled and waved Keenan out the door. His face brightened as his communications device came to life and he talked to his staff once more. As he walked out of building on his way to the rendezvous point where his lifter would pick him up, he downloaded the file from the vidcorder and sent it to all his contacts with a typed warning about the listening devices and instructions not to talk about it until further notice.

Miley stopped Ashley as she was getting ready to leave the room. "Not just yet," she said. "We need to talk about your son."

Ashley looked a little confused as Miley lead her back to the table. Ryan stood behind Ashley as Miley sat down in her chair.

"What is this about Michael?" Ashley asked.

"Your son was charged with murder. He was tried in absentia and found guilty. He has a death sentence on his head, one that will not be commuted," Miley stated.

"Michael was just defending himself against the mob your people sent against him." Ashley said.

"The mob took their chances," Miley continued, "I did not send them against him; they took it upon themselves to rid our territory of the intruders. I received an anonymous message that a paramilitary group might be inserted into our lands and that if I helped the United Nations military people catch them, my people would stop being harassed. I planned to guide your son and his team out of my territory and into UN hands." She looked down at the table top and said, "That didn't work out well."

Miley paused for a moment. She wiped a tear that formed in her eye and continued, "Walter Chavez was a guard, the first person killed when your son's unit entered New York last year, shot down in cold blood. He was my mother's closest friend. Walter died for nothing." Miley drew a deep breath. "Your son ordered the elimination of anyone who could compromise his mission, and Walter was executed without having the opportunity to fight back." She paused for effect. "The others died fighting. Walter was murdered."

"Collateral damage," Ryan said. "It happens in war,"

"Not for us!" Miley stood up and paced around the room. "Your son caused my people to rise and fight for freedom against the United Nations. He gave us what we have now," she waved her hands to indicate the Neo Luddite Territory. "I know why he did what he did, but my friends held a trial and judged him guilty. The punishment we all agreed upon is death."

"Why are you telling me this?" Ashley asked.

"To make sure your son never sets foot in Neo Luddite New York. We will not hunt him down, but if he enters our lands one of my people may recognize him and exact the punishment they voted for him. If I ever see him, I will kill him myself." Miley looked down at her feet and said, softly, "Walter was my father." She looked up into Ashley's eyes. "It is our way."

"I understand and thank you for telling me." Ashley held out her hand, but Miley would not take it. Ashley turned, and with Ryan following her, left the room and started back to her headquarters.

Chapter 7 - Discoveries

"Lunch time," Betty, blond and a still-trim forty-seven, called out as she walked into the lab carrying a plate of fresh fruit and cheese. The ranch the Whippettes owned outside of Dallas boasted a summer house, a pool and an old barn they had outfitted as a laboratory. Betty walked over to William, who was peering at the screen displaying the microscopic parts of the destroyed nanoprobes taken from the bodies of plague victims. She ran her fingers through his graying hair and he jumped.

"Sorry, Betty, I was just looking at something strange. What do you make of this?" William increased to the maximum the magnification.

Betty could see something that appeared to be etched onto the shell of the nanoprobe. It looked like a drawing. "I can't really tell. Could it be a logo of some type?" She stared again. "It would be a big breakthrough if we could find out who was behind all this. See if you can find more pieces."

Three hours later, the fruit had turned brown, and the cheese was getting hard. Both Whippettes stared into the monitor as William went through the fragments once more, capturing images and trying to piece together one complete shell. Finally, he leaned back and said, "I have it, but what does it mean?"

Betty squinted, trying to make out the markings on the microscopic shell, and then jerked back from the screen.

"Oh my God," she exclaimed. "That is a fox head!"

William looked once more at the scarred surface of the nanoprobe shell. It was mangled like all the other shells had been when the probe self-destructed. But the outline of a fox's head was clearly visible.

"You are right, that is a fox head. That means our architect for the plague probes is Julian Fox," he said.

Julian had been a co-worker of the Whippettes in Dallas; a bit of a pompous ass who always signed his work with a fox design on the shell. He bragged that he was so skilled he could write the entire NUS constitution on a nanoprobe shell. A few of the scientists took an offer from a start-up company to work on emerging nanotechnology about a year before the new plague hit New York. Julian left with a tremendous signing bonus and flew off in his brand new Mercedes lifter, yelling, "So long, suckers."

"No one heard from him after he left," William said. "And the company he worked for no longer exists, if it ever did. I saw nothing it produced. And I certainly think if he had been developing something great, he would have called us to rub it in our faces."

"Let's see if we can find anything else." Betty put more samples into the electron microscope.

Late the next day, William shook his sleeping wife's shoulder. She woke with a start. "What?"

William put his hand over her mouth and showed her the note he had written.

"The nanoprobes have transmitters in them do not talk."

Betty took the note and picked up a pen. She wrote, "Only Corvis has the resources to do this."

A flashing red light appeared on Steven Corvis' computer. He stopped mid-sentence and said, "Please excuse me for a moment, won't you?" The new executive in the room, Danny Corvis' replacement, looked confused. The other three attendees just gathered him up with their eyes and walked out of the room with him in tow.

"Computer, what is it?" Steven stared at the screen as the text of the Whippettes conversation scrolled across it.

Chapter 8 - First UN Mission

The German government's official position on Bohemia was that the land was abandoned when the Czech Republic ceased to exist; therefore, it could be settled by whoever got there first. The Poles had already taken over territory that was once Slovakia, Romania and Hungary, and the Germans began to expand to the southeast to keep Poland from becoming too large.

Poland had agreed to German occupation of the former Czech Republic in exchange for the German government's dropping of the claim that the space colony of New Germany become a part of their country. Unofficially, Poland and Germany agreed to allow German occupation of the land to stop Serbian expansion. There were no indigenous people in the area when German and Polish squatters moved in and set up settlements. There were a series of recent attacks against the squatters conducted by war lords operating in the area.

The war lords were from Serbia. Serbia was competing for the territory occupied by both Poland and Germany. Poland needed German support in Bohemia due to the low-level insurgency going on in the border regions along the Danube River between Serbia and Poland.

The fighting was often brutal, with atrocities being committed by both sides. Nationalism played an important role in the ethnic fighting. Because the members of the European Union dominated the UN and Serbia had never been a member, action was proposed to stop the Serbian advance.

The communicator buzzed.

Paine reached for the button and then looked at the screen to see who was calling. The sender was blocked.

"Colonel Martin here." Paine was still uneasy with his new rank and the chilling similarity to his father's. It bothered him.

"Oberstleutnant Martin, hier ist Generalmajor Jung." Paine remembered that his immediate commander was from the German Army, attached to the UN Military Forces Command. Paine was from the Army of New York.

Paine tried to remember his German as he answered, "Ich verstehe kein Deutsch."

"So sorry, Colonel," Major General Jung said. "I mean to speak more English, as that is the language of the UN. I have a mission for our special operations force." He asked Paine, "Can we do this in video chat?"

"Of course, General," Paine said as he set the communications' device on the stand and activated the camera.

Jung's face appeared on the screen. "Is it not true that most of your force is from the original United Nations Army?" he asked.

Paine had just reviewed the personnel records of all of his 500-person force with his adjutant, Lieutenant Trisha Jones, and discovered that except for the command group and his old scout platoon; most of the soldiers were UN recruits. He wanted to recruit more of the 82d troopers, who had stayed with now General Flagehty, and the Kentucky Regulars who stayed behind after the nuclear blast ended the fighting in the city into his new unit, but the UN bureaucracy was notoriously slow when it came to personnel actions. Trisha was working on getting more transfers, but had only managed to add thirty-five seasoned veterans to the force. She was being blocked by all the paperwork.

"Yes, Herr General, that is true," Paine said.

"And what is the status of their training and combat capability?" Jung asked.

Once again, Paine searched his memory for the operational readiness evaluation given to his subordinate units by Marcus Pace, his Command Sergeant Major; Major Rachel Miller, his new operations officer; and Major Yuri Kompaniyets, his executive officer.

"Sir, we need an intensive training program to bring all of our units up to standard. Most of the leadership is young and inexperienced. The soldiers need to be tested for drugs and psychological fitness, and our equipment is in sorry shape," Paine said. "I would say we could be marginally combat ready in about two months, if I am given a free hand to winnow out the undesirables in the unit."

"We do not have the time," General Jung stated. "We need to deploy forces to the Bohemian Mountains to stop the ethnic violence going on there. It has been noted that local Bohemian militia forces, back by Greater Serbia, have been attacking and killing ethnic German and Polish people who moved into the area after the start of the plague."

"Let me explain," General Jung began his history lesson. "At first, there was relative harmony between the people, but now that agriculture has returned and the locals can grow their own foodstuffs, they have launched a campaign to push out the settlers from the North and West. It seems we have not learned the lessons of the past, and the warlords claim that the Fourth Reich is being established in Central Europe." General Jung paused. "Nothing could be further from the truth. Since 1945, we Germans have been peace-loving people and have helped our neighbors, not tried to dominate them."

General Jung continued. "The Security Council has directed that a UN police force will deploy to the Bohemian region to stop the fighting there. I have instructions to put a combined UN and German military unit together to accomplish the mission. I even have a good name for it: the Joint United Nations and German Forces, or JUNGFOR for short." He paused and waited for a few seconds, but Paine did not respond. "Very clever, isn't it? You see, JUNGFOR commanded by me, General Jung?"

Paine politely smiled, all the while thinking that the Herr General either had a terrible sense of humor or was slightly demented – or both. He questioned his decision to join the UN military more every day.

"Very clever, indeed," Paine said. "And just what is it you want my unit to do in this deployment?"

"Your mission is to take out the leader of the warlords. Once we know where he is headquartered, it will be a simple insertion and extraction mission like your assignment last year to infiltrate into New York." General Jung smiled as he saw the look on Paine's face. "I have my sources. Every good military commander studies the tactics of others and improves their own ability to win battles. The German General Staff has been watching the operations of the Kentucky Regulars for years. We also have a good intelligence exchange program with the NUS government."

Paine made a mental note to check communications coming from all of his soldiers because only those on the mission could have talked about the tactics used. That meant one of the scout platoon members involved in the insertion must be selling information. Six of the original members died, killed in the fighting in New York, so not counting him and Marcus that left 22 possible leaks. All of them were in Paine's UN force. He would have to be careful.

"We need to make sure that there are no civilian casualties; nothing that would give the Serbians a reason to start a fight. You know how they are." Jung paused for a breath, "Always trying to grab territory and thinking that they have the best interests of the people in mind. Is history repeating itself? They will start a war in Europe to get what they want! Those verdammt Serbs. We have the opportunity to stop this madness from happening again."

Paine cringed at the vehemence in the last two sentences. This would not be an easy mission, and Paine would have to watch his back. "When do we deploy?" he asked.

General Jung composed himself. "You have two weeks to get your men ready to go. We leave New York on the first of October. Our destination is Plzen."

Chapter 9 – Elle

Elle walked into the home office at her parents' house and stood looking at them scribbling notes on pads of paper for a full minute before she spoke.

"Mom, Dad, what is going on?"

William put his finger to his lips and motioned her to come closer. He took a piece of paper and wrote, "Must not talk. We think we found all the cameras and microphones, but are not sure"

Elle took the note, read it and wrote one of her own, "What can I do to help?"

Betty came over to her daughter and put her arms around her. She handed her a sealed letter. She wrote on her pad of paper and showed it to Elle. "Just talk about what you are going to do. Then take this to Paine, he will get it to Ashley - important you keep this safe."

Elle nodded, a little confused but understanding it must be very important. She thought about what she needed to say before she spoke again.

"I just came by to tell you guys I am going to be taking a trip up north, back to New York. Dallas is way too hot this time of year. Besides, I really do want to see Paine again before he deploys." She walked over to her father and wrapped her arms around him.

William returned the hug and put his hand on hers, the one holding the letter. "I hope you have a safe trip, dear. We would come, but we have a lot of unfinished research to complete. Maybe we can join you later?"

"That would be nice; Paine would love to see you guys again." Elle gave her mother an embrace and then turned and walked out the door.

Ryan knocked on the door frame to Ashley's office. Once she arranged for the establishment of SUNY, she moved into the abandoned City Hall Building and declared it the State House. The Technos had assured her that radiation from the UN nuclear explosion was negligible and would harm no one who worked there.

"Come in, Ryan." Ashley welcomed the intrusion. She was tired of all the paperwork and conducting day-to-day operations of the new country. She had just finished discussing the future of the United Nations Building with the new secretary general, Andre Chevalier of France. He was working hard to move the UN from New York to Versailles in France, and she was just as determined to keep it in New York. A meeting was scheduled for the following week in the temporary UN Headquarters, in Madison Square Garden.

"We have a strange message from the Whippettes. It didn't come by electronic communications. The letter is hand written and brought by their daughter, Eleanor." He held up an old-fashioned envelope. "She said she had to get this to Paine, but when she couldn't find him, she brought it here. She seems to think it's pretty important."

Ashley became very official. She liked Ryan; they had a long history of friendship. But at a time like this she wanted to make sure he understood that this merited a serious approach.

"General Flagehty, could you please show Ms. Whippette in?" She switched to the patrol sign that Paine had taught both of them and signed "come back and tell me when the dampener field is on full power."

"Yes, Madame President, right away." Ryan winked at her. Damn him, he refused to take things seriously, but she smiled at him and waved her hand in dismissal.

Elle walked into the office and stopped short of the desk. "What do I do?" she asked. "I've never met a president. Do I courtesy or salute, maybe bow?" Elle laughed out loud and said, "I am so confused."

Ashley laughed with her as she walked from behind the desk with her arms opened wide. "A hug will do." She wrapped her arms around Elle and held her tight for a moment, then pushed her to arm's length and looked at her from head to toe. "Still as beautiful as ever," she said, viewing the petite blond.

Elle looked embarrassed and said, "You look pretty good, too. I haven't seen you since Michael's change of command."

Ashley laughed. "Us old folks need meditube technology to look good. It's amazing how easy it is to look beautiful when you're young," she said. "So, what have you been doing with yourself?"

"Well, since Paine was too busy to spend any time with me, I got fed up and went back home to Dallas to see my folks." Elle pouted a little as she continued, "I thought maybe he would ask me to stay in New York, but he said it was better if we waited," Elle shook her head. "I am not sure I have a future with Paine, he's married to his work."

Ashley motioned Elle into a seat and went back to her desk. "Michael, or Paine, since he prefers that name, just needs a little time. Let him get his feet on the ground and he just might surprise you one day." Ashley smiled at Elle and said, "Don't give up hope."

"I haven't, but I'm also not waiting for him to make a move," Elle said, "I will be going to study languages at the University of Texas, starting in the fall."

Ashley looked up as Ryan came to the door and gave her a thumbs up sign.

The change in the tenor of Ashley's voice was noticeable as she said, "General Flagehty just informed me we can talk freely. Tell me what is going on with your parents."

"They were acting really weird this morning." Elle looked troubled. "I was going in to tell them that I'd been accepted to the school I wanted, and they sent me away with instructions to get this to Paine." She pointed to the letter on Ashley's desk. "When I couldn't find him, I decided to bring it to you. I don't know what is in it, but it must be pretty important to have me hand carry it all the way here from Dallas."

"Well, let's see what it says together." Elle came around the desk and read the note over Ashley's shoulder.

Paine,
Thank you for saving our daughter when she came to New York to search for us. You can save her once again. We understand you have feelings for her but it would be best if she not see you after you read this.

Please do not let her read this letter as it will put her in mortal danger. Get it to your mother as soon as possible and tell her someone can listen in on conversations via a new batch of nanoprobes. I do not know for sure, but suspect they are manufactured by the Corvis Foundation. A former colleague of ours, Julian Fox, went to work for an undisclosed company and disappeared six months later. His family has also had a series of unexplained accidents and no one is left alive who knows where he might be. His signature is all over many of the probes that were causing the plague and on the nanoprobes with transmission capabilities.

Both Betty and I are infected, and we suspect you are, too, due to your treatment for radiation poisoning. Anyone you come into contact with who has been in a meditube in the past year may have the transmission probes. Be careful who you talk to and what you talk about.

Betty and I are working to block the transmissions, but haven't quite figured that out yet. See if the Technos in New York can do anything and please inform as soon as possible. Please tell Elle nothing and send off to school without letting her find out what is going on. That way, she may be safe until this is resolved, and you can be together again.

Your friend always, Will.

"Keenan was right. They can hear us." Ryan said. He had moved to where he could also read the letter.

Ashley shot him a look, started to snap at him and then changed her mind. She spoke slowly, "General, I trust you with my life, as I have many times before. But next time, ask me before you read over my shoulder."

Ryan looked chastised.

Ashley saw that Elle was upset and touched her hand. "This room is shielded from the listening devices in the nanoprobes, so we are the only ones who know what the letter says. As long as we keep it between ourselves, we shouldn't be in any danger." She stood up, refolded the letter and held it in her hand. "Don't worry, I won't tell Paine what your parents said about you being in danger. I'll let you decide what to tell him." She put the letter in the desktop incinerator and it disappeared in a flash.

Ashley turned to Ryan and said, "General, please get handwritten instructions to all of our top officials notifying them of this potential breach in security. Send a messenger to Keenan to increase production of the dampening devices like the one in this office." She paused and then said, "I want our country safe from eavesdropping by the end of the week."

Ryan saluted and said, "Right away, Madame President," and then walked out the door.

Ashley walked over to Elle, put her arm around her shoulder and escorted her to the door.

"You, my dear, have six days before Paine comes back from the field." Ashley said. "That should be more than enough time to get the Technos to develop a portable jammer and get this information to my son." She looked at Elle and said, "I don't have to tell you that this information is dangerous, but Paine must be told that someone can listen in on any plans the UN forces are making He needs to be careful."

Elle nodded as Ashley hugged her and said, "In the meantime, you can act like a tourist and enjoy the city. It's much safer that the last time you were here."

Chapter 10 – The Bad Part of Town

Elle had been alone in New York for three days, waiting for Paine to come home and feeling hemmed in. The door chime announced a visitor, and she pushed the intercom button.

"Yes, who is it?" she said.

"Elle, this is Katrina. I heard you were in the city and thought going out would be nice. I need company. I've just been sitting around moping since the boys left for training and want to do some shopping." Katrina's voice got more excited as she asked, "Are you up to a short excursion?"

Elle buzzed Katrina in and said, "Thank God you came. I think I'm ready to jump out the window." She asked, "Where do you want to go?"

Katrina settled herself in a chair and dangled her legs over the edge of her seat. She looked almost like a child sitting there.

"Since Ashley reopened the city to trade, Fifth Avenue shops are open again. I also heard there are a few good restaurants down there and I want to see what they have to offer." Katrina babbled on, "Marcus said as soon as he gets a place for us to live overseas, he's going to send for me. I thought about getting new high heels and surprising him by being a few inches taller when I get off the shuttle." Katrina laughed. "He's always teasing me about my height and I want to tease him back."

Elle looked at her friend and worried that maybe they should not go out. Paine had warned her that New York was a hazardous place, due to a few snarf addicts and free-lance criminals still roaming the city.

"I don't know. Maybe we should just stay in and talk. It could be too dangerous out there," Elle said.

Katrina snorted in disgust. "Elle, after everything we've been through, do you really think a few hours on the town are going to put us in more danger? I think not. I can take care of myself, and I can protect you, too, if it comes to that." Katrina paused and reached for her handbag. "I have a gun I can give you, if that will make you feel any better."

She pulled a small black semi-automatic pistol out of her purse and handed it to Elle. "This is just what you need to walk the streets of Manhattan! It's a nine millimeter, and it holds seven shots. Marcus got it for me as a going-away present. It's romantic, don't you think?" Katrina laughed.

Katrina pulled the slide back and locked it into place, then leaned over and showed Elle the safety. "Flip this down and it's ready to go." She pointed at the button on the handgrip and said, "Push this and the clip falls out. Watch."

Katrina ejected the magazine, catching it before it fell to the floor. "Just push a fresh one in and release the slide." Katrina inserted a full magazine in the pistol and loaded a round.

She handed the pistol to Elle and gave her instructions, "Just point it at center mass and pull the trigger. Be careful, there's one in the chamber."

Elle looked at the weapon. She understood how to use it but was still squeamish about handling pistols. Paine had taken her to the range several times and taught her how to shoot a handgun. Her father had insisted she learn how to shoot a wide variety of long guns. He wanted her to help him stop any unwanted visitors; two- or four-legged, approaching the ranch where they spent their summers. Although she had seen her fair share of dead bodies, she still did not like the thought of inflicting death or injury on anyone.

"What about you? How will you stay safe if we get split up and I have your gun?" Elle asked.

Katrina jumped from the chair and held out her clutch purse. "Take this from me, now," she said.

Elle grabbed the small bag and as she pulled it from Katrina's grasp, a small push knife appeared in Katrina's hand.

"I can do a lot of damage with this little thing," she said as she swept her arm in a wide arc and the knife swished through the air. "And I really need to get some fresh air. So either give me back my pistol or put it somewhere and come with me."

Elle hesitated. She had a premonition it was going to be perilous no matter what. Still, she did want to go out.

Katrina pleaded with her, "Come on, Elle. It'll be fun!"

Elle checked to make sure the safety was on, put the gun in her purse and stood up.

"OK, let's go." Elle led the way out of the apartment.

The restaurant was almost empty as Katrina pushed back her plate and sipped the last of the wine. Elle was picking at her food, worried because the sun was going down and the supply of power to the city was intermittent. The street lights were coming on, but there were still many shadows where trouble could be lurking.

Katrina picked up the high heels she had bought in the last store they stopped in. "These things hurt my feet!" She laughed as she stood up. "I guess we'd better get going; it's getting dark. I will call for a cab and we can wait here until it arrives. Or we can walk home."

Elle laughed at the thought of Katrina walking five blocks in her new heels. "I think we'd better call for that cab. You don't want to go to Marcus with a broken ankle, or blistered, swollen feet, do you?"

As Katrina made the call for a cab, Elle looked out at the street. There were five men standing across the street leaning on the wall of the building watching foot traffic go buy. For safety, most of the pedestrians were traveling in groups of at least ten. A few even openly carried a weapon. The men did not move away from the wall and tried to avoid eye contact with the passersby.

"Katrina, we may have complications. Look over there." Elle fingered the pistol in her purse and got nervous.

"No problem, the cab will be here in a few minutes. We can wait outside." She stood up and slipped the heels on her feet. When Elle stood up, Katrina noticed that even with the addition of the heels, she now barely reached Elle's shoulder. They walked out the door; she noted, "Hey, I'm almost as tall as you are now."

As soon as the door closed behind them, the five loungers pushed away from the wall and moved across the street. Due to the oncoming darkness, the sidewalks were empty of traffic. The men approached the two women.

"Good evening, ladies," the largest of the five said as he planted himself in front of the girls. "I would really appreciate it if you could please give us your purses and your jewelry."

Katrina grabbed Elle's hand as if in fear, stopping her from reaching into her purse for the gun. "You seem to have us outnumbered. However, I for one do not want to give up my belongings. And I don't think you can take them from me."

Katrina stepped out of her shoes, appearing even smaller. "But you are welcome to try."

The big man pulled a large knife out of his pocket and waved the others back. "I can take this little girl by myself. I don't need your help. When I am done, take what you want from the other one." As he stepped forward, Katrina handed her purse to Elle. She pulled out the knife, smiled and said to Elle, "This won't take too long. Once he is down, pull the gun."

The large man lunged toward Katrina, who sidestepped and slashed at his knife hand, cutting a shallow gash in his wrist. He looked down at his bleeding hand, bellowed and lunged again.

Katrina danced away, pirouetted, then darted in and slashed his other hand.

"You bitch, I'll kill you!" he yelled as he lunged once more.

Katrina had a grin on her face as she slashed once more, this time slicing open his shirt with a forehand slash and leaving a small cut just above his right eye with a backhand cut. She had to leave her feet to reach his face, but landed lightly, balancing on her toes as she looked at the thief bleeding in front of her.

"If you want to die, come at me again. Otherwise, I suggest you and your friends leave now." She waived the knife in front of his face. "Decide now, or they pick up your body in the morning."

The other four men were deciding what do because Elle had pulled out the pistol and was pointing it at the two toughs on her left. Katrina's eyes never left her primary opponent, but she sensed the other two men stepping closer from the right. The big man waved them in, and the fight was over in five seconds.

Elle fired all seven shots into the two men moving toward her, hitting the first in the chest three times then shifting to the second for the next four shots. They both died at Elle's feet.

Katrina slashed the throat of her first attacker, who dropped to the pavement, trying to stop the bleeding with both hands while gasping for air. Katrina then turned to stab the closest man in the groin as she ducked under his oncoming fist. The other man turned and ran.

Katrina looked at Elle, who was standing staring at the empty pistol in her hand; its slide locked in the open position. Katrina took it from her grasp, ejected the magazine and put in a fresh one.

She pushed down on the slide release and watched as a round loaded into the chamber.

Katrina handed the pistol back to Elle. "Please wait here. Tell the cabby to stay until I get back." She ran down the street after the fifth man, calling over her shoulder, "And don't forget to pick up my new shoes!"

Katrina easily caught up with the running thief and cut his hamstring just above the back of his knee. He fell to the ground and covered his face with his hands, begging for mercy.

"Move your hands, please." Katrina's voice came out softly, "Or I will hurt you more."

"What do you want?" He cried as he looked up into Katrina's cold eyes.

"I will let you live, but you spread the word. No one and I mean no one, messes with me or my friend. Got that?" The thief nodded in fear. "And I promise you this, anyone who does will get what your buddies got." Katrina kicked the man's sliced-open leg. He screamed in agony as she walked away.

When Katrina got back to Elle, the bodies were nowhere to be seen.

Elle was crying as she stood waiting for the cab to arrive. "The restaurant owner heard weapons fire and came outside with a shotgun. He had the wait staff take away the bodies. They put them into the dumpster in the alley." She closed her eyes and said, "At least I don't have to look at them anymore."

Elle drew in a deep, quivering breath. "That is the first time I ever killed anyone." She could still see the eyes of the first man she killed, wide open in pain and fear. She remembered the light leaving those eyes and was sure it would haunt her for the rest of her days. "How do you live with it?"

Katrina hesitated, took her shoes and her purse back from Elle's shaking hands, and then tried to explain. "You do not think about what you do, you think about what might happen to you and those you love." She moved in front of Elle and looked her in the eyes. "Elle, think about how Paine would feel if you let someone take your life without at least fighting back. I can tell you, Marcus would be really pissed off. He knows I can take care of myself, but there is always a chance I will die."

Katrina took Elle's hand and said, "Look at me. I learned about death a long time ago when my father was killed and my mother died from a simple infection. No one would help us because people blamed my father for the deaths of others. My father didn't kill them, but they died and so did he. We had to go on alone. I watched my brother die because the UN wanted to control New York and killing everyone seemed to be the best answer they could find to do that."

Katrina stared off into the distance and continued. "I know Carl died for me, and I promised that I would avenge his death." Her hair stood out from her head as she hissed, "And I did."

Katrina shook her head. "Maybe I'll tell you about it another time. Right now, we have a cab coming. We need to get off the street." She pointed at the pool of blood on the pavement in front of them. "Don't get that on your shoes, it makes the cabbies mad."

Chapter 11 – Reunion

Ryan activated the jamming device and left the room after ushering Elle into Ashley's office once more. Ashley was looking out the window at the park across the street.

"The street camera caught your little incident last night. I am sorry; I should have warned you that the streets aren't safe yet," Ashley turned around and looked at Elle. "I am just glad you had Katrina with you. Those guys got what they deserved."

Elle started to shake as she was reminded of what she had done.

Ashley put her hand on Elle's shoulder. "Don't worry, I won't be telling your parents about this. And I won't mention it to Paine, either. I told Katrina... well you need not hear what I told Katrina." Ashley thought Katrina would think twice about putting Elle into harm's way after the tongue lashing she'd received both from her and from Ryan.

"When you see Paine," Ashley saw Elle light up when she mentioned her son's name, "give him this and make sure you take one, too." She held out a small pill. "He should be back at his quarters tomorrow night. Command Sergeant Major Neel had a chat with his sergeant of the guard and arranged for you to have access to his apartment."

When Elle looked at the pills, Ashley said, "These are short-duration blocking devices that should keep the transmissions from any nanoprobes getting to wherever they are supposed to go. They only last for twenty-four hours; then the battery burns out. We haven't determined how the nanoprobes have enough power to transmit for such a long time. The Technos are working on a better battery solution, but haven't come up with one yet."

Elle just nodded her thanks, gave Ashley a hug and walked out.

Paine was hot and tired when he returned to his quarters. The unit had been out on the firing range for three days, sleeping in the field and working on night operations while not doing marksmanship training. He rubbed the stubble on his face and thought about the shower he badly needed. He hadn't slept for over three hours a night and was ready to clean up and go to bed. As he pushed the door open, he saw Elle standing in the living room.

Elle moved to the surprised Paine and threw her arms around him.

"I've missed you so much, my love!" She kissed him hard on the mouth, slipping a small pill into it and waiting for him to swallow. Then she bit him on the ear as she whispered, "Paine, hug me tight and don't let go. We need to talk. The pill you took is a jamming device. It will stop electronic transmissions, but there are probably more sensors and cameras in your apartment." Elle pulled away from Paine and wrinkled her nose and announced, "You stink, Michael, you need a bath!"

Elle took Paine by the hand and dragged the stunned man to the bathroom. She unbuttoned her blouse when Paine asked, "What..." and stopped him from talking with her finger on his lips. She continued undressing until she stood naked in front of him. Paine felt his heart race as she reached out and tugged his belt loose. Their hands worked together quickly to disrobe him and Elle pulled him into the shower and turned on the water.

Elle squirted soap on her body. She whispered into Paine's ear, "A little something I learned from my parents. This is how they kept from being overheard in their home in Houston," and then pressed herself against him to create a lather.

Paine almost fell over and could not help but have an involuntary reaction. Elle looked down and said, "Mother said this would happen, and that maybe we should make the best of it. After all, we've known each other for a long time." She kissed him again and pressed even tighter. "I've had my contraceptive implant. Besides, it makes the people watching us believe this is all we are in here for. Now you need to act like a man who hasn't seen his girlfriend in two months."

As they began their lovemaking, she told Paine what her parents had discovered. Paine had a difficult time concentrating on the conversation.

In the middle of the night, the communicator buzzed.

Paine reached for the button, careful not to wake Elle, who was curled up next to him. The sender was blocked, as usual, and Paine kept the camera off as he answered.

"Colonel Martin here," Paine said.

"Hey, Paine, time to get up. We got our orders to fly out within twenty-four hours. General Jung sent over the movement orders by courier." Marcus paused, and then said in an official voice, "Colonel Paine, we are officially in lock down as of now. All the officers and NCOs have been informed, and the soldiers are marshalling for pre-deployment checks. I have you scheduled to address the troops at the next formation which will be held at 0400 hours. That's only two hours from now."

"Thanks, Sergeant Major," Paine replied. "Please have the staff ready to meet with me in one hour. See you in the ready room then. Paine, out."

Paine gently shook Elle's shoulder and called out her name.

"What, again?" She smiled as she held out her arms. "OK!"

Paine put his hand on her shoulder and said, "I am sorry, Elle, but I just got orders to leave."

"When?" she asked.

"We leave by this time tomorrow, and I have to go to work right now." Paine got up, but Elle grabbed him, drew him close to her and hugged him tight for a few seconds. Then she released him and turned over, covering her head with her pillow.

Paine dressed as quickly as he could and then returned to the bed where Elle was sobbing into her pillow.

"I'm sorry, but I have to go now. I'm not sure when I'll be back, but I'll send you my communications information as soon as I can." Paine touched her shoulder, but Elle shrugged his hand away.

Elle's muffled voice came out from under the pillow, "Don't bother. I am going home to my parents."

Paine stood for a moment, then turned and walked out of the bedroom, picked up his alert bag and left the apartment. He did not hear Elle call out his name after he closed the door and walked down the hall to the elevators.

Chapter 12 - Home to Dallas

Elle was once again in Ashley's office.

"So you decided to go back to Dallas?" Ashley asked.

"I think I should go see my parents and figure out my next step with Paine," Elle replied. "Thanks for all your help, and for getting me together with Paine before he left."

"I think I may have made things worse between you two, and if I did I am truly sorry for the both of you," Ashley smiled a sad smile at Elle and continued. "Paine is not an easy person to get through to sometimes, but once you do, you have him for life. And I think you two are perfect together."

Not knowing what to say, Elle simply nodded.

Ashley handed Elle a small package and said, "There are three more dampening pills in the envelope. Two are in case you and Paine need to talk more, one is to give to your father. Maybe he can build a copy for himself."

Elle and Ashley hugged each other, and then Elle left for the spaceport.

Elle decided not to go home right away. She wanted time to think about what she and Paine had done, what he meant to her, and how she would handle him being gone all the time. She spent three weeks traveling by lifter through the New South, touring the coastal cities and enjoying the southern cuisine. The days were cooling off, but the weather was still nice enough to take long walks on the beach. The food was great, and she ate much more than usual.

Elle thought her parents looked a lot older than when she left.

"Welcome back, dear." Betty gave her daughter a hard hug and put her fingers to her lips. "Your father and I have been waiting for you to come home. How was your visit to New York?" She made a continue sign with her hands, showing she wanted Elle to talk.

"It was all right. They call it States United in New York or something like that. Everyone says SUNY for short. All three factions came up with the name which if you ask me is pretty lame. You should see their flag; black on top, to represent space, green in the middle, for the ground and blue on the bottom, representing the ocean. There are three stars in the upper left corner signifying the three states. A bit on the ugly side, I am sorry to say." Elle stopped and looked quizzically at her mother, who made a continue sign to her. "The new government is cleaning up the city and you wouldn't recognize the streets today. Things have changed since you were last here."

Elle shot her mother a quizzical look. Betty, exasperated, motioned for Elle to keep talking again.

"I saw Paine while I was there, but just briefly. He was gone most of the time, and then when I got to see him, he was called out and deployed the next day. So I took a little vacation before school starts and went to Savannah, Hilton Head, Beaufort and Charleston and then came on home. How is everything here?" Elle shrugged.

"Oh, just fine. Your father and I have decided to take a little vacation ourselves and would love it if you could come along." Betty once again indicated that Elle should talk.

"I guess I'm all ready for school, so I won't be coming with you guys." Elle stopped as her father came into the room.

William came over and hugged his daughter. "It's OK now. I have the field on. We can talk."

Elle looked up at the ceiling as if to point out the possibility of cameras being hidden there.

"I redid the drywall and ceilings myself." William wiped his brow. "It took some doing, but I got rid of three cameras and a bunch of microphones. This room is safe."

Elle turned to her mother, "Mom, what is wrong with you? You look terrible!"

"Your father put me in a modified meditube, one that extracted all the nanoprobes from our bodies. Age creeps up on you fast when you are as old as we are." Elizabeth smiled. "I still feel pretty good, but I look about forty now, and I may be at my real age in the next few months." She held up a mirror to look at the crow's feet around her eyes and said, "I remember these from before New York. It's nice to be back to normal."

William frowned. "If by normal you mean in danger, I agree. We have rudimentary knowledge of the nanoprobes used in the plague that killed so many in New York. We are working on the source, and we may be getting close. The closer we get, the more likely we are to become targets. Your mother and I want you to go to the university and start classes because our home may not be the safest place for you."

Elle looked at both her parents. "Sit down, please."

William and Betty sat down on the couch next to each other and joined hands.

"Something happened between me and Paine." Elle took a deep breath. "Mother, I took your advice and things got sort of physical."

Her parents were not shocked after all Elle was a grown woman.

Elle sat in the chair opposite them and continued. "Paine is a sweet guy. I like him a lot, no, I think I love him." She clasped her hands together and said, "But I am not sure I can live the life I would have with him."

Elle leaned forward and vehemently said, "They woke him up and he was gone within fifteen minutes! I don't even know where he is or what he is doing. That is not a life I can share because there is no sharing!"

William interrupted. "But Paine can at least protect you. He could have people to watch over you while he is gone."

"It's not worth it," Elle said. "So I'm home for now. I will not leave if you may be in danger. I can shoot and I can protect you." She stared down at her clenched hands for a moment, silent as she relived the moment she pulled the trigger in New York.

Betty looked at the expression on her daughter's face and asked, "Elle, what else happened in New York?"

"I had to kill two people who were threatening Katrina and me," Elle blurted out. She took a deep breath to calm her nerves and continued, "I felt bad, but now I don't. They would have taken my life, so I did what needed to be done. And I know now I can do it again. You are my life and I will not go. I'll die protecting you." Elle crossed her arms and planted both feet on the floor. "So there!"

William looked at his daughter with sad eyes. "It's always hard to take a life. I think the difficulty is figuring out how to deal with the memory. Just realize that you did the right thing." He got up from the couch, but did not let go of Betty's hand. "All right, we have to make arrangements. We will go to SUNY as soon as possible. I just need to get a shuttle scheduled from the Dallas Fort Worth Space Port with a pilot I trust. We'll be traveling incognito." William squeezed Betty's hand and said, "Looks like you can relax until I get everything set up." William left the room.

The communicator buzzed. Paine's number showed on the screen; Elle and her mother looked at each other, and then Betty answered the call.

"Hello? Oh, hello, Paine. Wait a moment; I'll see if she is here." Betty looked at Elle who shook her head no.

"Sorry, Paine, Elle must have stepped out. Can I take a message?" Betty listened for a few minutes, and then said, "All right, I will tell her. You take care of yourself, you hear?" She broke the connection.

Betty looked at her daughter. "He said to tell you he has been trying to get a hold of you for the last four weeks. He is worried about you."

Elle made a face.

"Oh come on, child, he sounded worried enough! He said he would be in Paris at a UN military conference on Tuesday and wants to know if you can come. He said, and I quote, 'Just tell her I miss her and want her to meet me. If she wants to see me, she is to come to the French Officer's Club on Place de Saint Augustine Wednesday evening. There is a space reserved for her on a UN shuttle leaving Dallas on Wednesday; all she has to do is show up.' That's what he said." She smiled at her daughter and said, "Trisha Jones will be there to get you on the flight."

Elle looked defiantly at her mother and said, "I'll have to think about it."

William returned as the conversation ended. "Wednesday would be great! That is when we fly to New York. You can wait until then to decide. Meanwhile, let's go sit by the pool and enjoy the day."

Chapter 13 - Deployed to Plzen

"Lieutenant Colonel Martin, reporting as ordered." Paine and Marcus stood in front of Major General Jung's desk at the position of attention. Even though they had spoken many times via communicators, it was the first time Paine was in his presence.

General Jung looked like someone from central casting gave him a role in a movie as a German officer. Tall, blond hair close-cropped and just showing a little grey at the temples, uniform tailored precisely so that it fit him like a glove, Jung reminded Paine of the pictures of Wehrmacht officers he'd seen when studying the 20th-Century War.

"Yes, Colonel Martin and Command Sergeant Major Pace. Do you mind if I call you by your given names?"

"Not at all, sir. The sergeant major goes by Marcus, and I am called Paine by my friends."

General Jung wrinkled his brow, "Then you are not called Michael? I read that that was your name."

Marcus broke in, "Excuse me sir, but that is a long story."

General Jung cocked his head to one side and said, "I think it is a soldier's story and one best told later, perhaps over some cognac?" Paine simply nodded. "Very well, Marcus and Paine, we must get down to business. Please come over to the map."

Central Europe was projected on the wall. Jung took up a laser pointer and began his briefing.

"As you will notice, the old boundaries pre-plague are shown here. Germany ended here, Austria here, and the Czech Republic here." Jung tapped the computer and the lines on the map changed. "Poland has claimed what had been Slovakia, and we moved settlers into our traditional German area of the Sudetenland. An agreement reached between us and the Poles enabled us to inhabit the rest of the Czech Republic. We reoccupied what had been rightfully ours and peacefully incorporated those few people still living there into the German Republic. I am being clear so far?"

Both Paine and Marcus shook their heads in agreement.

"Sehr Gut. Now we came to the not-such-good things. The Serbs, those bastards... excuse me, as you can tell I have a dislike toward them. Anyway, they moved paramilitary forces into the southern part of our lands, claiming that Serbs had been there all along and saying we were pushing Slavic people out of their homes. We, of course, are doing no such thing. When we arrived, a complete population survey was done, and no one was found to be living there." He paused for a moment. "But you already heard that in my earlier briefing."

"Now the Serbs are claiming this belongs to them." Jung almost broke the computer as he jabbed his finger at the key board and the map changed once more. The line on the map showed the country of Greater Serbia which included much of former Austria and the lower half of the Czech Republic.

"How they can justify this is not in my mind. They claim that former Austria-Hungary, a German Empire, belongs to them because of the defeat of the aforementioned country in phase one of the 20th-Century War! How absurd!"

Paine asked, "Just what are they doing in those areas that we need to be concerned about?"

"You know, but your Oberstabsfeldwebel does not. Good that you have not told Marcus, so I can have the honor." General Jung said, "You are a good commander, Colonel Paine Martin."

"My thanks to you, Herr General," Paine replied.

"Marcus, these Mischling send irregular troops into our German settlements and kill innocent women and children. I have films to prove it." General Jung leaned close to them and said, "I also have spies who tell me the Serb soldiers are also there, disguised as civilians, but giving arms and food to the guerrilla troops. Your mission will be to capture these Serb provocateurs and bring them in for justice."

General Jung turned back to the map as Paine and Marcus exchanged looks. This would be a very difficult mission.

Chapter 14 – Double Cross

"Mister Corvis, a call for you." The computer jarred Steven out of his thoughts. He was going over the transcripts of every conversation the Whippettes had for the last five months and could not find any clear indication they knew about his operation. Utilizing a shell company, he'd hired fifteen private investigators to track and record their every move. They found no hard evidence that the Whippettes knew anything. Still, he wanted to be sure they told no one else if they'd found out damaging information. The investigators discretely spread the word that any information on the Whippettes would be greatly appreciated and handsomely rewarded. Steven would have to be thorough in cleaning up this mess.

He activated the speaker and said, "Steven Corvis."

A mechanically disguised male voice came out of the speaker, "Mister Corvis, you do not know me, but I have information you may want to hear."

Steven was certain that was true; all communication was vetted by the computer before it got to him. This must be important.

"Go ahead, sir." Steven looked at the caller ID and saw the signal was blocked. He typed in a trace command and his password and then sat back as the computer identified the location of the caller. It flashed DALLAS SPACE PORT on the screen.

"A friend of yours told me you were looking into the Whippette family. I have been paid a great deal of money to fly as the co-pilot on a shuttle taking them to New York next Wednesday I am sure that someone in your position would pay even more if I were to alter our flight plans and land somewhere a little short of New York, say in New Jersey at the old Newark Airport?" The man paused for a moment. "In no-man's-land, so there will be no government to interfere with our little personnel transaction. This way, you can have them in your custody and no one will be the wiser."

"And just what do you think the authorities will say?" Steven asked as he typed in another command on his console, "They track every shuttle flight."

"Once the pilot is taken care of, I will declare an in-flight emergency. I will land and have the Whippettes handed over to whatever people you have on the ground there. I will then fly the shuttle to an undisclosed location and destroy it. All I ask is five hundred million dollars, wired to this Swiss account." Numbers appeared on the screen. "I believe that is a reasonable amount."

Steven snorted in disgust. That was pocket change for him, but then he realized this man didn't understand the gravity of the situation. He began to negotiate.

"I don't think so. I will offer one hundred million, not a penny more," Steven said.

The two men haggled back and forth for a few minutes.

Steven sat back with a sigh. "All right, three hundred-fifty million." He typed a few commands in his computer and said, "It should be in your account now."

There was a pause as the man checked his balance.

"All right, I will make the arrangements. We should be in Newark Wednesday by 1300 hours, and I will turn the Whippettes over to you there." The man chuckled. "You drive a hard bargain, Mister Corvis. But it was a pleasure doing business with you."

Steven shocked the co-pilot when he answered, "The pleasure is all mine, Flight Officer Baldwin. Just make sure you do what you agreed." He terminated the communications link. "Computer, send a message to my security chief to have a detail at the old Newark Airport Tuesday night. They are to wait further instruction." Corvis moved to change the screen, and then said, "And make sure that all the money in Mr. Baldwin's account is transferred to my personal bank by Wednesday at 1400 hours," he said, "He won't be needing it anymore."

The voice said, "Of course, Mister Corvis."

Chapter 15 – Josh's Turn

Josh woke from his dream as the chime sounded. The alarm kept ringing, even though he slapped the off switch several times. He looked around his room. Nothing had changed in the last six months. The treadmill and a weight bench were still in the center of the room, and the monitor hung from the wall in front of a desk with a single chair, taunting him. As he got up from the bed, it automatically closed into the wall, providing a little more space for him to move around. The chime rang again, and the monitor blinked off and on, signaling an incoming message. He thought about destroying the alarm, but he pushed the off button, gave up and moved to the monitor. He took a deep breath and touched the screen to activate the program.

A disembodied voice rang out in the close confines of the capsule. "You need to activate the outside sensors, now!"

Josh touched the activate blinking activate icon. The screen came alive, and he saw a piece of space junk not far from the capsule. Instructions appeared on the screen directing him to capture the disabled satellite and pull it close to the capsule. He complied with the instructions. As the object closed to within two meters of the capsule, his screen flickered and the image of a man appeared on the screen. His heart raced as he recognized the face.

"General Martin, you are a hard man to find." Josh was staring at a very young looking, fit man who appeared to be about thirty years old. It was the face of Steven Corvis, President and CEO of the Corvis Foundation. The nanotechnology that Corvis had access to, coupled with the latest in meditube advances in cosmetic surgery, made the ninety-four-year old Corvis appear to be in the prime of his life.

"You disappointed me, General. I had great plans for you and you had to ruin them. Didn't I tell you to do what I asked?" Corvis shook his head and glanced down at his notes for a moment. "I wanted you to get control of the UN forces, not take control of the UN. I would have made you famous, rich and powerful, but now you are doing nugg work for the very organization you tried to control."

Josh interrupted Corvis, "What exactly is a nugg?"

"Not unusually gifted guy." he yelled at Josh, "You acted like a complete idiot. You also ruined my plans." Corvis' voice returned to a normal tone as he continued, "But now I can use your position there to help me out of a predicament."

"What is in it for me? I'm stuck here on this piece of space junk with no way back to Earth." Josh spit out the words. "Besides, why should I help you?"

"I need a favor from you." Corvis' voice became much smoother as he laid out the plan. "There will be a launch from the Dallas Space Port tomorrow, a private shuttle to New York with only twelve people on board." Corvis sounded like he was talking to his board of directors as he said, "Since I control the software that pilots the vehicle, I will make sure it passes right by your station. It needs to run into this piece of space junk. You will make sure that happens. I do not want it to look like an accident; it needs to look like you intentionally rammed the space junk into the shuttle."

"I am already living under a death sentence. Why should I increase my chances of having it executed?" Josh leaned back in his chair and looked at the screen, waiting for an answer.

Corvis looked perplexed for a moment, then continued. "You are well acquainted with the people on the shuttle." Josh sat up straighter and leaned in toward the computer screen. "The Doctors Whippette and their daughter are traveling to New York from Dallas. They have very incriminating evidence that I was somehow involved in the New York plague." Corvis paused. "All fabricated, of course. But I cannot have any questions popping up right now, so it will be easier to eliminate the rumors at their source rather than spend my precious time refuting them."

"And after I execute your plan, what happens to me?" Josh asked.

"You will have to die." Corvis smiled as Josh moved to cut the transmission. "Listen for just a moment, will you please? The plan is simple and foolproof, just like your execution of Doctor Engle at UN Headquarters."

Josh moved his hand from the switch and leaned in. "You have my attention," he said.

"The ship you are on is designed for two people. The manifest for the craft shows two crew members, both of whom are fictitious. All you have to do is put on one of the vacuum suits, climb out of the airlock and wait for the UN Space Police." Steven leaned toward the camera and continued, "Once they get here, they will find an empty vessel and the second suit still on the rack. They will assume that you lost your mind and decided you could fly back to earth, and that your partner was sucked out when you decompressed the living module. It has happened before on many of the early farming platforms so it's conceivable that it could happen again."

Steven's hands typed something on his keyboard and two biographical sketches showed up on Josh's screen. "Pick whichever one you think will fit best. These are the profiles of the fictitious people assigned to that particular station." Steven continued with his instructions, "Leave a nice note saying you are going to walk home. That should make it more believable."

Josh stared into the screen, thinking. "What happens when I run out of oxygen? I don't mind dying; but I want to go down fighting. Suffocating in a space suit is not my idea of a glorious death."

Corvis smiled. "Once the police arrive, they will have to suit up themselves to come into the capsule. You will hide on the outside of your ship, away from the airlock. Place yourself in the center of the letter U etched on the outside of the ship. Your white suit will blend in with the outside skin and camouflage you enough to escape detection. As soon as the police vehicle is vacated, you will receive instructions on what to do next." There was a slight pause. "Fail me and I will make your life even more of a hell than it already is and do not think I can't do that."

Josh didn't react as Corvis finished his threat. He really didn't care what happened to him, but he wanted to get his revenge on those who put him in this prison. He decided to cooperate, at least for now, just as he had done with the UN debacle. The desired end was justification enough to agree to help.

Chapter 16 – Dallas Space Port

William came into the living room to find his wife and daughter waiting for him.

"Time to go, my ladies," William said. He was in a much better mood now that he felt he could get his family to a place where they would be relatively safe. "The lifter is loaded with our bags, and the only thing left to do is take our pills." He handed both of them the makeshift jamming devices Elle had brought from New York. "Wait until we get to the space port to take them. All anyone who tracks us will know is that we are flying, but they won't know exactly where we are going. I don't think whoever is running the show will try to shoot down all the flights scheduled for today!"

The trip to the space port was short, and the three of them kept their conversations to a minimum. When they arrived at the terminal, they swallowed their pills.

Elle was sick to her stomach. "Mother, I do not feel well," she said.

Elizabeth looked at their daughter. "You look a little flushed. It couldn't be anything you ate; we both had the same thing." She turned to her husband and said, "William, come have a look."

William checked Elle's vital signs with his pocket diagnostic sensor.

"Everything is normal. Maybe it was the pill?" He looked at Betty and asked, "How about you, are you OK?"

"I feel pretty good actually," Betty replied. "I was a little sick a few days ago, but that passed."

"Once we get to the ship, I want to get both of you into the meditube for a quick check-up. We will have at least thirty minutes before liftoff and the checks don't take more than a few minutes."

As they made their way through the terminal, a team of investigators shadowed them up to the terminal gates. The Whippettes were momentarily out of site as they entered the tunnel to the ground transportation area. Suddenly, seven identical vehicles moved out of the tunnel and headed for different parts of the space port. The investigators scrambled to keep up with them all.

"That should give us a little time," William said, as the family walked out of the tunnel. The women had put on hats and scarves, and William sported a large, black Stetson and a fake beard. The disguises were not designed to fool anyone for long, just enough to get into a small lifter and fly to where the private shuttle was waiting for them.

Once they arrived, William led the women into the passenger area. He looked at his wife, and said, "You first, my dear."

William opened the meditube door and ushered his wife inside. As soon as the door closed, he pushed the diagnosis button and waited for the machine to complete the physical exam. The results shocked him and he exclaimed, "Oh my God, your mother is pregnant! But how can that be?"

Elle was as shocked as her father, but said nothing as her mother exited the machine.

"You next, Elle," William said as he ushered her into the meditube and closed the door.

Betty said, "Do I have more nanoprobes, since this isn't our machine?"

"I don't know, but I have a sim card that will overwrite the meditubes program and eliminate any nanoprobes it might have injected into you," William replied.

As the meditube doors closed around her, she said a prayer that she was not pregnant. When the doors opened two minutes later, she realized her prayers had gone unanswered.

Her mother and father both wrapped their arms around her.

"The tube can't determine what gender they are yet, but you and I are both pregnant!" Betty squeezed her daughter, "and it looks like we are about a month along."

"But Paine and I only did it once, how can I be pregnant?" Elle was on the verge of tears. "I thought contraceptives were foolproof."

"Studies have shown the inoculations are only ninety-eight percent effective," William mused, "Elle, it could have been the dampening pill you took when you met with Paine."

He turned to Betty, "Our pregnancy must have happened after we purged ourselves to get the plague nanoprobes out of our systems. I didn't think about the probes in the birth-control inoculation. No wonder you got pregnant." William grinned and said, "The shower always was the perfect place to talk."

Both women blushed and Elle threw a half-hearted punch at her father.

"Bottom line is you both are with child, so now what do we do? I can put you both back in the machine if you want to abort…" William was interrupted with loud "NO," from both women.

William looked at his wife and daughter and said, "You have to go back in any way, and all nanoprobes must be removed from your body." He motioned his daughter toward the machine.

Elle stopped and turned to her mother. "Now what do I do about Paine?"

"You need to decide soon. The UN shuttle is scheduled to depart in fifteen minutes and we take off in twenty." Betty said.

William opened the meditube door once more and told his daughter to get inside. He adjusted the settings to eliminate all nanoprobes from her system. As he closed the door, he looked at her and said, "You have the next three minutes to think about it, and then you have to either go to Paine or stay with us."

He turned to Betty as the meditube drained the nanoprobes from Elle's blood. William picked up the vial of blood now full of nanoprobes and slipped it into his pocket.

Elle stepped out of the tube and said, "I made up my mind. I have to go to Paine." She hugged both of her parents and said, "I will see you both as soon as I can get to New York." She turned and headed for the international terminal.

As Elle walked away, William patted his pocket and said, "We have to keep these on the shuttle or they will track her down in Paris." Betty hugged her husband, then got into the meditube and closed the door.

The chief investigator scanned the shuttle leaving for New York and read the screen. He actuated the send button and flashed a message to an unlisted computer. "Parents and daughter are on board flight 45089. Transponder signal is 385.97. They were positively identified via nanoprobe signals. You may go ahead as planned."

William held Betty's hand as they flew toward their destination.

Chapter 17 – Paris

Paine and Marcus walked out of the meeting room and down the hall. What they heard was unsettling. JUNGFOR was only to be a small part of the military forces being deployed to the region.

The French military was deploying units into the former country of Slovenia, just south of Klagenfurt, Germany. French settlements were being attacked by warlords operating in what had been Croatia, now part of Greater Serbia. Serbian attackers had penetrated far in to the northern Italian peninsula which was now a part of France.

When asked about the rules of engagement, the French commander had emphatically stated that they were not there under United Nations rules of engagement; they were there to protect French interests and population and would do whatever needed to be done to accomplish that mission.

Polish troops were sent to the border of Serbia and the Polish state of Slovakia. Their orders were to patrol the boundary between the two countries and stop anyone from crossing the border into Polish lands. Their government directed them to use whatever force necessary to stop the raiding.

Ukraine also deployed its military forces. Units moved to its border with Serbia, near the Danube Delta south of Odessa. There were reports of sporadic fighting in that area every week.

JUNGFOR was the only authorized United Nations force deployed to help stop the violence. Stationed in Plzen, it was expected to operate within a five hundred-mile radius and come to the aid of anyone attacked by paramilitary forces. Paine could not have envisioned this when he signed up for the United Nations military.

"How in hell do they think we will do any good?" Paine said to Marcus as left the meeting. "I think Jung's plan is to have us be the fire brigade. He wants us to be ready to deploy to stop the other military forces from doing something that could start a general war." Paine and Marcus saluted a passing French general as they walked to a waiting lifter. "I don't see how that can help.

We can't get there in time to stop any confrontation between Serbs and anyone else."

They entered the lifter and fastened their seatbelts as the pilot started the engines. As soon as she saw that her passengers safely secured themselves, she took off and headed for the battalion headquarters location.

Marcus leaned over to Paine and said, "Not only that, but we are under such a restrictive ROE that we have to lose people to enemy fire before we can respond, and then only if we get permission from the headquarters." He shook his head in disgust. "We better impress that on our people. If we kill any of the Serbs without them shooting one of us first we may be in for a rough time."

Paine looked at his friend and Command Sergeant Major and wondered if he had made a mistake that could cost them both their lives.

"Marcus, if you want to back out of this, I will understand." Paine held up his hand as Marcus started to respond. "Hear me out. I got you into this, and I feel badly about it. I thought we would do a good thing for humanity when I agreed to take this job." Paine looked sad as he said, "I didn't realize what a sloppy mess we were stepping into."

Marcus leaned back into the nylon webbing of the seat and shook his head.

"Paine, you really think you had to talk me into this? I would go through the fires of Hell for you, and so would most of the people in the unit. You are my brother; you told me that once when I was confused about who I was. You made me realize that brothers stick together, no matter what." He reached out and put his massive arm on Paine's shoulder. "You want to do good, and will do good for the people of the United Nations, even if others don't think the same way."

Paine looked at his friend's scarred face and remembered all the things they had been through together. He really did love Marcus as a brother and knew that they would always have each other's back.

"The good news is, with the five-hundred mile limit on our area of operations, we won't have to face any Ukrainian troops," Paine said. "That might have been a problem for the XO." He could see Major Kompaniyets, his executive officer, standing in front of the unit for the morning formation.

Taller than Marcus, muscular and a stickler for details; Kompaniyets had already caused Paine a few problems. He was ten years older than Paine and did not hide the fact that he thought he was more experienced and would be a better commander. He insisted that United Nations Regulations be followed to the letter and insisted that Ukrainian regulations be used to decide disciplinary issues. Paine believed the regulations were too harsh and often suspended punishment to give the soldiers a chance to redeem themselves. Those who did straighten up were never punished for the first offense, but those who messed up again got double the punishment. That made Paine popular with the troops, but irritated Kompaniyets.

Kompaniyets made it clear after their first discussion that he would argue to the point of decision and then follow Paine's orders exactly. He would not sabotage the unit, but would only do what he was told to do if he disagreed with the orders.

United Nations personnel regulations did not allow Paine to ask for a replacement. The assignment was for two years, and Paine knew it would be a long tour of duty.

Marcus flashed Paine a broken-toothed grin. "Hey, at least we got the ops officer on our side."

Rachel Miller had been the adjutant of the Kentucky Regulars, then the unit's operations officer at the time of the UN takeover. Marcus had saved her from the nuclear explosion that destroyed the United Nations Building, and she had helped him get the delegates and ambassadors out before the blast. Paine remembered her as being a very good officer and offered to take her on as his operations officer. She had always liked and respected Paine; she readily agreed. Rachel was even better than Paine remembered and was instrumental in training the unit for this deployment.

"Send a copy of the ROE to Rachel and have her set up classes for tomorrow. We are operational in five days, and I want all our troops to understand the rules before we set foot on hostile soil." Paine tilted his head as his communicator chime sounded. "It's Trisha. I better take this. She hasn't gotten back to me about picking up Elle at Dallas yet." He answered the call, "Colonel Paine."

Trisha's voice was stern as it came over the airwaves. "Colonel Martin, I have someone who wants to talk to you. Please hold."

There was a momentary pause, and then Elle's voice came through the ear bug.

"Michael, both of my parents are dead!" She cried uncontrollably, and the call abruptly ended.

Paine sat there in shock for a moment. Marcus could see something was wrong and opened his mouth to speak when the chime went off again. Paine, still reeling from Elle's message, answered the call with a shouted, "What!"

Trisha, Paine's adjutant and long-time friend, came on the channel. "Paine, listen. I have Elle with me here and she is devastated. I had to give her a sedative. She should be OK for a while, but this really hit her hard."

Paine asked, "Just what in Hell happened?"

Trisha took a deep breath to settle her own nerves and began. "The shuttle carrying the Whippettes, which, by the way, Elle said she was supposed to on, ran into a piece of space debris and was completely destroyed. There were no survivors. Hold on," She stopped for a moment as she looked at the news feed coming into her communicator. "The update says it a crew member of a sweeper craft responsible for clearing out the space lanes went off his rocker and destroyed the craft. The shuttle was 300 kilometers off-course when the collision occurred." Trisha waited as she watched the news feed provided more information and then continued. "United Nations Space Police are on the way to the capsule to find out what happened. No communications have been established with the crew, but indications are that there was a massive decompression in the capsule seconds after the shuttle was destroyed."

Trisha paused to read the updated report. "Now the news is that the police can see the capsule airlock is open. I will keep you posted, but you better get here quickly. I will take Elle to your room and stay with her until you get there." There was a brief silence on the line and then Paine heard a strained, "Trisha out," from his adjutant.

Paine tapped the pilot on the shoulder to get her attention and said, "Take us back to Paris."

Chapter 18 - Josh Escapes

Josh Martin sat back in his command chair and watched the piece of space junk Steven Corvis had provided him hurtling toward the oncoming shuttle. Josh could almost see the face of the pilot as the alarms went off, signaling imminent collision with a foreign object. He felt nothing as he played the scenario out in his mind, the pilot trying to adjust his flight path, watching the junk match his course, the frantic distress call ending as the two objects met with a combined speed of over fifty thousand kilometers per hour. He watched dispassionately as both objects disintegrated.

Josh was already in his vacuum suit. He downloaded the message he'd prepared and waited, watching the display for the space police shuttle that would come soon. Once the police craft began its approach, he sealed the helmet. Attaching the tether to an anchor point in the wall, he cut the gravity generator and hit the emergency override switch that opened the hatch.

Josh flew to the end of the tether as the escaping air pushed him out of the airlock. He floated in weightlessness. Careful not to lose contact with the ship, he activated his magnetic boots and floated back to the outside of the capsule. After detaching the tether, he walked out onto the hull of the vessel to the black U of the UN etched into the side of the white spacecraft, and then lay down in its center, his white space suit blending into the hull of the ship. He reattached the tether to a portable magnetic anchor he had earlier placed on the skin of the capsule and settled down to wait for the police shuttle to arrive.

Josh calculated that he had about ten hours of oxygen if he breathed normally. He didn't think that would be enough, so he dialed down the regulator to deliver what an average person would breathe at ten thousand feet. He knew he could live on that and calculated that his air would last for maybe an extra hour.

Josh's suit stayed connected to the ship's computer so he could hear the proximity chime coming through the speakers in his helmet. He turned his head to put his face-plate away from the oncoming police shuttle and waited.

"Control, this is shuttle two thirteen approaching the sweeper." The pilot's voice rang out in the speakers. "The hatch is open, looks like we have a possible jumper. Scanning the area for any floating bodies or suits." The air waves were silent for a few minutes, and then the pilot's voice again rang out. "Negative on either one. Looks like whoever this was is floating back to Earth."

Josh was thinking this just might work. If the pilot would just get moving, he might have a chance.

"Firing tether." The spacecraft shuddered as the magnetic anchor hit the side of the ship. "Closing to within one meter, preparing to enter capsule."

Josh understood his only chance of being undetected was to move from his hiding place at the same time the policemen were entering the capsule. He unsnapped the tether and prepared to launch himself at the police shuttle.

"Entering now, no sign of either occupant."

Josh saw a small access port opening on the top side of the police shuttle. He had one chance to make it. If he missed, he would die floating in space, and become a brief flash of light in the sky as his dead body entered the atmosphere. He disengaged the anchor and used one finger to launch himself toward the police craft.

As he drifted toward the open hatch, he listened to the police report.

"Looks like we were right; there were two occupants, and one suit is missing. There seems to be a report on the console. Downloading now."

Josh was closing on the port as he reviewed the letter he'd written in his mind.

Dear Bethany,

Such a beautiful sight, Earth. I miss being home, and I know you and children miss seeing me. I need to get home soon because it's our son's birthday tomorrow. Jonathon doesn't care that we are missing our families. I hate his guts. I am sorry that he is no longer here. I sent him home first. It took all my strength to get him into that suit, and he protested a long time that he didn't want to go, but I helped him go home, don't you see? He has been gone long enough to be home by now, so now it's my turn. I just need to clean up this big piece of junk coming at me, and then I can go home, too. I love you guys and will be flying home to you soon.

"Nothing more we can do here. Returning to the shuttle and heading back to base." The two police officers exited the capsule just as Josh caught the edge of the hatch and pulled himself inside. There was a seat complete with shock harness fitted into the cargo port. He maneuvered himself into position as the seat activated, capturing him and holding him tightly in place with the harness. Josh reached down and pressed a blinking button and the hatch closed and locked it in place.

The shuttle's gravitational system came on as Josh thought, "So far, so good." He didn't feel the tiny needle go through the back of his suit and inject him. The suit automatically repaired the pin hole as the needle retracted.

Chapter 19 – Anguish

Paine and Marcus asked for and received permission to fly straight to the front door of the French Officer's Club. Their lifter landed in the middle of the street. Paine leapt out and with Marcus on his heels ran into the building. Trisha was at the front desk, trying to get the French soldier working there to understand she did not want the woman in room 603 to be disturbed.

"Trisha, how is she?" Paine asked.

"Not good. I understand what she is going through after watching my brother die in that bordello in San Francisco." Trisha had been a sex slave for six years before being saved by the Kentucky Regulars. She owed her life to Marcus and had been working for Paine for the last four years. She liked and respected her leader.

"I had to sedate her pretty heavily; she was coming apart at the seams and was threatening to do something drastic." Trisha recognized the signs of potential suicide; she'd been in that place several times in her life.

"Can you take me to her?" Paine asked.

"Follow me." Trisha led Paine up to the bank of elevators and ushered him into the express elevator.

Marcus called out from the lobby, "Let me know if there is anything I can do."

Paine reached out and stopped the door from closing. "There is something you can do. Find out what capsule caused the collision. I need the number of the ship as soon as possible."

As the door shut, Paine made a call to his mother's private line. When she did not answer, he left a message. "Mom, I am sure you heard about the Whippette's shuttle being destroyed. I am sorry for our friends and for your loss. You need to interview the UN police who investigated the capsule. It may be very important that we do that." Paine paused for a moment and then said something that made Trisha wonder if he was losing it. "I also heard Elle was on the shuttle." Paine's voice cracked as he finished the message with, "I love you mother. Make sure you and Carole stay safe."

Trisha started to ask Paine a question, but he flashed, "Not now" in patrol sign. He pointed at the camera in the corner of the elevator and tried to prepare himself to see Elle.

As the elevator doors opened, they were met by a rather strange sight. Elle was standing in the hallway in her nightgown, slowly swaying to back and forth. She did not appear to notice them as Trisha and Paine stepped out.

"Maybe I should talk to her first." Trisha said. She moved to Elle's side and took her arm.

Recognition appeared in Elle's eyes as she looked at Trisha's blond hair and stroked it. She cried out, "Mother, I've missed you so much." Elle threw her arms around Trisha, who hesitated and then returned the hug as she looked over Elle's shoulder at Paine.

Paine mouthed, "Her mother hand blond hair, too."

Trisha pushed Elle to arm's length, looked into her eyes and said, "Honey, Paine is here to help you. You remember Paine, don't you?"

Elle turned to Paine and stared at him for a full minute, then said in a little girl voice, "No, I don't think so. That is a funny name, Paine. Is it your real name?"

Paine, who had started toward Elle, stopped himself from taking her in his arms.

"That's my real name." Paine said.

"Well, I think it's a silly name," Elle said and turned back to Trisha. "Momma, can I go to my room, now? I am really tired and my tummy doesn't feel well."

Paine watched as they walked hand-in hand down the hall to his room and wondered how long Elle would be in this condition. Trisha stopped as Elle turned in the hall in front of the suite Paine had reserved for them and waved at him, then followed her inside and closed the door.

A few hours later, Trisha called Paine. "I gave her a pill to calm her. She has finally gone to sleep. I'm not sure how long this will last, but I've seen it many times. She may come out of it; she may never recover. The only thing we can do now is wait."

Paine asked, "Do you think you can leave her alone for a little while? We have a staff meeting to go over our training for the next three days and we have to be ready to move at a moment's notice starting Sunday."

Trisha looked at the sleeping Elle and said, "I believe she will be all right alone. She is out cold right now." She walked over to the young woman and brushed her hair. "You poor thing; I know just how you feel." Pulling the covers up to her shoulder, she turned and left the room, locking the door behind her.

As soon as the door clicked into place, Elle got out of the bed. She threw the pill she'd spit into her hand into the sink and flushed it down the drain by turning on the water. She walked over and activated the security lock. Then Elle moved to the desk and called up every news report possible on her parent's shuttle disaster.

Chapter 20 – Move to Plzen

Marcus knocked on the door to room 600.

"Come in." Paine was sitting at this desk, looking at the movement orders he'd just received.

"So we have our instructions?" Marcus asked.

"Looks like we move out at 0400 tomorrow; we will be flying in by lifter. We will be keeping only a quarter of our pilots and aircraft once we arrive at our base in Plzen." Paine studied the orders once again. "We will be staying in several of the refurbished buildings in the old city, right on the square. That means no way to provide good security. It's like we're being hung out to dry!" Paine shook his head. "Why doesn't General Jung realize this as a problem?"

"Not only that, but our aerial transportation will be outside the city," Marcus said. "That means they will either have to fly in to get us, or we will have to drive out to the lifters. That limits our ability to initiate an immediate response to unfriendly actions." Marcus was figuring out travel time. "That arrangement will add thirty minutes to our reaction time, and we will only be able to respond with minimal forces. If anything happens at the maximum range of the lifters, we will be on the ground for nearly four hours before we are at half strength, and sixteen hours before the entire unit is there." He scratched his head as he did the math. "And if we lose one or two of the lifters to maintenance problems, it gets even worse."

"I have sent a request to General Jung asking that we be allowed to keep the lift capability when we arrive." Paine was not happy as he said, "I haven't heard back from him yet."

They were interrupted by another knock.

"Enter." Paine called out.

Major Rachel Miller entered the room. "Sir, do you have time to discuss the lift issue?" she said.

"We were just going over the problem with transportation. Come and join the meeting. I want to hear your thoughts." Paine waved her over to the desk.

"I think we may have a solution, but it may not be what you want." Rachel moved to the side of the desk and laid out a paper.

Rachel produced a movement plan that calculated times for a five-hundred-kilometer trip. "See, we can send in the first troops by lifter. I would recommend that your old scout platoon and A Company under Captain Curtis be air lifted to whatever hot spot we are ordered to secure." She pointed out the ratings of A Company and continued. "Chris has done the best possible job getting his troops ready. They are the best-trained company in the battalion, and their marksmanship and maintenance scores are way above every other unit, except the scouts."

Paine had trained the scout platoon himself; they were the finest soldiers the Kentucky Regulars had. They'd volunteered to a man to come with Paine when he joined the United Nations Forces. Paine hand-picked the fourteen replacements he had to make from the veterans Trisha had managed to get into the battalion. He knew what they were capable of, and they had the combat power of both C Company and D Company combined.

"Anyway, we can lift the scouts and A Company, then have B and D companies move by road to back you up. They can get close enough to be in a position to help if needed. C Company will be brought in by our lifters from Plzen." Rachel stood straight and looked at both Marcus and Paine. "We can then use the lifters to move the other two companies from wherever they are along the route to the battalion's location."

"Have you figured the total time it will take to be at full strength?" Marcus asked.

"I estimate no more than five hours, assuming we launch the ground convoy the same time as the lifters." Rachel shook her head. "The biggest problem I foresee is the weather. It's already begun to snow in the higher elevations, and if we get a heavy snowfall, it will slow down the ground convoy. It's not perfect, but it's the best we can do with what they've given us to work with."

"Fine," Paine said to Rachel. "Develop a briefing for company commanders and have it ready as soon as we arrive in Plzen. We leave in one hour; you can put it together on the flight in." Paine returned Rachel's salute and watched her walk out the door.

"She is one smart staff officer. We are lucky to have her." Marcus stated the obvious.

Paine was looking at his hands, wondering what was going to happen next.

"Marcus, do you know when Katrina is supposed to arrive?" he asked.

"She should be landing in the next five minutes. Trisha flew to the space port to get her and is bringing her here." He smiled as he thought of her arrival, but was sad he would only see her for a few minutes before he had to leave. "A soldier's life is not an easy one, that's for sure!"

Paine stood up and straightened his uniform. "I suppose I better go see how Elle is doing."

He walked to the door across the hall and knocked. There was no answer. He knocked again and heard movement in the room. He was about to use his key to enter the room when the door opened and a pale, disheveled Elle answered the knock.

She walked away from the door in a stupor and fell back into the unmade bed. Untouched trays of food were stacked on the bedside table. Elle pulled the covers up and curled herself into a ball.

Paine made his way into the room, careful not to make any noise or disturb Elle. He walked over to the bed and reached out to touch her. She did not respond to the gentle hand he laid on her shoulder.

"Honey, I have to go away for a while." Paine said as he tried to get through to the tortured woman on the bed. "I have your friend coming to stay with you. Katrina should be here soon. She has promised to look after you while I am gone."

Elle did not say anything as Paine leaned down and softly kissed her hair. She waited until the door closed, then got up, re-locked the door and went back to the computer.

Chapter 21 – Elle and Katrina

Katrina had taken the first shuttle from New York to Paris as soon as Marcus called. The flight was delayed due to increased security after the Whippettes shuttle disaster. If Trisha hadn't been there to rush her through customs, she would still be in the Paris Space Port. Trisha got her to the hotel just in time to see Marcus loading his gear into the lifter parked in the Place de Saint Augustine. Katrina rushed over as Marcus was climbing in, jumped into his arms and gave him a quick hug, followed by a long kiss which generated a brief round of applause and cheering from the nearby soldiers until Marcus managed to pull away from Katrina to glare at them. Katrina took his massive head in her hands and pulled him to her, gave him one last kiss and then watched as Trisha and the rest of the staff climbed aboard the lifters and they flew away.

The concierge was waiting for Katrina when she walked in.

"You must be the guest for room 603." He took her bag and called for a bellhop. "Take this young lady to join her friend on the sixth floor."

Katrina was silent as she rode the elevator to the fourth floor and then followed the bellhop down the hall. When they got to the room, Katrina handed him a tip and said, "I can take it from here. Just give me the key."

She waited until he entered the elevator to put the keycard in the door. The security lock was on, but that was no match for a former thief like Katrina. She bypassed the system and quietly opened the door. She was surprised at what she found.

Elle did not hear the door open. She was staring intently at the monitor of the computer on the desk. Katrina softly moved up to a position behind her and read the screen over Elle's shoulder.

The news feed headline read, "Jillian Corvis to attend fund raiser at Paris Opera House."

Elle was talking to herself. "One today, four more to go." She jumped when Katrina touched her shoulder and spun the chair around to face her.

Katrina looked at the knife that seemed to appear in her hand and grinned at Elle. "Sorry, my reflexes are something I can't always control. Do you mind telling me what is going on?" She casually stuck the knife back into her purse. "Marcus made it sound like you were a nut-case. Trisha tried to fill me in as we flew here from the space port. I fully expected to see you hanging from a rope, the way they talked."

Wild-eyed, Elle jumped to her feet. She began to pull her hair and gibber like a madwoman until Katrina hit her across the face, lightly, with her open hand. "Cut it out and tell me what is going on or so help me I will slap you harder!"

Elle grabbed a piece of paper off the desk and feverishly wrote, "Have you had any meditube procedures in the past six months?" She practically threw it at Katrina.

Katrina read it and looked surprised. She said, "Are you crazy? I hate those things. They give me the creeps." She shuddered as she remembered Dr. Engle and the deaths of the people who'd surrounded her in the United Nations cleansing operation.

Elle ran her fingers through her tousled hair and sighed. "I have to ask. Corvis has found a way to record conversations using nanoprobes. That is what my parents found out." Her voice caught in her throat. "And that is why they were killed. I was supposed to be on the flight with them but came here instead." Elle looked at Katrina in horror and said, "I'm sorry, but if anyone finds out that you know the truth, you will be a target, too."

Katrina laughed. "I have been under a death sentence my whole life. I just wake up every day glad to still be walking around. Dying doesn't scare me; it's living that's hard."

Elle sat down on the edge of the bed. "I agree; living is hard." She looked at Katrina and reached out for her hand. "I want to die."

Katrina came over and put both of her hands around Elle's and looked deep into her eyes. "Think more about life than death."

"I am. That is why I am still here." Elle paused. "You see, I'm pregnant."

Katrina blurted out, "Is it Paine's?"

"Of course, but he doesn't know it yet. I wanted to see what he thought about being a father. If he hates the idea of children, I can go away before he finds out and have it and raise it on my own. I owe that much to the child and to my parents. I have to keep up this act or Paine will want me to go out somewhere with him, which will make him a target, too." Elle's eyes got hard. "And I have unfinished work to do."

"Does it have to do with the Corvis Foundation matriarch, or are you just looking to attend a fund raiser for orphans in Southern Spain?" Katrina asked.

Elle's eyes filled with tears as she said, "You wouldn't understand. My parents told me a secret that got them killed. They wanted to stop Corvis. And I have to finish what they started and take revenge on those who killed them."

Katrina bristled and snapped out, "You think I do not understand? Remember the story I said could wait? Well, listen to it now. Marcus brought me the snake that killed my brother and a lot of other innocent people. It took me a while to figure out what to do, but I got my revenge. I know what it's like to lose someone you love, and what it's like to watch them die." She walked close to Elle, reached up and wiped away the tear that was hanging from her eyelid. That brought on an avalanche of tears streaming down Elle's face.

Katrina put her arms around Elle and said, "It wasn't as satisfying as I had hoped, but at least I got to watch that bastard suffer for a long time. Your secret is safe with me. I will do whatever I can to help you."

Elle's voice was quivering as she answered, "Thank you, Katrina. You are a true friend." She shrugged out of Katrina's grasp, wiped her tears, and said, "But you don't get to kill anyone on my list. They are all mine."

Katrina's eyes narrowed to mere slits as she remembered Marcus bringing Engle to her. She would never have forgiven him if he'd deprived her of seeing Engle die. She hissed through clenched teeth. "Agreed! But that doesn't mean I can't help. So what can I do?"

Elle and Katrina discussed the plan until early evening and then got ready for the first revenge.

Later that evening, the manager came to room 306 and knocked softly at the door. The waiter behind him had a cart full of food that Katrina had ordered.

Katrina waved them into the room with her fingers to her lips. She whispered, "Just wheel it over here, if you please. And could you remove the uneaten food, please?" As the waiter piled the dishes on the cart and moved it out of the room, the manager glanced at the still form lying under the covers. Poor girl, he thought.

"She will be all right?" he asked.

Katrina looked at the bed and said, "I hope she will be better soon."

Elle, heavily made up and dressed in an elegant gown, walked down a hallway in the Paris Opera House and turned into the front left balcony. She listened to the music for a short while, wondering if she had it in her to do what she planned. She leaned against the wall for a moment, then steeled herself and stepped forward, thrusting the push knife Katrina had lent her into the back of Jillian Corvis' neck, straight into the medulla oblongata. Jillian slumped in her chair. Elle wiped the blood off her hand and dropped the cloth on the floor in the darkened hallway. She calmly left the balcony area and headed for the exit.

An alarm sounded in the Opera house as she was walking back to the French Officers Club. Elle turned and watched the emergency vehicles rush through the street to the scene of the crime. She continued on her way, and as she neared the front door of the Officer's Hotel, Katrina waved her into the shadows.

Elle stripped off the dress, used it to wipe the bloody knife clean and dropped the soiled gown down into the open sewer. She then let Katrina pick her up and carry her up the outside of the building back to room 603. As they closed the window behind them, Elle handed the push knife to Katrina.

"Thank you," Elle yawned. "I think I better go to sleep. We have to go to the Czech part of Germany tomorrow to see our men."

Elle dropped exhausted on the bed and was soon breathing deeply. Katrina opened the computer console and looked at the last page on the site. It was a list of all the Corvis family members, and one of them was in Plzen.

Chapter 22 – Hanger Seven

New York's Kennedy Space Port was busy. The tarmac and the runway that had been damaged in the Colonel Flagehty's assault had been repaired, and a new tower had been erected. The Technos had established the temporary space port at the old airfield and were working on developing a landing system for globes in New York Harbor. The plan was to have the ships splash down and be towed to the loading docks. With the increase in asteroid mining, the need for a port able to handle the half-mile diameter globes was growing every day. Shuttles were used to ferry down much smaller quantities of metals to feed the manufacturing plants on the Earth's surface. It wasn't cost effective, and the first space port to develop a better system would make a lot of money.

Josh was gasping for air as the UN Space Police shuttle finally coasted to touchdown. As the shuttle roll to a halt, he opened his visor and breathed in the cool air. He had forgotten how sweet fresh air was after living with recycled air for so long. He could taste the salt and smell the fumes from vehicles scurrying about moving space-produced goods to waiting businesses. He could feel the pull of real gravity and flexed his muscles. He knew it would take time for his full strength returned, but he had religiously used the exercise equipment on the shuttle and had not lost much of his impressive physique.

He could hear the police officers walking away from the shuttle. His helmet speakers came alive.

"General Martin, please stay where you are until you are told to move." Steven Corvis' voice rang in his ears. "I have taken the liberty of remotely locking the hatch which means if you do decide to leave you will make a lot of noise and be discovered." He paused for a moment. "We do not want that, now, do we?"

Josh grated his teeth so loudly Steven could hear the grinding sound in his speakers.

"Why must I wait?" Josh asked.

"Because, my difficult friend, you need to be taught to listen to me. I will not have you do anything that I do not condone. And believe me, I know everything that you have done and will know everything that you do." Steven laughed. "I found you when everyone else thought you were dead. I have brought you back to life, and I can just as easily end that life."

There was suddenly a crushing pressure in his chest and Josh could not catch his breath. He began to see stars.

"You see, even from my office in California, I can reach out and touch you. The pain should get less intense now." Steven tapped a few icons on his computer screen and said, "Just like poor Bob Brown, and the delegates you had killed during your brief, but rather exciting UN takeover, you have been infected. And I control the switch. Cross me again, and I will end your miserable existence."

Josh would do what Corvis wanted until his personal scores had been settled; after that, he didn't care if he lived or died. "Fine, I will sit quietly. But you may want to release me sooner rather than later because my suit's about full of secretions and excretions and I may stink so much they can find me by smell."

"No more than two hours, I promise. It will take that long to clear the hanger and get you decent transportation to the city. I hope you remember how to disappear into the woodwork because I fear your ex-wife may begin looking for you soon. While you wait, is there anything else you want?"

Josh had been planning a return to Earth for a long time and knew who would help him. "I need to contact my cousin, Albert Martin. He has to be at least forty by now. Arrange to have him called as soon as I get free. He owes me a lot of favors, and he may in a position to help both of us."

"Locating," Steven asked his computer to find Albert. "He is serving as a private soldier in the United Nations Forces in Plzen, Germany. He is assigned as a member of a squad in the Special Forces Battalion." Steven paused and then said, "Very interesting, his battalion is under the command of your son. Looks like you were right, he may be an asset. Let me know when you want to talk to him."

"Since I have nothing better to do for the next two hours, how about now?" Josh asked.

"I really don't want to hear what you are planning, because I may not approve. Besides, I will have plausible deniability this way. Give me a few minutes to set up a secure patch and I will leave you to your plans." Steven paused again. "Don't forget, I can always find you and kill you. Your ride will be there in one hour and forty minutes. Three knocks on the hatch, then one. Then you can enjoy your freedom and do what you will with your family. I know how difficult families can be." The communications link shifted from Corvis to Albert Martin.

Of course, Steven Corvis had the communications monitored and recorded for future reference. Corvis had no intention of letting Josh do whatever he wanted to do and already had a plan in place to undo the damage Josh had done. The world would be his in spite of General Martin.

Chapter 23 – Albert

Albert Martin was on the advanced party to Plzen. His first sergeant had asked for volunteers to do the heavy lifting, moving the office equipment that would be used by the headquarters staff in the new location. When he didn't get enough soldiers to offer to come, he called out Albert's name. Albert had been trying to hide in the back rank. He liked Paris. He had already found a sufficiently beautiful girl and had been following her every move for the past week. Now he would have to start all over again.

Albert sat in a metal chair outside a bistro in Plzen, sipping on what had to be the finest beer he had ever tasted. He watched as another unaccompanied good-looking woman slowly walked past. He thought that being on the advanced party for the battalion wasn't so bad after all.

Suddenly, the communication's device he was required to carry signaled an incoming call. He prayed it wasn't an alert; he just wanted to get close to that gorgeous woman.

"Private Martin," he answered.

A familiar voice came across the air waves. It sarcastically repeated, "Private Martin. You are still a private after all these years? I wonder if it's because you are basically worthless!"

A wave of nausea hit Albert, and he almost threw up. He swallowed several times and tried to keep his composure. He recognized the voice of a dead man, his first cousin, Josh.

"General Martin," he began.

"Shut your mouth. This is a secure communication but I don't know if anyone where you are may be listening." Josh snapped. "Do not use my name again; just listen and talk only when I tell you."

Albert immediately became silent.

"I don't need to remind you that the things I managed to keep secret for you will get you killed." Josh said.

Albert thought about the time he went to his cousin when Josh was commanding the Kentucky Regulars. Most of the Martin family had signed on with Josh when he established the mercenary group. They feared Josh, but respected his abilities and knew he would do whatever he could to protect them.

Albert had been a holdout. He lived in the compound because he was a family member, but never joined the force. Then one day he went to Josh's office. Albert begged Josh to let him join and send him far away on any mission that would get him out of the state. Josh noticed the blood under his fingernails and pressed Albert for details. Albert remembered the conversation as if it happened this morning.

"I need to be gone, far from here." Albert said.

"You need to tell me why, or I will call my guards and have them extract the truth," Josh said.

Albert knew from painful experience what Josh was capable of; he'd seen the results of retaliatory attacks against rival groups and did not want to end up like those who crossed the Regulars.

"I have a problem." Josh made a come on gesture with his hands, and Albert started to speak very quickly.

"My cousin, our cousin, Mirabelle, she comes over to help Ma with Big Al, ever since he had that stroke. She been flitting around the house for a long time, always wearing those tight shirts and short skirts, running around barefoot. Well, yesterday, she came over to me and bent over right in front of my face while I was sitting there on the couch not doing nothing. She was just teasing with me, but I wanted to teach her a lesson. When she went to go home, I followed her and caught up with her near the creek behind the house. I tried to hug her, but she slapped me." Albert looked down at his feet. "I can't stand being slapped. I might have punched her a little too hard, and she fell down in the creek. I guess I just went mad, all I could see as red. When I finally come to my senses, she was there, naked and bleeding. I had blood all over me, too. I don't know what happened."

Josh showed no emotion as he asked, "Then what?"

"She was crying and trying to gather her clothes so she could get dressed. She was saying how she was going to tell her Daddy and brothers and how they were going to come and kill me." Albert looked at his bloody nails then stared into Josh's cold eyes. Josh could see the emptiness, the lack of emotion as Albert said, "When she climbed the bank of the creek, she slipped and fell into the water." He took a deep breath. "I hit her with a rock and then held her down until she quit moving."

Josh didn't care about the death of his cousin. "All right, I will have my personal guards take care of the body. You can join the Regulars, and I will make sure none of this gets out. There are a group of squatters over in Cave City we can blame this on, and I want you to be in the unit that goes after them. Say you joined the Regulars to avenge Mirabelle's death, since everyone knows how fond you were of our dear cousin."

Albert winced at the last comment. He mumbled his thanks and stood up to leave.

Josh barked, "Sit back down, I am not through with your yet!"

Frightened, Albert plopped back into his seat.

"You will do whatever I want you to, no matter the consequences, no matter the circumstances. Do you understand?" Josh said in a cold, hard voice.

"Of course, I will. I promise." Albert was then dismissed.

Albert had a rather uneventful year with the Regulars. Although other recruits were advancing quickly through the ranks, he was still a private when he was called to Colonel Martin's office.

Josh waved Albert into the chair and leaned back in his own seat. "I have something for you to do. It involves my son, your cousin, Adam." Josh paused for effect. "Adam is planning to escape with Ashley. They have been secretly stockpiling food for more than a month. I tried to have this cleaned up before now, but his brother Michael is always there, watching his back. I had it set up so Adam would die in the last attack, but Michael shot the assassin before he could get the job done. In all the confusion, I convinced Michael that he had shot Adam and separated them. I think I can still control Michael, but Adam is beyond hope. Ashley has infected his thinking. With Michael assigned to a different squad, I want you to partner with Adam."

"What do you want me to do?" Albert asked.

"When the time is right, do what you did to Mirabelle. Killing family is what you seem to be good at." Josh turned back to his paperwork.

"But what about Ashley?" Albert asked. He had always had feelings toward Ashley; she was quite a beauty. Maybe Josh would let him...

His thoughts were interrupted when Josh interjected, "Not yet. If it comes to that, I will let you have Ashley, too. She won't suspect anything. I plan on getting roaring drunk after the death to convince her that I grieve our loss, too." Josh glared at Albert. "Make sure it's lethal. The meditube technology is too good and it would be very bad for you if Adam survives."

Albert thought about the look on Adam's face when he put six rounds through his combat vest and into his chest. Albert stood over his cousin until he was sure he had drawn his last breath and then cried out for a medic. The medic looked up at Albert and shook his head. It was too late.

Albert shuddered as he tried to rid his mind of the memories and turned his attention back to Josh. "What must I do now?" he asked.

"If Marcus is still babysitting your commander, I want him out of the picture. He is always there to watch Michael's back, and I need him to be gone so I can deal with my son," Josh said.

"You mean the command sergeant major?" Albert had a run in with Marcus once, a little barracks brawl when Marcus first arrived in the unit. Albert, the barracks bully, tried to jump Marcus from behind and beat him, just to show him who had control of the quarters after lights out. It didn't work out like Albert planned; he required a quick trip to the meditube for repairs to his broken ribs and nose. Albert was scared to death of Marcus and had steered clear of him.

"He will not suspect you. He knows what a coward you are." Josh's words stung Albert's pride.

Changing the subject, Albert asked, "By out of the picture, do you mean like Adam?"

"Of course, but wait until you can do it without being caught," Josh said. "And if you are caught, it will be completely on you. Mirabelle's two younger brothers are still mourning their sister after all these years," Josh said as the communications ended.

Chapter 24 – Goodbye Paris

Katrina walked up to the desk clerk and plopped her credit disk into the machine.

"Checking out, Mademoiselle?" he asked, smiling at the exotically beautiful young girl.

Katrina flashed her best smile at him and said, "Yes, could you please call a cab for my friend and me? We are going to the space port and flying back to New York." She pointed at the woman with the shawl and dark glasses sitting in the lobby. "My friend does not want to take the Metro. She has had a rough few days and wants to avoid the crowds."

"But of course." The clerk smiled and called the taxi company. As soon as the cab arrived, the clerk had the bellmen load the luggage into the cab and waved them goodbye. He then went into the lobby and called the number he had been given and said, "They are on the way to the space port for a New York flight. They should be arriving in about twenty minutes."

As the cabbie pulled away from the hotel, Katrina leaned over the backseat and said, "Slight change of plans. Drive us to the Gare de l'Est."

The cabbie took them to the East train station in Paris, just a few blocks away from the hotel. "This should give us time to disappear. The trip to the Charles de Gaulle Space Port is at least thirty-five minutes. We should be on our way to Germany by the time anyone who might be looking for us finds out we aren't going to fly." Katrina touched Elle's hand and said, "Are you sure you want to go to Paine?"

"Absolutely, but remember, I am still going to be mentally unbalanced. It's the only way I can keep him safe." Elle closed her eyes and reviewed the events of last night. She somehow did not feel the satisfaction she thought she would, but was as determined as ever to avenge her parents and her unborn sibling.

Katrina waved down a porter and got the bags loaded onto the train, with Elle following behind her. Once they were settled in first class, Elle put her head in Katrina's lap and pretended to sleep. The conductor asked if they were all right and Katrina simply nodded, pointing at Elle and then putting her finger to her temple and shaking her head.

Chapter 25 – Discovery

Ashley called Paine as soon as she got his message.

"Paine, Michael, son, whatever. What is going on?" Ashley was flustered after hearing Paine's recorded message.

"Mother, I need you to go to secure alpha two-two now!" Paine's voice cracked over the air.

"Stand by." Ashley took a scrambler out of her pocket and attached it to the communication's device she was using. She put in the combination and pressed the actuate button. She shook her head as the ear bug squealed. It finally stopped and the air waves were clear. "Ready."

Paine was calm as he reported what he knew to his mother. "The Whippettes shuttle has been destroyed. News reports also say that Elle was on board."

"Oh Michael, I am sorry," Ashley said.

"She wasn't, thank God. She is with Katrina in Paris, who will try to keep her safe until this is all over." Michael said.

"Until what is all over?" Ashley asked.

"Did you find out the number of the capsule that caused the accident?" Paine asked. "I had Marcus check into it, and he couldn't find out anything."

"I am sorry, I have been in the Neo Luddite area for the past day, and have been out of contact. I only just got your message." Ashley typed in a sixteen digit security code and opened her protected file on Josh. She gasped as the number of the sweeper craft appeared, "Oh, my God! It's your father, isn't it?"

"That's what I thought," Paine said. "We may be too late. If he somehow got onto the police shuttle, he has at least an hour head start. You have to send your people over to Kennedy and stop him from escaping." Paine paused. "Give them his description and a shoot-to-kill order. If he escapes, he'll be coming for you next!"

"Hold on for a moment." Ashley changed channels and got Ryan on the other frequency. "General Flagehty, I need you to send as many troops as possible to the Kennedy Space Port. Lock it down at once. Nothing goes in or out. I will call you back shortly. Ashley out." She switched back to her son. "Paine?"

"Here, Mother," Paine answered.

"I've got General Flagehty closing down the space port. I will get the description of your father to him as soon as we are done here. What else can you tell me?" Ashley asked.

"Elle didn't get on the shuttle with William and Betty; she flew to Paris to see me." Paine took a breath. "She was crushed by the news and had to be sedated. She doesn't even recognize me. I think she will need serious psychiatric help, but I don't want anyone to find out she is alive."

Ashley could sense the anguish in her son's voice. "Because she knows something about what caused the plague would be my guess."

"Mother, I'm afraid it's more than that. I don't know what she did or what she knows, but I do think that it has put her in danger. As long as people believe she is dead, I can keep her safe, with me." Paine said. "But if father escapes, none of us are safe. He has to be in New York, and that means he will be close enough to get to you. You need to watch your back, and keep Carole safe, too."

"Paine, do you still have nanoprobes in your system?" Ashley realized they had just made a tremendous blunder.

"I did. The last time I was in the tube was after the rescue at the UN bunker. Why do you ask?" Paine said.

"This conversation is compromised." Ashley could not believe she didn't tell Paine to watch what he said; the news about the Whippettes and Josh had been too much. It was hard for her to think clearly.

"But this is a secure line," Paine said.

"It's the nanoprobes. They are listening in via the nanoprobes." Ashley sighed. "I am sorry, so, I just put you in as much danger as the rest of the family."

"Mother, I don't have any nanoprobes in my system. When Elle came to visit me last month, she told me what her parents discovered. I am sorry I couldn't tell you, but I didn't know that you were already aware of the truth. She gave me a dampening device that blocked my signal, and she told me everything. When I left to come to Paris, I had all the nanotechnology removed from my body." Paine paused. "Nothing will be discovered through me, I promise. I've lived in danger all my life. I'll be fine. Just find father and we will all be safe again." Paine thought to himself, "If you kill him this time."

Paine continued, "I have people here who will protect Elle, and I'll keep doing my job as if nothing is wrong. As soon as Katrina thinks she can be moved, I'll be bringing her to join me in Plzen. I'll keep you informed."

Paine broke the connection right before Ashley murmured, "I love you, be safe my son."

Chapter 26 – Manhunt

General Flagehty sent his alert company to Kennedy Space Port and marshaled the rest of his troops for deployment. It was a ten-minute flight to the terminal where the UN Police shuttle was parked. Command Sergeant Major Neel arrived with the unit, carrying written orders for the SUNY Space Port Police from the general.

The space port was completely locked down within twenty minutes. General Flagehty ordered a complete identification check of all passengers, crews and support personnel on the premises. The search did not turn up Josh Martin.

"General, you'd better get over to the United Nations Police hanger." Sergeant Major Neel's voice came over Ryan's personal communicator.

As Ryan entered the hanger, he could see technicians going over a vacuum suit they had found stuffed inside a small storage compartment in the shuttle. The UN Police officers were being interviewed and one of Ryan's criminal investigators from the SUNY Police Department was reviewing the black box flight recorder for evidence.

Neel walked up and saluted Ryan. "General, this is what we have so far. DNA tests confirm that it was Joshua Martin in the vacuum suit." Ryan looked shocked. He watched them take the body out of the bunker and was there for the cremation and dumping of the ashes. Neel continued. "The black box indicates a hatch breech as the shuttle crew entered the capsule. It lasted for seventy seconds, long enough for Martin to get from the capsule to the shuttle and climb into the hidden compartment. We haven't been able to track him yet, but we're still working on finding him."

"Nothing leaves this port unless it's checked by SUNY personnel!" Ryan walked out of the hanger and called Ashley with the news.

Ashley did not seem surprised to find out Josh was alive. She issued orders. "Sit on the information. No one in the press is allowed to report what is happening. Understood?"

"Yes, Ma'am," Ryan answered, and then issued orders of his own. Every vehicle was to be checked thoroughly before being allowed to leave the spaceport.

An automated trash hauler slowly wormed its way through the sewers under the space port terminal. It passed unseen under the perimeter fence and trundled toward the dump four miles away. Josh had a hard time not throwing up from the smell of the stinking refuse. But at least he was out of the spaceport.

At the dump, the trash hauler opened its doors and Josh climbed out before he was ejected by the hydraulic plate that pushed the garbage out into the landfill. He noticed a small commercial lifter ten feet away from where he was standing. As he approached the vehicle, the door opened automatically, and the engine came to life. Wiping the garbage off his jumpsuit, Josh got in as the lifter rose into the sky, heading toward the city. He tried the controls, but they were locked. Josh settled back in the seat as the lifter flew toward its destination. At least he was free.

Chapter 27 – Madness

Katrina called Marcus from the speeding train.

"Hey, honey. I decided to get Elle out of the city and come to see you," Katrina looked over at Elle, who nodded. "She was having a really hard time staying in Paris. Do you think you could find time to pick us up?"

Marcus was in the middle of a meeting with the battalion's senior noncommissioned officers. He replied, "I need to know when you're going to be getting here, so I can rearrange my schedule. And how is Elle doing?" he asked, "Paine will want to see her."

"She is sleeping. She does that a lot. I have to keep her sedated, or she begins to babble about her childhood and keeps asking where her Mom and Dad are, poor thing." Katrina looked at Elle, who indicated that was a good lie. "If the schedule is correct, and with German efficiency being what it is, we will be there in about twenty minutes."

"I won't be able to get there, but I'll call Paine and see who he can send. I can't wait to see you!" Marcus ended the call before Katrina could reply.

"That man is all business. I will be lucky if I see him today." Katrina threw her hands up in the air. "Maybe that's why I love him; he is just as focused as I am."

"Paine's the same way. He gets that look on his face and you just can't get through to him." Elle sighed. "I just hope he is too busy to spend much time with me. It's been hard keeping up this facade."

Katrina's communicator buzzed. "Hello?" she said.

"Katrina, its Paine. How is Elle and how are you doing?" he said.

"As well as could be expected; Elle is sleeping, but I could try to wake her if you want to talk to her." Elle shook her head no. "I think that may not be the best idea." Katrina waited a few seconds and then said, "Sorry, Paine, she is completely out of it. She has been having a lot trouble and needs her rest."

"That is OK; I'll see her when she gets here." Paine paused and Katrina could hear him draw a deep breath and let it out. "I sent Trisha to the train station to get you. She should be there when you arrive. I have to get back to my meeting, maybe we can all have dinner later?"

"We'll have to see how she is. See you soon." Katrina cut the connection and filled Elle in on the details. "Trisha is coming to get us. Remember, she has been through something similar herself so she may be able to spot your charade. You have to be convincing, and act like you did when she picked you up in Dallas. Do you really want me to sedate you, or can you be believable enough?"

"I can't be unaware of what is happening around me. I have to play the part as best I can and hope she doesn't see through me." Elle grabbed Katrina's hand and looked her in the eyes. "I managed to convince Trisha I was crazy before, because I was shocked and devastated by my parent's death. You may have to help me convince Trisha. That may mean physical violence."

"I'll be ready for it if it comes to that." Katrina stretched and flexed her tired muscles. "You need to be ready, too."

Trisha was waiting with two soldiers and a lifter as the train pulled into the station. She watched as Katrina practically dragged Elle from the train and then grabbed her as Elle started to wander away. Katrina shook her to get her attention. Trisha sighed; it appeared as though Elle was still in a state of shock.

"Katrina, over here," Trisha called out. She pointed out the girls' bags to the waiting soldiers, who slung their weapons over their shoulders and carried the luggage to the waiting lifter. As they were putting the bags in the cargo compartment, Trisha shook Katrina's hand.

"Good to have you here. I thought you were going to take her to New York, but I'm glad you changed your plans," Trisha looked over at Elle. "She needs to be around people she knows, so when she does come out of it, she'll have all the support she needs to deal with what happened."

Elle was standing still, staring at the ground.

Katrina said, "Come on, Elle, we have to go." She did not move until Katrina took her arm and pulled her to the waiting lifter.

The flight to the hotel was silent. Once they arrived, they landed in the square next to the gothic Cathedral of Saint Bartholomew. "I got you both rooms at the Hotel Central. It should be all right, it's the best hotel in the city." Trisha pointed at the Renaissance Town Hall, the building the German government used as their administrative offices. "Our headquarters is just across the square. The third floor has been turned over to the United Nations as a temporary headquarters. If you get a chance, come for a visit. Marcus should be out of his meeting in about an hour."

The soldiers carried the girl's bags into the hotel as Trisha walked across the square to her office.

Elle, head down and shuffling, followed Katrina to the room. She waited until the soldiers left before asking, "Is there a computer here I can use?"

Katrina pulled a tablet out of her bag and gave it to Elle.

"I have to go stretch out my legs," Katrina said. "Then I'm going to meet with Marcus." She looked at the text Marcus had sent her, "He told me he would be out of his meeting soon."

Elle started the computer and called up a search engine.

Katrina said, "Paine said he wanted us all to get together for dinner later."

Elle shook her head as she looked intently at the screen.

Katrina changed into her new clothes, remembering the shopping trip she and Elle had been on in SUNY. She thought that this woman in the room with her was significantly different than the girl who killed someone in self-defense a few short months ago. She walked over to Elle to tell her goodbye, waited for a second, and then gently squeezed her friend's shoulder and left the room.

Chapter 28 – Ambushed

The battalion had been in the new location for four days, but Albert hadn't been able to get to Marcus yet. There had been too many meetings, and Marcus was always at the headquarters. Albert was back at his place at the Bistro. He enjoyed sitting there, even though it was a little cold. He liked watching the women strolling down the street. There wasn't much foot traffic, but the sun was bright and the crisp air felt good. He sipped more beer and then noticed something that made him sit up straighter.

"My God, she is beautiful," he whispered to himself.

Katrina, newly arrived from Paris, was walking from the hotel toward the United Nations Barracks area. Albert stared as she passed. She had almond-shaped eyes and a tiny but shapely body. She was wearing a tight skirt and short leather jacket and appeared to be about twenty-five years old. Albert watched as she walked by on six-inch heels and noticed how muscular her calves looked. She looked so much like his dead cousin. He watched her walk up to the gate and talk to the sergeant of the guard. She disappeared inside the compound. Albert nursed his beer as he waited for her to reappear.

Albert looked across the square as the beautiful girl he'd seen came out of the headquarters, walking hand-in-hand with Command Sergeant Major Marcus Pace. Albert thought this was going to be the perfect mission. He would get rid of Marcus, and after killing him, enjoy the pleasure of dealing with the only witness, that wisp of a girl on his arm. He caressed the pistol he had concealed in his waistband and fantasied about what he was going to do to the girl.

Two hours later, Marcus and Katrina stepped out of the restaurant and walked arm-in-arm toward the UN compound. Marcus was deep in thought as they came out of the side street and walked into the square.

Albert was really enjoying this. He would finally get the revenge he'd always hoped for on Marcus. He pulled the pistol out of his waistband and flipped off the safety. He approached the unsuspecting couple. He thought about shooting Marcus in the back, but that wouldn't allow him to see the surprise on Marcus's face right before he died.

He called out as he extended the pistol to arms-length.

"Marcus?"

They turned around as Albert squeezed the trigger and said, "From General Martin."

Katrina's left hand struck the man's outstretched arm as the pistol fired. She continued her attack with her right hand, fingers locked as they knifed into his abdomen with enough force to break through skin and muscle and reach into his chest. His face registered shock as she clutched at his heart, pulled it out and threw it, still beating, into the dying assassin's face.

She picked up the gun and turned only to see Marcus down on the pavement in a pool of blood. Katrina kicked off her high heels, picked him up, threw him over her shoulder and ran toward the aid station two blocks away.

Marcus was drifting in and out of consciousness. Suddenly, he was five years old, standing in an alley in a pool of blood. The gang fight was raging around him as he fell down, only to be picked up by his mother. She ran with him in her arms, all the way back to the apartment where she held him close. She rocked him gently and said over and over, "Marcus, it will be all right. Don't worry, Mama is here for you. Mama is always here for you." Marcus could feel her heart pounding in his ears as she held him to her breast, but her heart started skipping beats and began to slow. When he could no longer hear her heart blackness overtook him.

Katrina saw the red cross on the third floor of the old apothecary located on the square. It had been chosen as the sight for the medical aid station for that reason. She kicked in the door and yelled at the tech.

"Open the meditube, now!" she screamed.

The tech saw a blood-covered woman carrying a large man who appeared to be dead. He slapped the emergency open on the meditube and Katrina threw Marcus in as the door opened. The machine was already beginning to perform emergency operations as the door closed.

The tech watched the medical status indicators on the machine blink on one by one. All of them came up red and the machine began to return to standby mode. He took a deep breath and said, "I am sorry, miss but your friend is dead."

"Manual override," was all he heard.

"The man is dead, lady; there is nothing I can do", he said. He turned to comfort the woman only to see a bloody hand holding a heavy pistol inches from his face.

Katrina's voice came out as a whisper. "You have ten seconds restart the meditube or the machine won't be able to help you, either."

The tech punched in his personal code and restarted the trauma sequence. He and Katrina both stared at the console as the machine whirred back into action. Thirty seconds later, the lights began to come on again, one at a time, red, red, red, then a flickering red that changed to yellow. The tech stared at the console for a second, then jumped into action, pushing packaged supplies into the machines access doors as it called for more nanoprobes, blood and plastiskin.

Marcus was hallucinating. He felt an ache in his chest as he heard soft jazz music playing in the background. He thought he could hear his mother as she rocked him in her arms. "Marcus, you're going to be all right, baby. You can go back to sleep now. I will see you later." Her lips brush his forehead as he passed out from the returning pain.

"I don't understand it," the tech said as he read the indicators. "Brain function is normal, kidneys are working, liver is normal, all his blood levels are close to normal, but there is no heartbeat. It looks like he is being kept alive by the machine, just as if he were on life support. Either that or the heart monitor is broken, but the machine went through a thorough maintenance check last week," he shook his head and peered at the display again. "Everything was fine."

Katrina wiped away a tear that had formed in her left eye and looked over his shoulder, then almost jumped out of her skin as a loud knock came from the meditube. She and the tech stared at each other, and then the tech quickly opened the tube door.

Marcus was lying naked on the table, breathing heavily as he ran his hands across his chest. He swung his legs over the side of the slab and then stood up on shaky legs. He drew a deep breath, let it out in a whoosh and said, "Man, I thought I was dead." He reached out and wrapped Katrina in his arms, pulling her close to his chest. "Thank you for saving my life. I love you." He kissed her on top of her head.

Katrina's ear was pressed against Marcus' chest. She heard no heartbeat. She pushed away from him and said, "How can you be alive? Your heart is not working. I can't hear a pulse."

Marcus put his fingers against his neck and tried to find his carotid artery. There was no pulse.

The tech took out an old-fashioned blood-pressure monitor and put the cuff on Marcus' arm. After he pushed the start button, the machine inflated the cuff until it popped off Marcus' arm. "He has no blood pressure. Technically, you are dead." The tech, weary from all the stress of the last few minutes, passed out cold and hit the floor with a thud.

Katrina looked at the comatose tech dispassionately and then turned to Marcus.

"Baby, how do you feel?" Katrina asked.

"I hurt here," Marcus pointed at his chest, "And here." He reached around to his back with his left hand. "But otherwise I'm fine."

"The nanoprobes," Katrina exclaimed. "We pumped you full of nanoprobes, more than I have ever seen. They must be moving your blood through your system and keeping you alive!"

She shoved Marcus back into the machine and pushed the diagnostic button once again. The indicators all showed green except for the heartbeat, Marcus's heart monitor was flat-lined and the alarm was sounding. Katrina punched the off button.

"We need to get you out of here before the tech comes to," Katrina said, hurrying to gather clothes for Marcus to wear. "You need to be gone, so he thinks this was all just a dream. Put these on," she threw a set of medium coveralls at him, "then get into this and stay perfectly still."

Marcus looked at the open body bag Katrina threw on the table, and then hurriedly got dressed.

The tech was coming to before Katrina could get Marcus out of the building. She motioned him into the body bag.

Katrina kissed him full on the lips as she zipped the bag closed. "Please stay quiet and I will have you out of here in a minute." She dropped to the tile floor.

The tech awoke to see Katrina sitting on the floor, sobbing.

"I can't believe he is dead," she said as she angrily brushed tears from her cheeks with both hands. "I feel lost without him!"

Katrina wailed as she threw herself across the body bag.

She looked up at the tech who was standing there confused and dazed from the events of the day and from hitting his head on the floor and said, "Thank you for trying to save him. I am sorry I waved the gun in your face; you were only trying to do your job." Katrina got down from the table and hefted the bag over her shoulder. "I need to give him a proper burial. Thank you for trying." She reached out a bloodstained hand and patted the tech on the cheek and then walked out the door. She heard him hit the floor once again.

Chapter 29 - Disappearance

Paine was confused when Marcus called and asked to meet him at the motor pool office. They had just conducted an inspection of all the vehicles and equipment needed to provide ground transport for the two supporting companies. Everything was in decent shape, with only one vehicle requiring extensive maintenance and another four that would be ready by 1100 hours the next day. The entire unit would be prepared to respond to any enemy action by then. As he hurried to the meeting, Paine hoped it wasn't bad news.

When he walked in the door, Marcus was wearing a jump suit that was two sizes too small. Katrina was just coming out of the bathroom, barefoot and drying her hair with a towel. She had dried blood on her shirt front, and her leather jacket, covered with blood, was hanging from the back of one of the chairs at the conference table.

Paine blurted out "What the hell happened?" He looked at his friend and said, "Marcus, report."

"Albert Martin, that nasty little weasel, is our mole." Marcus began. "He followed Katrina and me to dinner and then shot me in the chest."

Paine looked at Marcus in disbelief. "How can you still be alive?" he asked.

Marcus shook his head and pointed to Katrina. "She saved my life. Private Martin did not survive the encounter. Then Katrina got me to the aid station, and I got a mega dose of nanoprobes…"

Paine flashed the danger sign at Marcus, who instantly stopped speaking.

"We are going to have to get you back to a decent medical facility to be checked out." Paine said as he continued in patrol sign, "the nanoprobes are how we are tracked. You have to leave or all our plans will be compromised."

"I'm doing pretty good right now." Marcus said as he flashed "I can't just leave you here alone, you need me. That rat said that it was from General Martin."

"I'm afraid that is out of the question. I'll be sending you to New York on the next available flight," Paine said. He signed "I figured my father is behind this. He must be getting help form Corvis. We can't afford to have our United Nations mission compromised. Talk to my mother, tell her what you know. She may be able to get the Technos to figure out a way for you to come back." He reached out and touched Marcus on the shoulder. "That is an order."

Paine shook hands with his friend. "I will take care of everything else," he said.

Marcus signed, "If they are listening in, they know I am still alive."

"I understand. I still have to work that out." Paine gestured for Marcus to leave, then signed when he stopped at the door, "At least for now, you have to go."

Marcus walked out the door, but Paine held Katrina back. "Katrina, I realize how much you hate the meditubes, so you shouldn't have any nanoprobes in you."

She nodded. "You want know how much I love them now? A meditube just saved his life!"

Paine looked at her and said, "You're the one who saved his life. Now I need you to keep him alive until we can figure out what happened." Paine gave her instructions, "You need to take Marcus and hide him somewhere after he gets seen by the doctors in New York. You know the city well enough to find a good hole to crawl into. I will send word to my mother to help you out."

Katrina nodded.

"We also need to spread the word that he died in the attack, and you are taking the body back for burial," Paine said. "Can you pull that off?"

Katrina explained what she'd already told the med tech.

"Great," Paine said, "Then you need to go now. Marcus still does not look good and I can't bear to think that he might really die." Paine handed her the remote starter for a scout lifter and asked, "Katrina, can you fly one of these? It's bigger and a lot heavier than your standard lifter and takes a lot of muscle to fly."

"I'm sure I can," Katrina snorted. "How do you want me to get it back to you? Won't you need it for the movement of the unit?" Katrina asked.

"Just leave it at the space port. I'll have Major Miller bring an extra driver and pick it up when she goes to the JUNGFOR staff meeting in Paris scheduled for tomorrow. You just need to get Marcus out of here, and quickly."

As Katrina left the building, she thought about all the brand new clothing she was leaving behind in the room. She'd paid a lot of money for those dresses in New York when she and Elle had gone shopping. She stopped short and Marcus walked back to her. "What about our mutual friend?" he asked.

Marcus said, "I am sure Paine can find someone to help her out; probably Trisha." They continued to the vehicle park.

Katrina wondered what Elle was going to do now that she was on her own. Then she shook her head and climbed into the lifter with Marcus. Elle wasn't her problem anymore. She needed to keep her man alive.

Chapter 30 – Bobby Lee

A cold wind blew across the parade ground as Paine stood in front of the formation and listened to Trisha read the eulogy for Marcus. A bayoneted assault rifle, stuck muzzle down in the ground in front of a pair of boots, was at Marcus' normal position for a parade. A blue beret with command sergeant major rank pinned on it was hanging from the butt of the weapon.

Paine's mind was racing, trying to process all the information he'd gathered over the last few days. He was half listening to the eulogy. "Born in New Orleans... Rose through the ranks... ultimately achieving the rank of sergeant major... will be missed by all. Battalion, attention!"

Paine snapped to attention and out of his reverie as echo taps was played. As the last note echoed across the old town square, he commanded, "Company commanders take charge of your units," returned their salutes and walked back to the headquarters. It was just beginning to snow as First Sergeant Bobby Lee joined Paine on the walk to the Renaissance Town Hall building.

"Sir, thank you for choosing me to be the acting sergeant major; but I have a concern. My replacement as first sergeant of A Company is not ready for the job." Lee wanted to make sure that A Company was still the best in the battalion.

"Don't worry sergeant major. Captain Curtis will keep everything going well, and you are in a position to make sure the company gets everything it needs. I have to have a good sergeant major, and I picked you because you are the best!" Paine started in the front door as Lee held it open and then followed him.

"I knew your mother, she was my friend," Paine continued. Gabby Lee had been Paine's squad leader when the Kentucky Regulars were hired to clean out the squatters near the Florida space station. She'd been caught in a trap and was killed when General Martin ordered Paine to leave her behind and continue the mission. "She was a great NCO and taught me an awful lot about how to live in the field. She showed me how to be a good leader." Paine paused as he remembered finding her after the mission was completed. "I was there when she died."

"I know," Lee said as they entered the conference room.

Paine sat down in the chair at the head of the table and said, "I need you to be my eyes and ears with the men, just like you did for Captain Curtis. You also need to tell me if you think something needs to be done with training, supplies or discipline. Once we deploy, the staff and I will be going in with the first company, A Company." Paine continued his instructions. "I need you to be with the follow-on units. Work with Major Kompaniyets to coordinate the movement of the rest of the battalion and keep the supply lines open. Once we are reconstituted as a unit, you stay with me."

"Understood," Lee said. "Would you like me to get the rest of the staff at this time, sir?"

"Round them up, Sergeant Major; the meeting starts in ten minutes." Paine got up to go to his office and said, "And bring me old-fashioned writing materials, please."

The staff and commanders filed into the meeting room and stood at their places, waiting for Paine to walk in and take his seat. Once Paine sat down, the rest followed suit. He signaled that everyone stay silent as the note he had written was passed around the table.

"All members of the unit will undergo pre-deployment checks, including a full medical evaluation," Paine said. "That includes all of you and right down to the lowest-ranking private in the unit. I expect that to be done before 0800 hours tomorrow. We have to be ready for action by then."

The note had reached Sergeant Major Lee by that time, and he handed it back to Paine after reading "All nanotechnology must be removed prior to deployment."

Paine continued, "All right, let's get the meeting started."

Chapter 31 – Change of Mission

The worst part was waiting for the call.

Paine's battalion had been alerted five times in the last month, ready to move to a hot spot but told to stand down each time.

The first alert had been for the Italian area, but the French responded to the attack with overwhelming force, fighting a pitched battle with the insurgents. That resulted in ten French soldiers dead and an estimated thirty five insurgents killed in the fighting.

The other four alerts were false alarms. No insurgent attacks occurred. The local police overreacted to reports of enemy activity and called for UN support.

Paine was sitting in his office when his intelligence officer, Captain Reynolds and his operations officer, Major Miller, knocked at the door.

"Come," Paine said.

"Colonel Martin, I think you want to hear this." Rachael Miller waved Captain Reynolds over to the desk.

Reynolds, short, dark-skinned and built like a small tank, put his tablet on the desk. He began his briefing by pulling up all the incidents recorded for the region in the past month.

"Look here, sir." Reynolds pointed at the weather reports listed on the left side of a split screen. The incidents were on the right. "The attacks and threats coincide with a period of good weather lasting more than three days after a period of bad weather." He scrolled down the page. "The pattern holds for the past year. That is all the data I have, but it seems to be pretty consistent."

"So what are your thoughts on this?" Paine asked.

"By my calculations, given the weather reports are correct, the next attack will come somewhere in the Tirol Region today, the 28th of December. I would bet my life on it." Reynolds stood up from the screen.

"You are betting the lives of this unit on your analysis; you understand that, don't you?" Paine said.

"I do, sir. I believe my analysis is correct." Reynolds touched the screen and the weather for the past five days appeared, along with the reports of enemy activity for the past week. "See here, the movement of the enemy forces coincides with the snow that has been falling across the region. They move only when they can't be tracked, then they hunker down and wait for the next round of bad weather. The French and German units stay in garrison during the storms, allowing the insurgent's freedom to move."

Rachel Miller prompted Reynolds. "Can you project where they might make their attack?"

"Ethnic Serbs have established a settlement in German territory near Mittersill on the Salzbach." He pointed out the town on the map. "I think that may be where the insurgents are heading. They will have a place to hide out during the next storm and resupply. From there, they could strike the settlement at Zell am See." Reynolds ran his hand over his shaved head. "There are only a handful of Germans settlers there and they could easily be overrun and killed. I think we can stop the insurgents if we get there first."

"Major Miller, send a report to General Jung. Tell him we are acting on good intelligence and are on our way to Mittersill to prevent an enemy attack. To delay might be fatal to the German's in the settlement." Paine pulled out his communicator and set it to all frequencies. "Alert, Alert, Alert," he said into the microphone. He grabbed his combat vest and headed for the lifter park.

As Paine walked out the door, he called Captain Curtis. "Chris, I need your company ready for liftoff in twenty minutes. Tell them if we see any enemy forces, they are to hold their fire unless fired upon."

The UN forces weren't the only ones who'd heard the alert notification.

Chapter 32 – Video Feed

Command Sergeant Major Lee walked down the line of vehicles. He stopped at the command vehicle that was being prepared for sling loading. Paine's driver, Sergeant Lukas Kligemann, one of the German soldiers assigned to the battalion, was getting the vehicle ready to be lifted with the unit as a part of the initial deployment.

Lee motioned him over and said "I need you to provide me a video feed of everything that happens once you get on the ground. It will come to us," Lee paused, "Major Kompaniyets and me, so we can follow the situation on the ground." He handed Kligemann a small camera. "The old cameras have been cutting in and out, so I want you to replace your video feed with this one. Make sure it's on at all times. Understood?"

Kligemann said, "Jawohl." He replaced his old camera with the new one. After he turned it on, he looked at Sergeant Major Lee.

Lee pulled down the small screen attached to his helmet and saw himself on the screen. He called out, "Testing, one, two, three." His voice echoed in his ears. "Perfect. Remember to keep it recording."

Paine gave one last set of instructions to his executive officer. "Yuri, please get there as soon as you can. I need to have the entire unit in place within four hours. Move along this route." Paine traced the road with his finger, "But watch out for these choke points. Any action encountered, you need to try to fight through." Paine had circled the choke points along the mountain roads.

Kompaniyets did not have a good feeling about this; there were too many places where the convoy could be stopped. He spoke. "Colonel Paine, I must protest this move."

Yuri was very formal in his speech and mannerisms when he made his displeasure known.

"We have the intelligence, and as the commander in the field, I am making the decision to go." Paine liked Major Kompaniyets despite his penchant for following orders to the letter and not taking the initiative. "Yuri, I take full responsibility for the actions of the unit. I just need you to follow orders." Yuri nodded.

Paine continued, "If you are stopped, set up a perimeter and wait for the lifters to return, and then get to us as soon as possible. I will need to protect the civilian population; if the insurgents are threatened, they may go after them to cover their escape." Paine shook Yuri's hand then stepped back and returned Yuri's salute. "See you soon!" he said as he entered the lifter.

Sergeant Major Lee walked over to Major Kompaniyets. "Sir, I have the feed from the unit; if you would give me your communicator, please." Lee made the adjustments and Paine's face appeared in the screen. Then the scene shifted to the window and Yuri saw the snowy terrain flashing by beneath the lifter. He could hear the rush of air through the ear bug, and heard Paine say to his driver, "Looks like we are making good time, Kligemann. We should be on the ground in fifteen minutes."

Major Kompaniyets waved his arm, and the convoy sped off down the Autobahn toward the mountains ahead.

Chapter 33 – The 28 December Massacre

Vuk Slobodanic, a Serbian secret police colonel, led his detachment of forty soldiers down the snowy slope to an abandoned barn just outside of Mittersill. He had several of his soldiers, clad in white camouflage, post themselves as sentries and had the rest go inside the building. Huddled together for warmth, the NCOs took off their rucksacks and dug out the small squad stoves. Soon, the hum of burning gas filled the air which was warming rapidly. Vuk took out his radio and tried to make contact with his agent in Mittersill, but was rewarded with only static.

"I need to go into the village myself," he told his second in command. "This weather is playing havoc with our communications." He took off the white coveralls he was wearing and put his rucksack on the ground. Then he took off the shoulder holster containing an antique pistol and placed it beside the pack. "You need to make sure you stay hidden, and no matter what, do not come to the village. If I do not return in four hours, break camp and head for the next rendezvous point."

Vuk pulled up the hood, wrapped the scarf around his neck and headed out into the growing storm. He trudged through the deep snow until he reached the outskirts of the village and then moved toward the lights of the Gasthaus near the center of town. As he neared the inn's front door, he was confronted by four armed men.

"Good evening, sir." A pleasant voice said in English.

Vuk stopped and opened his arms wide. In his best German, he said, "Nicht verstehen"

"This one is not German; this is a Serbian town. He doesn't belong here." Sergeant Kligemann said to Paine, who was standing in the shadows. "And although his German is good, it's classical German, not the dialect spoken by the people who live in these parts."

The feed from Kligemann's helmet camera was going to Kompaniyets' communicator.

"Tell me where your men are, so we can get them out of the cold," Paine said.

Vuk dropped his hands and said nothing.

"We can track you back to the general area of your troops, the snow is not falling that fast. We mean you no harm and do not wish to kill anyone." Paine moved out of the shadows. "I am a soldier, too, and understand what you must be feeling now. I have been in a no-win situation myself, and I tried to resist as long as possible, but when it came down to the lives of my people, I gave in to the inevitable. And as you can see, I am here today. I do not want to fight your men. If I do, then we will kill them. You do not want your men killed, do you?"

Vuk spit on the ground. "You will have to kill us all." He turned to run back out of town, but was tackled by the soldiers who had crept up behind him.

"Take care of him," Paine said. He called Captain Curtis. "Chris, leave two platoons here under command of your executive officer. I want you to bring your best platoon and the scout platoon with us."

Paine could hear Captain Curtis issuing his orders, and then he started backtracking Vuk, his scout platoon moving with him. Second platoon of Alpha Company, with Captain Curtis at its head, followed.

Major Kompaniyets could not believe what he was hearing. The feed from Kligemann's helmet caused him to tell the driver to increase his speed. He looked at Sergeant Major Lee and asked him to play it back for him. He believed what he was seeing was true; he had no idea that the Corvis Foundation was able to alter the video feed as the event was happening.

The sergeant major backed the recorded footage to where Paine stopped the man walking into the light. "It is ready any time, sir."

"Play it again," Kompaniyets said.

"Tell me where your men are, so we can get them." Paine said.

Vuk dropped his hands and said nothing.

"We can track you back to the general area of your troops, the snow is not falling that fast. We mean to kill everyone." Paine moved out of the shadows. "I am a soldier, too, and you must understand what I have, a no-win situation. Try to resist as long as possible, when it came down to the lives of people, I give in to the inevitable. I want to fight your men; we will kill them. You want your men killed, do you?"

Vuk spit on the ground. "You will have to kill us all." He turned to run back out of town, but was tackled by the soldiers who had crept up behind him.

"Take care of him." Paine said, and spoke into his communicator, "Chris, I need your company ready. Tell them if we see any enemy forces, they are to fire."

Kompaniyets could not believe that Paine would do this. He did not personally like Paine, but the commander he had come to know and respect was not the man he saw on the screen, and yet he was watching him issue orders to kill innocent people in real time.

Paine moved out, backtracking Vuk as the camera followed him into the snow.

"Just what is the colonel doing? Is he insane?" Kompaniyets urged the driver to move faster. He turned to Sergeant Major Lee and said, "Forward that to headquarters, to General Jung. Do it right now!"

The Serbian forces never saw the soldiers coming. The guards were taken out by long-range sniper fire, and the doors of the barn were locked from the outside. Three men with plasma weapons unleashed the fury of hell on the small barn and it burned to the ground, killing all those inside.

Paine could see the skyline light up in the distance and urged his force to move faster.

Joaquim Corvis wrinkled his nose at the smell of burnt flesh and turned to his mercenary commander. "Set the remote weapons stations in place and get your people loaded. Make sure we get Serbian weapons out of the rubble and take good footage of the bodies in the barn before we go. The UN troops will be here soon."

The mercenaries scurried about, setting the scene of a massacre.

Joaquim sat at the monitor in the lifter circling the burning barn at a high altitude, in the heart of the snow storm. He looked at the video feed from the commander's driver's helmet camera as the UN reaction force entered the area. This was going to be good.

The feed was being patched through the main computer at Corvis Foundation, which modified it in a split second based on the program that Joaquim had written. It was changing whatever was said to incriminate the commander, Lieutenant Colonel Paine Martin.

Paine ran up to the burning building and shouted "Is anyone left alive?" just as the remote weapons stations began to fire at the scout platoon. They returned fire with a vengeance, shooting at the weapon flashes with rifle, carbine and plasma fire, all recorded by the helmet camera. The platforms the weapons were on shot into the sky as soon as the firing from the UN forces ceased.

Paine yelled, "Cease fire! Captain Curtis, take your Alpha Team and go see if there are any casualties in the attacking force. If anyone is left alive, I want to talk to them." Paine turned to his driver and said, "Kligemann, see if there are any survivors."

Kligemann surveyed the inside of the barn and recorded the dead soldiers. He returned to Paine and said, "Sir, no one alive here. They are all dead."

Captain Curtis returned from the perimeter and reported, "No bodies were found. It's as if the attackers disappeared."

Just then, the command net was alive with the voice of General Jung screaming, "Cease fire, you idiots. Cease fire." He had just seen the feed modified by Corvis. General Jung could not believe his eyes as he saw the scout platoon firing all their weapons. Through the smoke drifting from the burning barn, he heard his subordinate commander ask, "Is anyone left alive. Fire. See if there are any survivors" and then the sergeant reporting, "No one is alive, they are all dead."

"Colonel Paine, you will return to the village at once." General Jung commanded. "You are to put all your weapons on safe, and not shoot, even if you are fired upon. Major Kompaniyets, you will hold the main body in place. Send three lifters to the village to pull the rest of A Company out of there. That is an order!" General Jung cut the transmission.

"When will we be arriving at the village?" Major Kompaniyets said.

Sergeant Major Lee looked at the GPS data on the vehicles heads up display and said, "About twenty minutes at our present speed."

Still in shock, Major Kompaniyets gave Lee orders. "You will take the lifters to the village. When you get there, you will place your commander under arrest for crimes against humanity."

"Major, I will arrest the Colonel," Sergeant Major Lee said.

"Very well, you take whoever you need and make it so. I do not know what happened and really do not want to know." Kompaniyets turned his head to the window of the vehicle and looked at the falling snow as the convoy went into a defensive herringbone formation ten miles short of the village. He muttered under his breath, "I told him not to do this!"

Lee passed the instructions to the two companies in the convoy to dismount and secure the perimeter. He ordered the soldiers to stay where they were and was the lone occupant of the lead lifter. As it landed in the village square, he jumped out and ran to the Gasthaus past the confused executive officer of A Company. "Stay where you are, Lieutenant." He went inside and shouted to the three men left to guard the captive. "Where is the prisoner?"

One of the private soldiers pointed to the locked door to the cellar. "We put him down there, Sergeant Major. He was yelling about his rights under the Geneva Convention and demanded to be released." He nodded at the other soldiers in the room. "We got tired of listening to him."

Lee waved the soldiers back and drew his sidearm. "Stay here, I will deal with this." As he entered the basement, he saw Vuk sitting on a bag of potatoes. Lee motioned for him to get up and then tossed him a small pistol. Vuk caught it by reflex. Lee shot him five times, all the while yelling, "He has a gun!" The soldiers ran down the stairs and found Sergeant Major Lee slapping a quick heal patch on the worst of the wounds. He turned and reached for the first aid kit of the nearest soldier.

The private said, "Forget it, Sergeant Major. Only a meditube could save this guy." They stood and watched as the prisoner breathed his last.

Lee wiped the blood from his gloved hand with a rag and shook his head.

"Whatever you guys remember about the prisoner, I want you to write down now." He picked up the pistol Vuk had caught and waited until the men had their heads down, working on their statements, and then shot each of them once in the head in rapid succession. He fired the remaining rounds into the door frame. "UN idiots," he said, as he put the pistol back into Yuk's cold hand, collected the papers and threw them into the stove. Then he ran up the stairs and into the courtyard, yelling that the prisoner had tried to kill him. He deployed the remaining platoons of the company around the village and got back into the lifter.

Chapter 34 – Newsworthy

Paine wiped the snow off his goggles as he trekked back to the village. He heard his communicator buzz, but no image appeared on his screen. Sergeant Major Lee's voice came over the air.

"Sir, you better not come here. Something has happened to our communications. Whatever you did out there was recorded and is now with both the executive officer and with General Jung." The modified recordings began to play on Paine's display.

"That is not what happened," Paine said.

"I know, sir. You would never do what this shows." Lee stated emphatically. "Someone must be messing with the feed, modifying the communications; someone who is out to get you."

Paine thought that his father must have friends in high places to be able to do this. "I have to come in to clear my name," Paine said.

Lee shook his head. "You can't count on the scouts to back your story; the images show they were firing on the barn. Any prosecutor would say they are lying, just trying to avoid trial themselves." Lee paused. "I think you may want to run away and try to get to the bottom of this mess, while you still can."

"And just how are we supposed to get away?" Paine asked. "I won't leave my scouts or Captain Curtis behind to face trumped-up charges."

"Two lifters will be there shortly. I personally picked pilots you trust. They will take you wherever you want to go and say you hijacked them once you release them. You really have no choice, you have to do this," Lee said insistently.

Paine could hear the lifters' engines whining in the night. "Very well, I will be in touch with you, but for now, do not try to make contact. I don't want you to be implicated in all this. Paine, out," He broke the communications.

Paine took his private communications device out and called his mother. "Go secure," he said.

"Paine, what is going on over there?" Ashley said. "I'm looking at Brian Watters of CNB reporting breaking news out of

Germany that a massacre of civilians has taken place. He said a UN source confirmed it was the special operations' battalion, commanded by you, that you have killed an entire village of unarmed civilians."

"I located a group of Serbian nationals hiding in a barn who were killed before we even arrived." Paine thought for a moment. "How could the news people get the information so quickly? I just found the bodies fifteen minutes ago."

"I do not know, but the press is calling for your head. Waters has even renamed your group the German and United Nations Force, calling it GUNFOR, since that is what the press is saying you are doing. General Jung is already under arrest; they showed video of him giving the orders." Ashley paused. "Let me show you the news feed."

As Ashley focused her camera on the monitor in her office, the lifters arrived. Paine recognized the pilot as the one who had flown him into New York during the insertion. Lee was right; Paine trusted these people. He jumped on board and waited until he got a green light from his scout platoon leader and then gave the pilot a thumbs up. The lifters took off into the storm.

"Paine, watch this," Ashley said.

"Brian Watters, back after a short break. We have obtained exclusive footage of German soldiers attacking a village and completely destroying it after a fierce firefight." The screen showed soldiers in cold-weather gear landing outside Mittersill and firing into people positioned around the village. There was return fire, but not much as the soldiers swept through the village, setting fire to vehicles and houses and shooting anyone visible. "As you can see, the Germans had no regard for the local population. Previously, the lead element, under the command of Colonel Paine Martin, attacked an unarmed group of woodcutters outside of town and mowed them all down." The modified footage of Paine at the barn played.

"Mother, those are my A Company troops being gunned down in Mittersill." He turned to the pilot who was intent on keeping the lifter flying in the high winds and switched to his frequency. "Who sent you?" Paine asked.

"The sergeant major ordered us to take you out of the area of operations, then return to pick up him and the rest of the unit," the pilot replied.

"How far are you supposed to take us?" Paine asked.

"An old airfield nearby," he said. "There is a shuttle there big enough to take your entire unit to New York. Sergeant Major Lee saw it on the intelligence report from Captain Reynolds."

"Alert me when we get close." Paine switched back to Ashley.

"Mother, I've been framed. I haven't figured out how he did it, but father is the one doing this," Paine said.

"He just got out of the capsule; there is no way he could have set up something this complicated in a few days. I think it's just one part of a bigger plan. What are you doing now?" Ashley asked.

"Going to an airfield and getting on a shuttle to New York. I think whoever is doing this wants all of us in one place," Paine mused.

"I agree, so let's not disappoint them. It would be better if we can fight this thing out together." Ashley sighed and said, "Looks like we will have to defend New York all over again. Come home safely, son."

Paine broke the connection as the lifters set down on an old runway. The blowing snow abated enough to reveal a large shuttle parked at the end of the strip, lights on and hatchways open. Paine waved his scout and infantry platoons off the lifters and into the waiting shuttle. He stood at the front of the lifter and saluted the pilot as he lifted off and flew back into the snow. The crew chief for the shuttle waived him onboard as the plasma engines started.

Paine strapped himself in his seat and wondered what was coming next.

Lee looked at the video feed coming into his heads-up display. The mercenary leader panned to show the burned bodies of the company executive officer and the rest of the command group lying in grotesque positions on the ground. The feed cut off as Lee landed in the battalion perimeter. He called the lifters he had assigned to fly the scouts and Alpha Team to the airfield. The communicator squealed at the pilot of the lead lifter. "Have you dropped off the scout platoon?" Lee's voice came over the channel.

"The shuttle has already lifted off, sergeant major," the lead pilot replied.

Lee pressed the actuator switch on a hand-held device and two fireballs appeared in the sky as the explosives Lee had placed on the shuttles detonated.

Chapter 35 – Another Corvis

Joaquim Corvis walked into his room in Hotel Central and threw his backpack in the corner. What a night this had been! First, destroying the barn and killing those Serbian irregulars, and then attacking the United Nations soldiers left to guard Mittersill. Too bad all those civilians had to die, but it was part of the plan. All in a night's work, he thought. His secure communicator buzzed.

"Corvis," he answered.

"Nice work, grandson!" Steven Corvis' voice came out of the speaker. "We have managed to make Colonel Martin the devil and ruined the credibility of the United Nations military all in one night. I still have more work to do, but your part was certainly well done. You deserve a break."

"Thank you, grandfather. I enjoy the field work, but this cold weather is almost more than I can bear." Joaquim shivered and moved to the thermostat to turn up the heat.

"I will be sending you a present soon. Try to get some sleep; you will need it!" Steven signed off.

Joaquim stripped off his outer garment to reveal a German uniform which he stuffed into a portable incinerator. He carefully placed the communicator on the table and continued to disrobe as he walked to the bathroom. He luxuriated in the hot water that was soon pouring over his half-frozen body.

Twenty minutes later, a waiter entered the room with the meal and bottle of a very fine Chateau Neuf De Pape Joaquim had ordered. He poured a glass, sniffed the fine aroma, took a sip and allowed it to dissipate in his mouth. After he swallowed, he took a deep breath and enjoyed the richness of the wine. He turned on the video and began watching the news as he ate.

"This is Brian Watters with continuing coverage of a special report out of Germany. It seems the perpetrator of the massacres of not only Serbian but also German and United Nations troops has been identified as Michael Paine Martin, son of the madman who caused the destruction of the United Nations last year." Paine's likeness appeared on the screen. "Martin is the son of General

Martin and the so-called President of New York, Ashley Miller. It seems like the apple doesn't fall far from the tree, so to speak. Miller has been accused of inciting the uprising against the United Nations that caused her husband to attack New Yorkers, and rumors are that she fabricated evidence of a plague to drum up support among the factions living in New York. The son, Michael Martin, who prefers to go by Paine, was then given command of a special unit in the United Nations."

Chris Schohymer, the political analyst for CNB News, took up the narrative. "It seems that the family is working together to keep the world government from being established."

"Why do you say that, Chris?" Brian prompted.

Schohymer leaned back in his chair and interlocked his fingers. "First, General Martin tried to take over the United Nations, an attempt that failed due to squabbles within the family. His ex-wife, Miller, was able to co-opt the NUS commander on the ground, one Colonel Flagehty, by promising to give him command of his own army in the new country of SUNY. With Flagehty's help, the New Yorkers defeated the United Nations Forces. General Martin then perished when he destroyed the United Nations Building with a nuclear weapon. Now that the United Nations is located in France and no longer headquartered in New York, Miller fears another takeover is being planned. What better way to keep that from happening than starting a war between Serbia and Germany in Europe?"

"I can't believe that is true," Brian said.

"One need only look at the facts. SUNY, as they call themselves, are on the verge of creating one of the best and most-efficient space ports on the planet. They already have taken steps to sign contracts with the space nations New Germany, New Quebec and Luna for landing rights, which will undermine the authority of the United Nations and increase their own power. I have it on good authority from an unnamed SUNY source that they are telling the off-planet nations that the UN is only for Earth countries."

"What about this man we now know as Paine?"

"He has been groomed as an assassin and killer his entire life." Schohymer paused and said into the camera, "If you have small children, they should leave the room at this time." Schohymer pointed at the screen behind him. "Just look at this footage of an operation he conducted in Atlanta two years ago."

The screen changed to show Paine in a long coat walking down a littered street. He fired a burst that shredded what appeared to be an unarmed man. The darts from his weapon continued into a second man who was trailing his partner too closely. A third man literally came apart as a grenade went off right next to him. Three more unarmed men tried to shield themselves from the flying metal and debris. Paine got into a kneeling position and calmly targeted the heads of them. They died quickly.

Schohymer turned back to the camera and said, "Of course, we edited out the gruesome parts."

Joaquim was impressed that his people were able to remove the weapons the gang members were carrying from the video. He was enjoying the scene when he was interrupted by a knock on the door. He pulled his robe around him and opened it to reveal a stunningly beautiful red-haired girl in a very short, very tight dress with a pair of high heels in her hand, ready to knock on the door again.

"May I help you?" Joaquim asked.

"I believe I can help you!" The woman said, in a low, seductive voice. "I was told there was a party being held in this room. I have come all the way from New York, and I wouldn't want to waste a good party."

Joaquim laughed and thought that his grandfather was getting generous in his old age. A woman like this must be very expensive, especially if she was a New York call girl, but he did do a good job with the video, the village and the Serbs. He deserved the reward. "Come on in, we can party all night if you can keep up with me." He waived the woman inside the room.

"Can I get you something to drink?" Joaquim asked.

The girl flowed into the room and walked over to the table. She picked up the half-empty bottle of wine and poured two glasses full. "I don't need much to get me going, just wine with a little touch of erotic corpus."

Erotic corpus was an extremely potent aphrodisiac that high-class call girls had been using for years. It made both partners insatiable for hours. The girl looked Joaquim up and down and said, "You don't look like you will need too much, so maybe only one drop for you." She took out a bottle and let a small amount drip into his glass. She swirled it slightly and handed it to Joaquim. "Just slug it down; the effect is more potent that way."

Joaquim took the glass and raised it in salute. "Thanks, Grandfather," he said as he swallowed it in one gulp. He looked at the girl and asked, "How long before I get the full effect?"

Elle took a sip of her own wine, and said, "Just a few seconds, sweetheart; just a few seconds."

The paralytic Elle put in his glass acted quickly, causing Joaquim to hit the floor hard.

Elle stood over him as he tried to move. Taking a wet wipe from her brassiere, she wiped the heavily caked-on make-up off her face, scrubbing it until her cheeks glowed. Elle pulled off the red wig she was wearing to reveal her blonde hair, pulled tightly in a bun. She put the wig into the incinerator Joaquim had used to destroy his uniform and pushed the start button. The hair was gone in a flash. She removed the band from her hair and shook it free, then ran her fingers through it to make it as messy as possible. She stripped off the dress she'd taken from Katrina's baggage, removed her undergarments, including the piece of shapewear she'd put on to hide her condition and threw them around the room.

Joaquim couldn't help but notice that her belly was a little large for the average hooker. Elle struggled to get the robe off of Joaquim's body; finally managing to do so and put in on, tying the belt securely at her waist. She tossed the shoes in two different directions in the room, and then bent over the still conscious Joaquim. He was able to follow her with his eyes as the effects of the short-acting paralytic began to wear off.

"You know, the authorities will be looking for a girl about four feet tall after picking up these clothes. I was right after all, I thought you would be too busy thinking about me without any clothes on to notice how ridiculously small they were." Elle patted Joaquim on the cheek, and then turned him onto his back.

She took a vial of snarf out of her purse, one she had scored in a back alley off the main square earlier that day. "The dealer who gave me this said it was eighty percent pure, which means if you take it all at once, chances are you will die. I can see the headlines now; Heir to Corvis Foundation found dead of drug overdose in his hotel room after a wild sex party."

"I really hope you like snarf," Elle said as she broke the vial open and grabbed his chin. Joaquim was unable to resist as she pried his mouth open and the entire contents of the vial into his mouth. She watched as the drug took effect.

Euphoria came first and changed to fear as Joaquim began to go into convulsions. Elle watched dispassionately as the man on the floor gasped for air. She reached down to check his pulse and once she was sure he was dead, whispered, "For my parents."

Elle pulled the robe tightly around her after his body stopped moving body, and walked to the door, "Two dead, three to go," she said under her breath and with her head down, stepped out of the room.

She was once again the crazy lady, wandering the hallways.

Chapter 36 – Orders

Steven Corvis called his grandson for the third time, still no response. He activated his computer console and asked, "Find Joaquim Corvis." Fifteen seconds later the response came, "Subject not found. Should I continue searching?"

"I need recordings of Joaquim for the last twenty-four hours." He scrolled right to the end, listening to the death rattle of his grandson's last breath. He moved the indicator back, playing the recorded audio five minutes at a time, until he heard what the woman said about being from New York.

"Computer, check the woman for nanoprobes." Corvis waited.

The computer responded, "There were no nanoprobes detected in the female."

"So you know about me, President Miller. Then this means you have to die." Corvis said aloud.

Josh's communicator buzzed. He got up from the cot where he was sleeping and stretched. He didn't want to talk to anyone today, so he walked over to the window to look out on the East River, flowing a few yards from the building where he was hiding. As he took a sip of water, he felt pressure building in his chest. The communicator buzzed again.

"Martin," he said.

"You really need to pick up whenever you are called, or bad things could happen to you." Steven Corvis' voice was cold. "When I need you, I expect an immediate answer. Next time, you will hurt for a week." He paused for effect, "There will be no third time."

Corvis could not see the veins pop in Josh's forehead or hear the impact as he smashed his fist into the wall.

Josh calmly asked "Very well. What can I do for you?"

"I believe that someone from New York is killing my family members. Jillian, my wife, was murdered in Paris last week. One of my grandsons, Joaquim, died of an overdose of scarf today in Plzen. The only common denominator in those two deaths is the UN Force commanded by your son." Steven paused. "Another grandson was killed in an elevator accident five months ago; one I believe was not an accident at all. I think it was either a Techno attack or a spy sent by your ex-wife. All I know is that someone is killing my family. I want them all dead," Steven said in a low voice.

"I think I understand you well enough to think you want them dead because you are afraid. It's fear, not revenge." Josh said. "You are not at all like me; you seem to care about your own life. What do they have on you?"

"That is none of your concern," Corvis said. "Your son is on his way to New York as we speak, he should be there shortly. You know where your ex-wife is. Just do not kill either your wife or your son right away."

Josh asked, "Why can't I just get rid of them now?"

"Because I'm commanding you not to!" Corvis pushed the button once more and Josh almost collapsed with the pain surging through his entire body. "Now shut up and listen. What I plan to do is use all in my power to make SUNY out as a rogue state, one that needs to be destroyed. I need them alive in order to accomplish that. In spite of your bungling attempts, I still have connections in the UN. I will get them to do my bidding."

Josh listened intently to what Steven had to say.

"Once the battle for New York begins, then I want you to do everything you can to disrupt their operations inside the city. Is that clear enough for you?" Steven twitched his hand and another pain shot through Josh's left arm.

"Crystal clear; I will do what I can to help." Josh broke the communications.

Steven thought about killing Josh right then, but knew he needed him to succeed. He thought, "Soon, I will be rid of you and your entire family."

Chapter 37 - Back in New York

The shuttle Paine was riding in was in a holding pattern in low-Earth orbit. Paine was waiting for a call from his mother to make sure no one was in the landing area when the shuttle landed. He was simultaneously listening in on air traffic control, waiting to hear landing instructions. He wanted to know when they were going to land and told his troopers to be prepared for anything.

Ashley answered the communicator with a grim look on her face. She had become more haggard in appearance since the meditube was no longer available to her, but she didn't care. She was sure this was going to be another fight for survival. "President Miller," she said.

"Ashley, it's Ryan. I have the space port secured." He paused. "We never did find out how General Martin escaped our cordon." Ryan shook his head. "I made sure nothing got in or out after we arrived. He must have already been gone when we closed the space port."

"Don't worry, Ryan, you did your best." Ashley checked to make sure they were on a secure channel and said, "I have another mission for you. A shuttle will be landing soon. I need transportation for fifty available; covered transportation. And I want the occupants of the shuttle taken to the old Chrysler Building. Tell them to go into the basement levels. There's already food and water there for them."

"Who is on the shuttle?" Ryan asked.

"You will see soon enough. Just get them there safely. And under no circumstances are you to go through any Neo Luddite territory." Ashley cut the connection.

"Government Center to Shuttle 151." The voice crackled in Paine's ear bug. "You are cleared to land on runway 3 South."

"Get your people ready to move as soon as we touch down," Paine said to Chris Curtis.

Curtis, no stranger to being in a tough spot, just grinned and unslung his carbine. "This is a little easier than the last time we flew into New York. I hope it turns out as well."

Paine laughed. "Last time we got taken prisoner! At least no one will be trying to kill us when we land."

Curtis tightened the grip on his weapon as the wheels touched down and whispered, "Let's hope not."

The shuttle coasted to a stop at the end of the runway. A "Follow Me" vehicle was waiting there, and the pilot taxied the shuttle to a nearby hanger. Paine tensed as the shuttle bay doors opened, and he saw that it was surrounded by SUNY forces. He relaxed as he realized they were all facing away from the open doors of the aircraft.

Paine was the first one out of the shuttle, then stopped and saluted the oncoming soldier. "General Flagehty," he said.

Ryan returned Paine's salute with a sloppy movement and then reached out to shake Paine's hand. "I thought it was you! Welcome back to New York. Your mother informed me of what's going on with your father, but the briefing can wait. I need to get you out of here and into the city as quickly as possible."

Paine waved the troopers out of the shuttle and followed Ryan to the waiting lifters. As they flew to the Chrysler Building, Paine filled his commander in on what had happened during the last twenty-four hours.

Chapter 38 – All the Eggs in One Basket

Trisha knocked on Elle's door. There was no answer, so she let herself into the room. Elle was lying face down on the bed, gently snoring.

Trisha thought she was going to go mad. It was one thing to have to live in the bordello, considering the hell that she'd been through there. It was bad when she first joined the Kentucky Regulars, dealing with her demons and repeatedly visiting the psychiatrists with thoughts of suicide almost winning over reason. It was hard to give in to feelings of love for a man after her experiences in the past, but she did and was glad she'd found Chris. Now he was a fugitive, and she feared she would never see him again. She didn't think she could live without him. Suicidal thoughts were once again gnawing at her mind.

She woke from her trance as Elle yawned and stretched. Elle didn't know she was there, so Trisha, not wanting to startle her, backed up against the wall and stood still.

Trisha watched as Elle stood up and moved to the desk to look at the computer screen.

"Elle, just what the hell is going on?" Trisha asked.

"Damn, again!" Elle swore. "Why don't you people ever make any noise?" She glared at Trisha. "The truth is I'm not crazy. You know how hard the news of my parent's death hit me, you were there. I almost did go insane and then I just got angry. I decided I wasn't going to die until I got back at whoever killed my mother and father." Elle shook her head and continued, "Katrina knows I'm faking my insanity and has been helping me hide it."

"Katrina found out just like you did, by skulking around while I wasn't looking. I have to learn to be more careful." Elle looked at Trisha and said, "Now that Katrina is gone, I can use your support."

Trisha, happy to have something to keep her mind occupied and suppress her suicidal thoughts, told Elle, "I'm listening," and sat down on the bed.

Elle waved her finger in a circle near her temple as she said, "This is just a ruse to get people to leave me alone, so I can avenge my parent's." She lowered her hand and spoke softly. "I need assistance, but if I tell you what is going on, you'll be in mortal danger."

"How much more danger can I get myself into?" Trisha asked.

"Have you used a meditube lately?" Elle asked. When Trisha shook her head no, Elle continued, "What I am about to tell you will get you killed if it ever gets out." Elle continued, "The Corvis Foundation has probes that can track your whereabouts and record your conversations."

Trisha now understood Paine's insistence that all nanoprobes be removed from the troopers and leaders in the battalion before leaving for Plzen. "Paine had us all scrubbed clean of nanoprobes before we deployed."

"Then you're safe, at least until they find out I'm alive." Elle looked at Trisha and asked, "So, will you help me?"

"No one in the unit will talk to me; they think I had something to do with the massacre because of my connection to Chris Curtis and my loyalty to Paine." Trisha continued. "Major Kompaniyets relieved me of my duties. My new assignment is to act as your guardian until Katrina shows up again. And for some reason, I don't think that is going to happen. She hasn't been seen nor heard from since Marcus died. The unit has been looking for her because of the death of Private Martin. They think she had something to do with it. Rumor is that she killed herself after Marcus was shot." Trisha paused. "She doesn't strike me as suicidal, but one can never be too sure."

"Katrina wouldn't kill herself; she would just go on with her life. I know her well enough to know that." Elle continued. "And as for you, I need your help to get out of here. I think a change of scenery would be good for us both. How would you like to go to New York?"

"That's where they tracked both Paine and Chris." A surge of hope ran through Trisha as she thought about being reunited with Chris. "What makes you think they'll let me go there?" Trisha asked, "If I do go there, won't that imply that I had something to do with the massacre?"

Kompaniyets directed that an investigation begin; he was looking into any possible connection Trisha might have had to the massacre. Trisha yearned to be back with Chris, and though she wanted to go to New York, she was convinced that she would be arrested if she tried.

"We have to go to Dallas, first. My parents have," Elle's voice caught in her throat and she paused to clear it, "an antique vehicle that can make it from Dallas to New York on one charge. It was an experimental electric-powered car that was made right before the hydrogen revolution. It uses a new-and-improved battery pack, like the one used in the hand grips of our accelerator weapons. I used to drive it around the lake on our property back at the ranch outside Dallas. Once my parents moved us to the city to be near work, we kept the farm and put the car in the barn."

Trisha thought for a moment and asked, "Why would Major Kompaniyets let us go to Dallas?"

"Because I am going to try to kill myself," Elle said, matter-of-factly. "Then you will insist I be transported to Dallas to see my personal physician. We go to the farm, get in the car and drive to New York." Elle smiled at the shocked look on Trisha's face.

"We'd have to travel through some pretty rough areas," Trisha said.

"I took a trip through the New South before all this mess got started. It's much safer now that it was. We'll be going through the New South and will only have to worry when we leave NUS territory and pass through what used to be New Jersey. Gangs still rule parts of that former state."

"I'll help you in any way I can," Trisha said, "especially if it will get me back to Chris." Trisha lowered her head and stared at her feet for a few seconds, and then said, "I've thought about it a lot and I discovered lots of foolproof ways to kill oneself," she looked Elle in the eyes and continued, "even though I never went through with it. I always held out hope that things would get better. You just made me reconsider what I thought was my only other choice."

Elle reached out and briefly touched Trisha's hand.

Trisha trembled at the contact, but did not pull back. She looked at Elle and asked, "So how do you plan to do it?" Elle said, "I just need something that only requires quick heal. I can't go into a meditube."

"OK, nothing that requires major medical help," Trisha said.

Trisha knocked on Lieutenant Colonel Kompaniyets' door and waited until he looked up from his work. When he saw who was there, he waved for her to enter. She stopped three feet from the desk and saluted. Kompaniyets returned the salute and said, "Take a seat, lieutenant. I will be with you in a moment."

Trisha thought Kompaniyets looked more comfortable than he had the last time she'd seen him. His promotion and subsequent assumption of command gave him a tremendous confidence boost.

He finished reading the latest report and said, "What can I do for you, lieutenant?"

"I have disturbing news. It seems the lady that Katrina brought with her and left here on her own, the one I have been tasked to watch over, has tried to end her life," Trisha said.

"I see. And what must we do about this?" Kompaniyets leaned back in his chair and thought about his options for a second before asking, "Should I have a full-time guard placed on her? I am not sure I can spare the men, as we are in heavy training right now, but I can see what I can do." He reached for the communicator.

"That is not necessary, sir. She was babbling a name as I patched up the slashes on her wrist, so I ran a search on it. He is a doctor of psychiatric medicine in Dallas, NUS." She paused. "I was wondering if I should take her there and turn her over to his care. I would then return here to resume my duties."

"I will check and see what I can do." Just then, Sergeant Major Lee knocked on the door. He nodded to Trisha, and said, "Excuse me, sir, but the woman Lieutenant Jones is talking about is a drain on resources. I think it would be best if she were out of the unit's hair once and for all."

"Very well, have the travel documents cut and send them on their way." Kompaniyets turned back to his paperwork.

After Trisha left the room, she stopped at Sergeant Major Lee's desk and said, "Thank you."

Lee responded with, "No problem." He had received a secure communication from a blocked station earlier that morning with the following text message, "Get Jones out of the unit, it's all part of the plan."

Chapter 39 – Blocking Marcus

Katrina stood behind a glass wall and watched as Marcus went through a full meditube body scan with the best doctors in New York in attendance. She was worried as they poured over the results flashing on the screen, a doctor gesturing at a key report while another waived at a different one. They finally all calmed down as the chief of medicine for the hospital stamped his foot and yelled at them all to keep quiet. He set up the printout for the machine which then literally rained paper. They collected the papers and left the room as the technician opened up the tube.

Marcus emerged looking fit and rested. The machine had fixed a few minor problems that surfaced after his emergency surgery in Plzen. Marcus felt great. The tech was staring at him as he put on his clothes and walked out to rejoin Katrina.

"I guess everything is OK," he said as he gave her a big hug.

Katrina put her head against his chest and listened for his heart. "Honey, it's still not there. No heartbeat."

Marcus joked about it. "Paine always accused me of not having a heart. I guess it was prophetic."

Katrina took out a pad of paper and wrote, "This means Corvis can track you wherever you go."

Marcus shook his massive head up and down, and said, "I've been thinking about taking a vacation; somewhere tropical; a place where I can lie in the sun and relax a bit." He wrote on the paper, "I can't leave you and Paine alone."

Katrina wrote, "I am glad you include me in such good company. Just kidding. I know you love both of us, but you love him more."

Marcus laughed out loud.

Katrina grinned and wrote, "I will have to talk to Paine and the Technos. Maybe we can find a solution." She said, "We'll have to wait and see what the doctors say."

Three hours in the waiting room just made Marcus more convinced that there was no hope for him at all. Every time the doors opened, Katrina and Marcus jumped because they thought the doctors were coming back with news of his condition. Finally, the door opened and the chief physician entered.

"I have some very good news for you." He paused.

Marcus wanted to strangle the news out of him, but held his anger in check. He also had a good grip on Katrina, who was about to rip the doctors' head off and spit down his throat. Marcus knew she could do that easily.

Through clenched teeth, Katrina finally asked, "Well?"

"There is nothing physically wrong with him, except his heart was completely destroyed by the bullet. The nanoprobes are doing the work of the heart, circulating the blood and keeping you alive. Marcus, as long as you go in for regular maintenance, you could conceivably live forever without your heart." He smiled.

Marcus did not return the doctor's smile. "I want a heart. What about a transplant?"

"I suppose if we could find the right suitable donor you could have a transplant, but why would you want one?" The doctor asked. "You are healthy, and with the number of nanoprobes in your system, you're virtually indestructible."

"Yeah, as long as I don't run into any kind of electrical interference, something that shuts off all the probes." Marcus continued. "And what if I can't get to a meditube? Am I going to be tied to meditechnology for the rest of my existence?"

"We have been discussing that, the doctors here and I," he looked at Marcus, "we want you to stay close to our facility so we can study you and determine why you, among all people with cardiac issues, managed to survive with nanoprobes alone." The doctor seemed eager to have Marcus as a test subject. "You are a special case, and we want to learn more."

Marcus stood up, towering over the doctor. "I am not a lab rat. I'll go through my life the way I want to live." He turned to Katrina and took her hand, "Come on, baby, let's get the hell out of here." They brushed by the startled doctor and walked out of the waiting room.

As Marcus and Katrina emerged from the front door of the hospital, they were confronted by three hooded figures. Marcus reached for his pistol and then stopped as Katrina grabbed his arm. The lead figured flashed "Welcome home," in patrol sign and the hood was pulled back enough to reveal Paine's face. Chris and

Sergeant Kligemann also showed their faces briefly. They flanked Marcus and Katrina as they moved down the street toward the State House.

As they got close to Ashley's government offices, Paine stopped the group. He handed Marcus a piece of paper.

"Marcus, your nanoprobes are being tracked by the Corvis people, and probably using you to feed information to the UN." Marcus looked at Paine, who indicated that he continue to read. "We need to try to get them blocked. There are four of us who will carry you out if the dampening device shuts down your nanoprobes. Katrina could do it herself, but we're here to help her."

Marcus grinned and pointed out that line with his finger to Katrina, whose eyes were shining, "If you want to try it, the field starts at the doorway."

Marcus put the note in his pocket and strode into the building. He collapsed two feet inside the door.

Marcus woke to Paine shaking him and asking him if he was all right. A half a dozen Technos were standing over him, furiously typing code into their computers. Paine signaled that Marcus was awake, and they looked at their data and started walking back into the building.

Paine signed, "That was pretty close, Marcus."

Katrina showered him with kisses.

Inside the building, Walter Biddle was furiously typing code into the permanent dampener he had installed the day prior. He looked at the new program and called Paine.

Paine tilted his head to the right as his ear bug delivered a message.

"Time to try again," he said out loud.

Marcus struggled to get his hands free of Katrina and signed, "They can hear you."

"No, they can't. Our friends inside informed me that the frequencies your nanoprobes use to transmit messages are now being blocked. Everything that you have said since you came out of the meditube was downloaded into our computer banks here, and its generating random conversation from you. You are convincing Katrina to go with you to Aruba as we speak." Paine listened again. "You guys are leaving on the 1900 hour shuttle and are planning to be soaking up rays on the beach tomorrow morning."

Paine helped Marcus to his feet. "I think the Technos are using a similar program that Corvis used to convict me of genocide." He smiled. "Thank God for the Technos. Two can play that game."

That evening, as Marcus and Paine sat down to a cold beer, Walter Biddle came in and asked Marcus how he felt.

"I'm fine, why, what's wrong?" Marcus asked.

The Techno looked at Marcus with sad eyes. "You went down in the Caribbean today at 2100 hours, just short of the runway." He continued, "I guess when you were no longer going to feed them information, they decided to terminate you. We will have to keep you in New York and under Techno protection for a while. You and Katrina are no more, along with sixteen other passengers, I am sorry to say."

Marcus was furious and exploded, "You let sixteen people die so I could be safe?" He stood up and was stopped by Paine before he could attack the Techno.

"Nobody died, Marcus. The lifter was loaded with nanoprobes, yours and Katrina's included, and was remotely piloted by our friend, here." Paine pointed at the trembling Techno. "I think you owe him a drink."

Walter said, "No thanks, I have to go back to work," as he scurried out of the bar and away from the wrath of the giant, angry man.

Marcus sat back down and took a sip of ice-cold beer. He said, "Paine, I really want to find out who is doing this and terminate them!"

"Amen to that, brother," Paine responded.

Chapter 40 – Show Trial

Paine was already convicted by the court of public opinion, but officially went on trial at the United Nations. It had taken a few weeks to put the tribunal together; the UN Secretary General wanted to make sure there was an impartial set of judges on the panel. No judge was from a country with a large space presence. Madagascar, Kenya and Pakistan provided the tribunes.

The tribunal at the International War Crimes Commission reviewed the video evidence presented by the prosecutor. It was certainly damning. Command Sergeant Major Lee and newly promoted Lieutenant Colonel Kompaniyets, the first two witnesses called to testify, confirmed that they had seen the video evidence. Major Miller also was called.

"What were the instructions given by Colonel Martin on the day of the attack?" The prosecutor asked.

"Captain Reynolds discovered a pattern in the movements of the insurgents," Major Miller began.

The prosecutor cut her off abruptly. "I specifically asked what the instructions were!"

"I believe that you need to know the situation." Major Miller was again cut off, this time by the chief tribune.

He gave her instructions. "Major Miller, Please answer the question and only the question."

Rachel Miller used all of her self-control to keep her composure. "He told Captain Curtis, 'Chris, I need your company ready for lift-off in twenty minutes. Tell them if we see any enemy forces, they are to hold their fire unless fired upon.' That is all I heard," she answered.

The prosecutor spoke to the tribunal directly. "That would be the same Captain Curtis who is a co-defendant in these proceedings!" He looked back at Major Miller and asked, "And did you hear Colonel Martin issue any other orders?"

Major Miller looked down at her folded hands.

"Please answer the question," the tribune said.

"I only heard those orders that came over the video feed. But they may have been tampered with," she finished.

"Major Miller, you are in contempt of court." The chief tribune turned to the guard standing behind the witness stand and said, "Remove the witness."

The prosecutor sat back down and reviewed his files as they escorted Major Miller out of the courtroom. He stood up and asked, "May we have a brief recess?" The chief tribune nodded. "After we reconvene, I would like to call General Jung to the stand." He sat back down after the tribunes left the courtroom and typed in a message to bring Jung to the stand.

General Jung paced in his private witness room in the basement of the courthouse. He was planning on what he would say when the bolts were electronically released in the door. He turned and straightened his uniform jacket, took a deep breath and waited for the door to open. He was determined to fight these trumped-up charges all the way, and he had enough evidence in his office files to debunk the videos of him giving illegal orders.

Two United Nations guards entered the room and flanked him as they walked with him down the hall. A junior officer was in the hallway and stepped against the wall to allow them to go by. Just before Jung passed the officer, the guards stopped and Jung took one step forward. The officer placed a small caliber pistol against the general's temple and pulled the trigger. Jung died instantly.

The guards caught the collapsing general under the arms and pulled him back to his cell. The officer followed them into the room, placed a suicide note on the bed and put the pistol they'd taken from Jung's office in his hand. Then they left and locked the door behind them.

Two hours later, the prosecutor stood before the tribunal.

"General Jung will not be able to testify, he was found dead in his cell just a few short minute ago." The prosecutor held a piece of paper up and said, "Lady and Gentlemen, I have proof beyond a shadow of a doubt that General Jung, Colonel Martin and Captain Curtis are all guilty of crimes against humanity. The evidence is overwhelming; especially with the confession of General Jung," he shook the paper clenched in his fist at the video camera for effect, "that this was an attempt to cause war to break out in Europe. Jung admitted it was engineered by Lieutenant Colonel Michael Paine Martin and his mother, Ashley Miller, President of the Sovereign United New York."

The prosecutor set the paper down and walked forward to stand before the tribunal. "Therefore, I ask that a verdict of guilty be rendered by this court, and that Ashley Miller be convicted of the same crime, as the mastermind of the operation!"

The tribunal stood and left the room to deliberate. The assembled gallery was just beginning to clear out when the court room was called to order. The press and the dignitaries rushed to get back to their seats as the tribunal returned to their seats.

The chief tribune stood up and announced to the court, "After careful deliberation, this tribunal finds all the defendants, including President Miller," a murmur went through the courtroom as he paused for effect, "guilty of all charges. The punishment is death."

Steven Corvis sat back in his chair and changed the computer screen to the project he had been working on before the verdict was issued. Foundations were already being poured for the new factories going up in Madagascar, Pakistan and Kenya. Steven thought the trial went well, and that he now needed to start the wheels in motion for the actual executions to take place. He sent a message to his contact in the United Nations.

Chapter 41 - United Nations Orders

Andre Chevalier of France, Secretary General of the United Nations, called the Security Council to order. John Gutenberg was still the NUS ambassador to the United Nations and was blowing his moustache out as he took his seat. Ian Burns was now serving as the President of the Irish republic and had been replaced by Sean Fergusson as the ambassador. Oshara Tdacki from Japan and Lin Chow Tsing, from China, were seated across from each other. There was still a bad feeling in China toward the Japanese, something the Japanese ambassador did not understand. The history of China and Japan was one of cooperation and friendship, according to the history Tdacki had learned. He did not know why the Chinese diplomat held him in contempt. John Wilson Smythe of Australia was still puffing furiously on his pipe, and a pall of smoke filled the air. The French, German, and Polish representatives were there, and for once, the Ukrainian ambassador graced the meeting with his presence.

Chevalier opened the meeting by banging the gavel. "The first order of business is to stop the smoke from choking us all! Ambassador Smythe, please put out that damned pipe!" Chevalier turned up the ventilation in the room and the smoke was drawn out by powerful fans.

"Thank you." He turned to his computer screen and indicated that the others do the same. "As you all know, President Miller and her son have been found guilty of plotting to create a state of war among the governments in Europe, making it difficult for the United Nations to stop their plans of strengthening their position in New York."

Tdacki spoke, "Why should that concern us? We have no quarrel with the New Yorkers. We have already begun construction of our own space port in Tokyo Bay and should be able to receive shipments from the space colonies soon."

Chevalier started to respond, but was interrupted by Tsing. "You Japanese are trying to undercut the resources of China once again, with your space port. We also have a port being built, one that will surpass yours, in Hong Kong."

Chevalier tried to inject his own comments, but was again interrupted by Fergusson, who said, "My people have an operational port in the Irish Sea, with facilities going into the coast by Dublin. We don't have a problem with a New York Port; it's none of our concern."

Chevalier banged the gavel once more, and the room fell silent. "Look at your computer consoles."

All the members turned their attention to the documents scrolling on their screens. Contract after contract, all with space mining companies, began to show on the screens. Even Luna and New Germany were represented in the list of businesses and governments that agreed to use New York as their exclusive port of entry to Earth's marketplace.

"We have no problem with this," Juri Navolska, the Ukrainian ambassador, stated.

"Juri, my friend, you do not have any idea what this means," Gutenberg said. "It means that SUNY, as they call themselves, will have a monopoly on space trade." He held up his hand as Juri started to reply. "They will control what comes down to the planet, not what goes up to space. We can send new platforms and mining stations up into space, but to make them operationally profitable will take years, years that SUNY will have to get stronger. Once their economy grows, it will be very difficult for us to break that monopoly."

Juri scratched his head and said, "But we in Ukraine primarily deal in food, why should this space trade bother us?"

"Because, old friend, the ones who have the money control the market," Tdacki said. "Now I begin to see what they are trying to do. The plan must be to get the great nations of the world like China and Japan to fight with each other, over the trade that is left, so we are helpless against the rise of New York."

Chevalier nodded his head. "That was the plan they used in Europe; to get you good people to fight and weaken each other so that SUNY could grow stronger." Chevalier looked around the room at the faces of the diplomats; he was convinced he had them right where he wanted them.

"So, gentlemen, you can see that we have to do something. My plan is to ask the government of SUNY to turn over the convicted murderers Paine Martin and Chris Curtis to the United

Nations for justice. Ashley Miller will also be asked to surrender." Chevalier paused and looked around the table. "When they refuse, as I am sure they will, we can place sanctions on them and refuse to let any trade go through there."

"I think we can do better than that," Gerhard Schmidt, the new German ambassador, said.

Chevalier made a come-on motion with his hand.

"Germany has been insulted and disgraced by the actions of these people. They turned one of our best generals against his people. They also killed innocent German settlers in an attempt to start a war." Schmidt shook his head and said, "I would like to introduce a UN resolution that the fugitives, including President Miller, be immediately turned over to the Security Council for execution of the sentence. If they refuse, we should go in and get them. Germany must have justice, and now!"

"I second the resolution," Fergusson said. He knew that a strong New York would threaten the Irish annexation of the upstate part of New York, promised by the SUNY constitution to the Neo Luddites.

"I agree, we should do that," Gutenberg readily agreed. The NUS was still stinging from the defection of Colonel Flagehty and the loss of New York to the new government and were afraid the expansion of the Technos into what had been New Jersey would stop their effort to reclaim it.

The Japanese and Chinese ambassadors had exchanged notes. They were competitors, but they both wanted SUNY out of the shipping business so they only had each other to compete with. Tsing spoke for them both, "We agree."

Chevalier nodded "Yes" to his ambassador, who had stepped in to take his place when Chevalier had been selected as Secretary General. The ambassador said, "Je suis d'accord!"

Juri once again shook his head. "I do not understand all of this bickering. Why can't we all just get along? I thought our mission statement here at the UN was to create and keep a lasting peace. It makes no sense to do this, as they will not turn over their leader or her son to us so that we can put them to death, and that means we will have to go to war."

Chevalier looked at his fiend and said, "They will not, you are right. Therefore, when they do not turn the criminals over to us, we will have no choice but to conduct military operations against SUNY. We must give them sufficient time to comply with an ultimatum, and then pass a second resolution, in the General Assembly, that authorizes the use of force to go and get them out of New York."

Juri pondered the enormity of the statement and mused, "Then I must have assurances, from all here, that Ukrainian goods will have free passage on any ships taking supplies anywhere on the planet, and to the space colonies." As he looked around the table, he got nods from everyone.

Juri had made sure that the list of countries dealing with SUNY did not include his own as Ukraine had concluded a secret treaty with Ashley not ten days before. In one simple move, Juri had gotten all shipping costs waived by the assembled parties and by SUNY. Ukraine would win not matter what the outcome of the war. He smiled at his success and said, "Very well, I too, agree."

As Chevalier looked back at his screen, the resolution he had already prepared for the council appeared. "Let's look over what has been proposed and finalize it today," he said. The UN Security Council Resolution began to scroll down the screens of each ambassador's computer. As Chevalier started to read it, a small box appeared in the upper right corner of the page. A text message began to run. "Good job, Andre. Now let's make sure that SUNY does not comply. S. C."

Chapter 42 – Ultimatum

"Madame President, I received a call a few minutes ago to from a UN Security Council aide, who used to be my neighbor here in New York. He told me he thought you would want to see this," Ashley's secretary said as he turned the video monitor toward her.

Ashley was conducting a meeting with her staff. Paine was there as an observer as were Chris Curtis and Marcus. Carley Squires; General Flagehty; Keenan Revis, representing the Technos state; and Carole, Ashley's daughter, who was an excellent note taker, were around the table. Carole began to write rapidly as the news show came on. Her notes were to be sent to Miley Pickers, head of the Neo Luddites, at the end of the meeting.

"This is Brian Watters, CNB News. I have just been informed that the UN Security Council, voting unanimously, has decided to issue the Sovereign United New York or SUNY as they like to be called, an ultimatum. You may read the full text on our home page, but it basically tells SUNY to hand the convicted criminals of the 28 December Massacre over to the United Nations and to allow the UN basically to take control of the country's government. I don't know how this is going to play out, but I will be here to keep you in the loop."

An incoming message light blinked on the computer of Ashley's Chief of Staff. Carley linked her screen to the others so everyone could read the ultimatum.

Ultimatum to the Government of the Sovereign United New York – 31 January 2052

Now the history of the past year, and particularly the painful events of the 28th of December in the town of Mittersill, have proved the existence of a subversive movement in United Nations Forces, whose object it is to separate certain portions of the nations from this peace-keeping organization. This movement, which came into being under the very eyes of the Sovereign United New York Government (SUNY), subsequently found expression outside of the territory of the nation in acts of terrorism, in a number of attempts at assassination, and in murders.

The Government of SUNY has done nothing to suppress this movement. It has tolerated the criminal activities of the various unions and associations directed against the United Nations, the unchecked utterances of the press, the assassination of both government and private individuals, and the participation of its officers and officials in subversive intrigues.

This toleration, of which the SUNY Government was guilty, was still in evidence at that moment when the events of the twenty-eighth of December exhibited to the whole world the dreadful consequences of such tolerance.

You are hereby instructed by United Nations Security Council Resolution 498 to remove from the military and administrative service in general all officers and officials who have been guilty of carrying on the subversive activities, whose names the Security Council reserves the right to make known to the SUNY Government when communicating the material evidence now in its possession;

To agree to the cooperation in SUNY of the organs of the United Nations in the suppression of the subversive movement directed against the integrity of the United Nations;

To institute a judicial inquiry against every participant in the conspiracy of the twenty-eighth of December who may be found in SUNY territory; the organs of the United Nations delegated for this purpose will take part in the proceedings held for this purpose;

To undertake with all haste the arrest of Lieutenant Colonel Michael Paine Martin and of Captain Chris Curtis, who have been compromised by the results of the inquiry.

The room was silent as each of the members of Ashley's staff read the ultimatum. Several snorts of disgust were emitted and one choked off, "What the..." broke the silence. Ashley was the first one finished reading. She watched the faces of her son and her inner circle as they finished the document.

Paine was the first to speak. "I will surrender myself to the United Nations if it keeps SUNY safe."

Carley laughed out loud, a rather ironic laugh. "Paine, don't you see? The United Nations is basically telling us we are all criminals, and that Ashley has to turn the country over to their control." She laughed again, "We are right back to where we were; do what the United Nations says or die."

"Not only that, but we've been implicated in the attack on Mittersill, so we will all assuredly face the same punishment as Paine and Chris." Ryan said. "I left one back-stabbing organization to join you here, and I will not go without a fight."

"How can they get away with this?" Keenan said. "We were fighting for our very existence against a couple of madmen who tried their best to kill the members of the United Nations and take over the world! We stopped that from happening." Keenan shook his head in wonder. "What are these people thinking?"

Paine interjected, "How soon they forget that we saved their sorry asses the last time someone made a power play. All the countries who voted on this ultimatum had delegates here in New York when the bomb went off, and most of them were locked in the meeting room until Marcus and Major Miller got them out."

Marcus grumbled, "See if I ever save anyone I don't personally know again."

Chris chimed in, "At least they think that you are dead. The rest of us will be soon enough if we give in to this ultimatum."

"I am not so sure they think I am dead," Marcus argued. "The Corvis Foundation or whoever is running the nanoprobe program there understands we can block the signals. They may think that I'm still alive. They may be smart enough to try to use me later. I think we need to plan for that."

Carole raised her hand like a schoolgirl and asked, "May I say something?"

Ashley said, "I told you when you asked for this job, speak up any time you need to find out things you think the Neo Luddites would like to be briefed on, what they would find interesting or helpful. You lived with them as one of them for five years, acting as a spy for me, for the Technos, and for the drug cartel. You know their intelligence needs better than anyone and have given us valuable insight into their thinking." Ashley looked at her daughter and demanded, "Say whatever you think!"

"Thanks, Mother. It's just sometimes I forget," Carole said. She thought for a moment, formulating her remarks and then continued, "I believe the Neo Luddites will want to hear what needs to be done. I am sure they will not allow the United Nations to come in and take over their territory, any more than they will allow us to bring our technology to their part of our united country. And don't forget, they may not have modern weapons, but the can still fight."

Paine agreed. "They do need to be in on our planning, on what we're going to do, and I know how well they can fight. The problem is going to be who we are fighting. What countries are going to be involved in the attack when it comes?"

Ashley said, "Paine, you said 'when' not 'if' it comes."

"The way this conversation is going, we're going to fight and not accept the ultimatum." Paine insisted. "That means we'd better start planning for war."

"One more thing," Ryan said, "They didn't give us a deadline for the response."

"Poor choice of words, General," Carley responded, "But you're right. They didn't give a time. That means they either are already planning an attack or they haven't decided who is going to be involved in the actual fighting."

"Let's hope the latter, because we're not prepared to repulse any assault at this time." Ryan replied.

Paine stood up and said, "I've been working with the United Nations Forces for six months now, and I can tell you, they can't take this city, even against the Neo Luddites." He turned to Carole and said, "Tell whoever at Neo Luddite headquarters that reads this that I meant it as a compliment to them."

Paine continued, "My biggest fear is that they go back to the old UN Charter and ask member states to send their armed forces in as a part of a coalition. That would mean facing real troops, not the UN forces. If that happens, we are in for a hell of a fight."

Ashley's aide, who had been watching for any developing news, broke in on the conversation. "The news guy is talking again," he said as everyone turned to their screens.

"Brian Watters once again; The United Nations General Assembly has been called into session tomorrow morning to begin discussions on revoking the amendment to the charter that allowed the formation of the United Nations Military Force. If that amendment is repealed, then the UN Security Council will disband the UN Military and then can invoke Article 41 or 42 of the charter. In Article 41, the Security Council may decide to interrupt economic relations, stop rail, sea, air, postal, telegraphic, radio, and other means of communication, including I suppose, space shuttles, and possibly sever diplomatic relations. If that doesn't work, it can escalate to Article 42, and take such action by air, sea, or land forces as may be necessary to maintain or restore international peace and security. Such action may include demonstrations; blockade; and other operations by air, sea, or land forces of the Members of the United Nations. By other operations, one can only assume invasion. Once again, I will be here to keep you in the know." Watters looked into the camera and said, "Now we return you to the regularly scheduled broadcast."

Ryan swore. "Damn, so much for facing the UN troops."

Ashley started ticking off the countries who could be involved. "NUS is a given, since they pulled Ryan's division from the fight so we would lose and they could just walk in and take New York over our dead bodies. The Irish will be in it, too. They want Connecticut and upstate New York and already have had a few clashes with the Neo Luddites over squatter's rights. Germany will definitely be involved; they blame Paine for the 28 December Massacre." She had a hard time keeping the contempt out of her voice as she continued, "France has to be the instigator; they wanted the United Nations to move to Versailles anyway and this will give them the perfect excuse to keep it there."

Carley chimed in, "The French also think they should be in charge of everything. They want to make the UN an extension of the European Union. And don't forget China and Japan. They want control of the space trade and have also been making treaties with the space colonies."

"Are we ready for a fight that may cost not only our lives, but the lives of our people?" Carole asked. Every head turned toward her after she spoke. Carole blushed and said, "I was told to ask what I thought the Neo Luddites would want to know."

"And I agree, they should be asked that question. And so should our people." Ashley said. "I think we should put it to a vote."

Keenan tapped a few words on his keyboard and stared at the screen in silence for ten seconds. "The Technos vote 96 to 4 percent for fighting for our freedom."

Ashley laughed and said, "We mere mortals may have to wait a little longer before we can tally our votes, but we'll get back to you as soon as we complete the count!" She turned to Carole and Carley. "Let's get the word out and see what our constituents think. I'd like to have an answer by Friday. Remember, we have thirty days to decide."

Paine mused for a moment and said, "And probably another thirty to ninety days to get ready. The UN won't be able to do anything faster than that."

Ryan replied, "Let's hope we have that long!"

Chapter 43 - Back in Dallas

Elle walked off the shuttle under her own power. Trisha had been helping her during the flight, holding her arm on the way to the toilet, feeding her when the in-flight meal was served and generally taking care of her every need. Trisha refused the help of the flight attendants, saying if her charge did not get the special care only Trisha could provide, she would have to be heavily sedated or be restrained. One wild look from Elle when a male attendant got too close was enough to keep the others away. Both passengers and crew gave them a wide berth as they deplaned in Dallas.

Trisha held Elle tightly until they entered the automated taxi at the curb.

"Whew, I am glad that's over, so we can finally relax." Trisha said.

"It isn't over yet," Elle said as she pulled up the touch screen and changed the destination of the cab from her parent's apartment to a downtown hotel. The hotel was just across the street from the local Corvis Corporation Headquarters.

After settling in their room, Elle walked to the widow and looked across the avenue into the building on the other side of the street. Elle mused out loud, "I can do a lot from here, but I need to pick up a few things at the ranch first." She turned to Trisha and asked, "Are you up for a little road trip?"

Trisha arranged for a rental car to be delivered to the front door of the hotel. When it arrived, she helped her invalid patient down to the vehicle, once again waiving off any of the hotel staff who tried to help. Once she got Elle in the backseat of the car, she took the controls and lifted off into Dallas rush-hour traffic.

"Get into the HOV lane and head out of the city. Go to Rockwall. I can get you to the house from there." Elle settled back in her seat, not watching the city pass beneath them.

Trisha checked the GPS and headed east out of Dallas, flying slightly higher than the posted speed limit. It had been her experience that air traffic controllers paid more attention to craft flying below or exactly at the posted air speed than above it. As they neared the designated beacon for Rockwall, the destination indicator beeped at her.

Elle shook herself from her memories and looked out the window. "Put it down on State Street and shut off the GPS. Drive to Bowles Lake. Just past the old airport runway, take a right onto the access road and drive to the end."

Trisha drove the car along a bumpy road to the end of the runway which then turned into a dirt path that led to a small farmhouse and barn near the dam for Bowles Lake. When she pulled up to the front of the house, she noticed a swimming pool, its bottom green with algae.

Elle got out of the car and wiped away a tear. "This was my parent's place. It's not much, but we enjoyed it on the weekends." She looked at the farmhouse for a minute and then began walking toward the barn. "Come with me."

When they entered the barn, Trisha was amazed at all the equipment.

"My father was big on experiments. He always said he didn't have enough time to do all the things he wanted to do, so when anyone came out with a new product or invention, he had to have it." Elle had to steady herself by grabbing the edge of a workbench, and then she took a deep breath and continued. "The car I was talking about is over there," she pointed at a tarpaulin covering a cigar-shaped object beneath it. "We have to hook it up to the generator to get it up to full charge."

Trisha pulled the tarp off to reveal a sleek, aerodynamic three-wheeled vehicle with a cramped crew compartment. The seating was tandem, with the driver guiding the vehicle from the rear seat. The passenger seat in the front was not more than four inches off the ground.

"I realize it looks funny, but it's a blast to drive, and it gets great mileage." Elle said, "My dad and I," there was another catch in her voice, "used to take it all the way to Corpus Christie and back in a day. It can really move!"

"OK, we have the means to get to New York. So when do we leave?" Trisha asked.

"We will leave as soon as I take care of a little business back at the hotel," Elle said. "You stay here and make sure the charger does not overheat. I am going back into the city for a meeting, and

I will return no later than six o'clock tomorrow morning. Once I get back, we leave immediately."

"I don't feel comfortable leaving you alone anywhere, much less in the city." Trisha said. "And the Corvis security people are going to be on high alert looking for a woman trying to get in to see any member of the family. What happens if you don't come back?"

"I will get back, don't worry," Elle replied, "But if I'm not back by six thirty, you get on the road and head for SUNY." She looked a Trisha and asked, "Do you understand?"

Trisha nodded. "So how do you think you are going to get to them?" she asked.

"My father took over the airfield when he bought this place. Did you notice the berm at the North end of the runway? He set up a range to test all the exotic weapons he bought." Elle walked over to another bench and pulled off another tarp to expose a long-barreled, sleek looking rifle. Elle picked up a five-inch projectile lying on the table and held it out.

Trisha, who studied early 21st-century weapons in her spare time, whistled. "Wow, I never thought I would ever see one of these. That's a Barrett M500, isn't it?"

"A little more kick than the previous model, but accurate as all get out." Elle smiled. "Ten rounds in this magazine, and I can take the wings off a fly at fifteen hundred meters and get a coyote in the head at two thousand." There was a catch in her voice as she finished, "My father taught me how to shoot."

Trisha did not notice as she hefted the rifle and said, "I bet this thing kicks like a mule!"

"Want to find out?" Elle led the excited Trisha out to the makeshift range.

Later that evening, Trisha, ice bag on her shoulder, waved goodbye to Elle as she headed back into Dallas.

Just after midnight, Elle landed the rental car on the top of the hotel and opened the door. She had a jammer her father had been using at the ranch blocking the computer signals emanating from the vehicle. She also pre-programmed it to block the video feed from the roof-top cameras.

J. B. Durbin

She pulled on a pair of skin-tight gloves and rolled a mask down to cover her face. The black jumpsuit she was wearing made her almost invisible in the darkness of the night.

Elle quickly got out of the car and pulled the Barrett from the cargo compartment. She had spent several hours cleaning and inspecting the weapon after she and Trisha made sure the sights were properly aligned. Elle walked to the edge of the roof, extended the bipod legs and turned on the infrared sight for the weapon. She scanned the penthouse floor of the Corvis building where the corporation kept a suite for visiting family members.

Elle's research identified five potential targets that would be in Dallas that day. Haley Corvis Buffett, wife of the heir to 20th – century billionaire Warren Buffett was in town with her two children. Richard Corvis, the oldest of the grandsons of Steven Corvis, was at a business convention in the downtown area, and could be using the apartment. The last target was Corvis himself, guest speaker at a fund raiser for the Luna Relief Program, designed to increase technical education for the Indian-Pakistani colony on Luna. The Corvis Foundation hired many of the residents of the Luna colony to work as programmers and tech support personnel.

Elle realized she didn't have much time, so she would take whoever she could get. She prayed it would be Corvis himself. As she scanned for heat signatures in the apartment, she identified four bodyguards on the floor. They were easy to spot due to the reduced infrared signature of their torsos where the body armor blocked their body heat. She also could see the outlines of their weapons; assault carbines usually only allowed in the NUS military. She would have to move fast once the shot was taken. Two of the guards moved to the private elevator and flanked it as the doors opened. A lone figure of a man walked into the spacious living room.

Elle took up the slack on the trigger as she breathed out and thought, "It's either Richard or Steven." She gently pulled the trigger.

Elle had chosen the 800-grain bullet for maximum effect. The bullet traveled less than two hundred yards before penetrating the glass window and striking its target with fourteen-thousand-foot-pounds of force. Richard Corvis disintegrated, and his body parts disabled the two guards who were flanking him. Elle shifted from them to the most dangerous guard, the one near the window who had his carbine pointed in her general direction. He literally blew up as the round hit him center-mass. Elle was counting down in her head as she looked for the fourth guard; he was on the floor, hands covering his head. She decided to let him live.

Elle ejected the magazine and threw it over the side of the building, then broke the weapon down, flinging the barrel onto the roof and taking the receiver with her to the car. As she lifted off and flew away, she turned off the dampener and threw the weapon's receiver out of the open window. Elle removed the gloves and mask she wore and dropped them over the city. Then she punched in the ranch's GPS location and settled down in her seat. Elle was fast asleep in three minutes.

Chapter 44 – Get Out the Vote

Josh put on a knit cap and a heavy coat. He had to get out of the apartment he'd been holed up in since his escape. He had let his beard grow, knowing how much that that would change his appearance. It itched; the irritation made him think about how much he hated the beard and Steven Corvis.

Josh was limited to one video screen and no computer access. He thought to himself, "Corvis could have at least put in more technology." The nanoprobes Steven Corvis had injected in him were activated any time he got near a computer station. Josh was stubborn enough to try it more than a few times and then realized he was not going to find a way to get network access unless Steven decided he needed it. The one thing the nanoprobes could not do was read minds, or Steven would be cowering under his desk.

The communicator buzzed in his pocket. Josh immediately pulled it out.

"Yes, Steven," Josh answered.

"I need you to make sure that you get no closer than five blocks to the headquarters of the SUNY government, but I do want you to do something for me," Steven said.

"I hope it involves more than walking around in disguise," Josh said.

"No, not really," Steven responded. "I want you to vote as often as possible in the referendum on the war. Use your excellent persuasive skills to get as many people as possible to do the same."

Josh sneered, "You know they make the citizens without proper identification dip their fingers in ink to make sure they do not vote more than once, don't you? And since I do not believe in any government that doesn't have me as the leader why should I vote?" The now-familiar pain returned to his chest.

"OK, I will do what I can." Josh thought for a moment and said, "I'll need a lot of money to make my plan work."

"Go to the nearest credit dispenser," Steven directed.

Josh walked up to the corner credit machine and put his hand on the palm reader. The machine began to dump $100.00 SUNY chips out at a rapid rate. Once Josh thought he had enough, he removed his hand and walked down the street looking for the nearest open bank so he could get change. After he got a bag of ten-credit coins, he headed for the nearest bar.

Four hours later, a man ran up to Josh and said, "Did you hear about the crazy guy buying drinks for anybody who votes for the war? I hear he's in this area," he showed Josh his ink-stained finger. "I just voted and want to get in on it!"

Josh smiled and handed the man a credit chip. "Have a drink on me, my friend." His plan was working.

Ashley looked at the returns and was amazed. There had not been a turnout like this since before the plague, and the votes were overwhelmingly for war.

Chapter 45 – Reunion

The trip to SUNY was uneventful. Elle let Trisha drive the last four hundred miles; she was tired from her night out in Dallas. As they passed through New South territory and re-entered NUS control, Trisha was a little nervous, she kept her personal weapon in her lap with a round in the chamber. Luckily, no one was on any of the roads going toward New York. As they got closer to the city, they saw an increase in traffic going south.

"Looks like people are jumping ship," Trisha said.

The GPS indicated that they were entering SUNY-controlled land. Suddenly, the whine of the electric engines stopped, and they coasted to a stop. Elle, in the front passenger's seat, looked at the power readout and asked, "Trisha, did you shut down the engine for a reason?"

Trisha replied, "I think you may want to show your hands right now."

The car had coasted to a stop in the middle of the road, and Trisha could see the barrels of three rifles pointing at them from the side of the road. She waved both hands in the window on that side and then opened the gull-wing doors, allowing her weapon to slide off her lap and onto the floor of the vehicle. Elle got out first, hands in the air, and Trisha followed.

A sergeant in SUNY military uniform walked up to them. He relaxed as he saw they were not carrying weapons and asked, "Just what are you two ladies doing, joy-riding?"

He was looking at the odd vehicle they had been driving.

"Lieutenant Trisha Jones, SUNY Armed Forces," she said, "on detached duty to the United Nations, at least until a few days ago." Trisha pointed at something in her jacket pocket she wanted him to see.

The sergeant lifted his weapon and then indicated she could reach inside her jacket. "Please move slowly," he said.

Still training his weapon on the women, he reached out and took the identity disk from Trisha. "Hands on your heads, please," he said as he took the reader from his cargo pocket and put the disk inside the port. A picture of Trisha appeared in his heads-up display. "Hold out your hand, Lieutenant," he said. He took a step closer and ran the reader over Trisha's outstretched wrist. "So you remember the drill," he mused as he compared the data in the mainframe at Techno headquarters with the information on the disk and the chip buried under Trisha's skin. His display blinked red for a second, and the read out indicated that a priority message was being sent to Trisha.

"Sorry, Ma'am, we can't be too careful these days. Sergeant Lew Seddon, at your service." the soldier said as he slung the weapon and saluted. "You have a message. Would you like to take it here or would you prefer a monitor?"

"I'll use your helmet, thanks," Trisha said. He took off his helmet and handed it to her.

As Trisha pulled on the helmet, the heads-up display changed to a video screen, and Captain Chris Curtis' face floated in front of her eyes.

"I was getting concerned, leaving you there with the United Nations Forces," Chris said.

"The sergeant major arranged to have me take Elle home. She is with me now," Trisha said. "She decided to come here; Dallas was too hard for her."

"Tell Elle Paine is worried about her. I was worried about you, too." Chris looked hard at Trisha and asked, "Are you two all right?"

Trisha smiled at him and said, "I'm much better now, because you're safe. I can't wait to see you!"

"Let me talk to Sergeant Seddon. See you soon!" Chris said.

Trisha handed the helmet back to the sergeant as the other three soldiers came out of hiding and moved onto the road. One was carrying a strange tablet, with several antennas sticking out of it that looked out of place.

"What is this thing?" The Techno with the tablet asked, pointing to the car.

"An electric prototype my father bought at an auction in Dallas." Elle replied.

The Techno looked at the screen of the tablet and said, "Thanks. This is only designed to keep weapons from working, but it stopped the car from getting the juice it needed to run. I will have to report this to my supervisor," he mumbled to himself, furiously typing as he walked back toward the side of the road.

"The Technos are in a world of their own. Give them something that they don't understand and they burry their faces in a computer screen and try to figure it out." Seddon laughed. "I just saw you stopped and figured you were out of juice. To each his own."

Sergeant Seddon waved the women back to their car. "You need to go ahead and drive to the city." He turned and yelled at the Techno who was sitting on the ground pouring over the data streaming to his tablet, "Johnson, turn it back on and let them get on their way!"

The Techno touched the screen a few times, and the car purred back to life.

Sergeant Seddon saluted Trisha again as she drove toward the city skyline in the distance.

Once they entered Manhattan, they saw a lot of activities. People were going about their business as if nothing was wrong, even though the country was about to go to war with what seemed like the rest of the world.

Trisha pulled up to the curb in front of the State House and cut the power. "You were right," she said to Elle as she looked at the battery level. "We had just enough to get us here. Ten more miles and we'd have been walking." She opened the gull wing doors and stepped out.

Chris saw her coming from the upstairs window and ran down the stairs and across the park to the vehicle. Trisha barely got out in time to be swept up in his arms. He kissed her and hugged her tightly until she yelled, "Put me down, you idiot!"

Chris released her and looked at her. He was confused.

Trisha stepped back, drew herself up and saluted, saying, "Lieutenant Jones, reporting for duty." She held her salute until Chris returned it, then jumped back in his arms. "Now we can hug." She whispered in his ear, "We have a lot of catching up to do."

Paine, as befitted his rank, only ran down the stairs. He then composed himself enough to walk at a brisk pace out to the waiting Elle.

"Paine, I am sorry I had to lie to you about being crazy. But I had to protect you." Elle looked down at her feet and asked, "Can you forgive me?"

"Of course, I forgive you!" He released her after a quick hug and held her at arm's length. He looked into her eyes and asked, "I know what it's like to lose someone you love. How are you feeling?"

"It will take more time for me to get over my loss, but I am much better." Elle made a mental count of the Corvis family members she'd killed and thought to herself, "Three down, and two more to go."

"I think I may have to make one or two more trips to get myself in a better place," she said. "After things settle down, I want to visit California," Elle mused. "My parents always loved California." It was also where the highest concentration of Corvis family members lived.

"That will have to wait until this is all over," Paine said. "The United Nations just put an embargo and travel restrictions on all of SUNY. Nothing can go in or out, according to the restrictions placed on us as of today. They also changed the ultimatum. They want an answer from us by the end of the month." Paine took Elle's hand and asked her, "Where do you want to stay?"

Elle thought about Paine's veiled offer and silently thanked him for not inviting her to stay with him. It was too soon, and she was grateful the heavy coat she was wearing was hiding her growing baby bump. "I need to find a safe, quiet place where I can be alone."

"I really do not want you to be by yourself, after Paris. I'm still not convinced that craziness was an act." Paine thought for a moment and said, "Trisha will want to stay with Chris, obviously." Trisha was snuggled in Chris' arms as they walked toward the State House. "Marcus and Katrina have their own place."

Trisha interrupted, "I thought Marcus was dead?"

"It's a long story that I am sure Katrina will tell you later." Paine looked thoughtful for a moment and said, "How about staying with Carole? You like her, and she has grown enough that her clothes may actually fit you."

J. B. Durbin

Elle laughed as she remembered giving a scraggly waif named Joy some of her clothes in a sewer here in New York. It seemed like an eternity ago. "Staying with Carole will be fine," she said.

"I'll take you there," Paine said as he took her hand and they walked down the avenue toward Neo Luddite territory.

Paine stopped at the imaginary dividing line between the Neo-Luddite State and the rest of SUNY. "This is as far as I can go." He pointed toward the three people working on digging up the sidewalk in front of an unused building. "They would beat me to death if I cross into their territory." Paine told Elle what Miley threatened to do to him if she ever saw him, and about the death sentence of he was under.

As they were talking, one of the men approached them with his digging pole in hand. "Paine, come on over the line and see what I can do with this," he said as he drove the pointed steel rod down into the asphalt and ripped up a chunk.

Paine smiled a sad smile and said, "Maybe another time." Paine called out as the man turned and walked away. "But you could do me a favor."

He stopped and looked back. "Could you please escort this lady safely to Carole Bean's apartment?" Paine asked.

"Why do you want her to go there?" the man asked as he spit on the ground in front of Paine's feet, daring him to come into the forbidden zone.

"She is a friend of Carole's and wants to join her, if that is all right with you." Paine said.

The man looked Elle up and down, scrutinizing her appearance and looking for devices she might have on her person. "Got any tech stuff on you?" he asked.

"Just a communicator, but I plan on leaving it with Paine." Elle took out the small communication's device and handed it to Paine. She gave Paine a hug and started into Neo Luddite territory.

"Stop, now," the man said. "Take off that time piece and hand it over to him before you come on our land." Elle unstrapped the electronic watch and tossed it to Paine. "Now you're OK. I'll get her to Carole, you don't have to worry about her," he yelled to Paine as they walked away. He turned to Elle and said, "Name's Zach. Follow me."

Chapter 46 - Carole's Place

As Elle walked with Zach down the street, she was amazed at how quiet it was. At first, she thought it was because there were no people around, and then she noticed many individuals walking or riding bicycles around the city walkways. She couldn't call them streets because they had no vehicular traffic whatsoever. The cement and asphalt was missing from most of the former boulevards, replace over the years by a grassy surface.

Zach led her through Times Square, now devoid of asphalt and concrete. Even though it was frozen, she could feel the earth beneath her feet. She wondered at the tall buildings slowly being dismantled from the top down, by hand. Chutes from the lower floors of the buildings allowed materials to be dropped to street level safely where work crews hauled off pieces of former high-rise buildings off to fill in the subway tunnels under Neo Luddite territory.

Zach saw her wondering what was going on and laughed. "Not used to seeing things coming down, are you? You people only want to build and we want to go back to a simple life. All this junk we sell to you people so you can take it somewhere else. What you do with it is your business as long as you get it out of here."

"I never built anything in my life, so I don't understand what you are talking about." Elle retorted.

"The house you live in, the cars you drive, the things you wear, all are made by a factory somewhere. That just destroys the world. And the science you guys love so much, it almost killed everybody here in New York, and for what? So rich guys could have somewhere to do business with space people." He spat on the ground. "Why don't you all go up in space and leave us simple folk alone?"

"That is a very good question. I guess people don't want to live like you do. They prefer modern medicine and comforts," Elle said.

"There is just no talking to you people. You don't listen." Zach fell silent and stayed that way until they got to a small building just off 42nd Street. "Go in, Carole should be home."

J. B. Durbin

Elle walked into what must have been a restaurant at one time. The kitchen was still intact, and Carole was standing over the stove, cooking something that smelled terrific. She was flipping over a piece of meat and checking the temperature with her thumb. "Perfect," she said to herself as she slid the rare meat onto a plate already holding steamed green vegetables and a salad. She picked up the plate and almost dropped it when she turned around and saw Elle standing there. She set it down carefully and went over to Elle and gave her a big hug.

"I haven't seen you since the last big fight." She stood back and asked, "Have you eaten? I can make more."

Elle shook her head "no", not trusting herself to speak.

Carole laughed, "Is that 'no' you haven't eaten or 'no' I don't want anything?"

"I am really not that hungry," Elle said as she took off her coat.

Carole stared at her for a moment and blurted out, "You better eat something, because you are eating for two!"

"How could you tell?" Elle asked.

Carole hugged her again, holding Elle close as she spoke into her shoulder. "Your face, your smell, and now your growing belly told me." She pulled away from Elle, but still held onto one arm. "You look vibrant! I have to ask," she looked into Elle's eyes, "am I going to be a true aunt or have you found someone else?"

"I'm sure it's Paine's," Elle said, her head down. "He doesn't know, and neither does your mother. I'd like to keep it that way."

Carole laughed out loud. "You have my word, but you can't keep this hidden for the next six months!" She put her hand on Elle stomach. "Heavy coats are fine right now, but the farmers in the Neo Luddite community are predicting an early spring. They've been pretty close in their forecasts for as long as I can remember. That means no more bulky clothing after the first of April." She pulled Elle over to the table. "Sit down and eat something. You need to keep that baby healthy."

Carole put the plate in front of Elle. It smelled good, and Elle took a small forkful of the meat and put it in her mouth. It was so tender it practically melted and teased her taste buds with a rich, full flavor.

"Wow, this is great! What is it?" Elle asked.

"Do you really want to know?" Carole smiled as Elle took another bite, this time with greens on top of the meat. "I take that as a yes. Very well, it's a cow's cheek, marinated in white wine for two days, then lightly seared on a very hot stove. I also put on a little salt and pepper. The greens are spinach in butter with onions. We grow the vegetables in hot houses during the winter. The meat comes from our cattle ranches in Central Park."

"This meat is really good." Elle wiped her mouth with a napkin and asked, "A cow's cheek; why that particular cut of meat?"

"We don't waste any part of the animals we raise for food. Anything edible is used to feed the people here. Even the contents of the intestines are used as fertilizer once the cattle are slaughtered." Carole smiled. "I won't tell you what we do with the blood, because you seem to be enjoying your meal. Maybe later."

"Why are you living here in Neo Luddite lands, Carole? I thought you would want to be closer to your mother and brother," Elle asked.

"I can see them any time I want and live anywhere I want. To these people," she waved her hand toward the field outside the door, "I'm Carole Bean, one of them. Oh, they see me when I leave the Neo Luddite territory and go to what they call the other side, but they don't really care. I am the eyes and ears of the Neo Luddite leader. If she accepts you, you are one of them. If she doesn't, then you aren't allowed anywhere in the territory."

"Then why am I here?" Elle asked around a mouth full of food.

"Because Paine sent you to me," Carole made it sound so simple.

"The Neo Luddites will kill Paine if he comes into their territory. He told me himself." Elle shook her head. "I guess I don't understand."

Carole laughed again. "I have lived among these people for years and I don't understand them either. I think they respect Paine for what he did for New York after he killed Walter Chavez." She paused. "He saved the city from UN control. But the verdict was already in, so they had to leave it stand. They could have sent someone after him, or not warned mother about the sentence and killed Paine when he wandered into the wrong part of the city, but they didn't." Carole shook her head and said, "They will kill him if he does cross the line, unless they all decide to let him come into their lands." Carole laughed again as Elle looked confused. "They are odd folk, but I honestly like them."

It was Elle's turn to laugh. "Is there anyone you don't like?"

She sat down and took a sip of water from the glass on the table, then said, "I've lived with or worked for every group in the city. Mother had me spying for her for years, ever since I was seven years old. I like the Technos, although they are a bit caught up in their technology and because of that, they seem like they're aloof. Basically, they are good people. I learned a lot about computers from them. I have been in the general population to report to my mother what the people think about the city and the factions fighting for power. Most of the non-aligned people in the city are just trying to get by and they like it that things are getting better."

Carole's eyes turned dark as she continued, "The drug cartel is full of dirt bags, but I worked for them for a short while I was living with Bannick. I don't like them at all." She shuddered at the thought of what they could have done to her. "I think they are leaving SUNY for New Jersey, mostly because mother is running them out, but they might try something foolish so we keep tabs on them."

"Once this is over, what will you do and where will you live?" Elle asked.

Carole shook her head and said, "I really don't know. It seems I like every place I have lived and could easily fit into any lifestyle. Maybe I'll stay the ambassador at large for the Neo Luddites, since they trust me and my opinions. Right now, I just want to make sure SUNY stays safe."

They were interrupted by a knock on the door.

"Come in," Carole called out.

A grey-haired woman limped into the room.

Carole stood up and Elle quickly followed her example.

"Miley, how good to see you," Carole shook hands with the woman and then turned to Elle. "Miley, may I introduce Elle Whippette. Elle, Miley Pickers, leader of the Neo Luddites."

"Miss Whippette, it's a pleasure. I am sorry to hear about the loss of your parents. I also have lost a loved one before their time." Miley took Elle's hand, her skin rough from manual labor, but her grip light. Elle could feel the strength in that hand.

"I will never get over their deaths," Elle said.

"My sources tell me you are trying to get back at those who did this to you," Miley noticed Elle turning red. "We may be without technology, but we aren't ignorant. We stay aware of what goes on in the world. The newspapers have reported several rather spectacular high-profile deaths recently. They seemed to have happened in places you visited." Miley looked intently into Elle's eyes and said, "The madness your friends reported seems to have left you suddenly, so what else can I surmise?"

Elle's face was returning to normal. "I have nothing to say."

"Very well, have it your way. But if I can figure this out, I am guessing your enemies can, too." Miley said.

"They don't know that I'm alive. The technology they rely upon told them I died in the shuttle crash that killed my parents," Elle said, defiantly. "And they depend on that technology to tell them everything."

Miley looked at the young woman standing before her and suddenly grinned widely.

"That's it!" Miley yelled so loud that both of the women jumped. "I owe you a debt of gratitude, Miss Whippette. I really want to hate you because you are close to Paine, but I find I can't."

Miley turned to Carole. "I want a meeting with your mother and the Technos as soon as possible. And I want Paine to be there, too."

When Elle gasped, Miley reached over to pat her hand and said, "Tell him he has safe passage into Neo Luddite territory until the end of the battle that I am sure is coming. Then we shall see what happens."

Miley turned on her heel and hobbled out the door.

Chapter 47 – Back in Radio City Music Hall

Miley grinned as Keenan Revis came through the conference room door. Even though he was prepared for the assault on his senses, he practically fainted as he entered, because the link to his data stream was severed when he walked into the shielded room.

Keenan looked dazed for a few moments, and then he seemed to collect himself and opened his eyes to what was for him a silent existence. He took the cup of chamomile tea Miley offered him with a weak smile.

Miley did not smile as Paine walked in with his mother, the president of SUNY. General Ryan Flagehty was with them as was Carole. Elle had decided it was not time to tell Paine and his mother she was carrying his child so she was waiting back at Carole's place. She asked Carole to tell her what transpired at the meeting.

Miley waived Ashley to the head of the table. Hand-drawn placards designated where the others would be sitting, and she had placed Paine's seat as far from her as the table allowed. She really did want to kill him where he stood, but controlled her impulse. "Not yet," she said to herself.

"Welcome, everyone. I called this meeting as a war council, and we are here because it's the safest place to talk in all of SUNY." Everyone nodded in agreement as Miley continued.

"We all understand that the United Nations wrote the ultimatum so that we would have no choice but to refuse it. That will result in a war we can ill afford to fight. We do not have the resources to defend ourselves, a fact which General Flagehty will no doubt confirm." Miley nodded to Ryan, who began his briefing.

"We might be able to stop the UN from taking SUNY, as demonstrated by my unit defeating, with the help of many New Yorkers, your people included, the combined United Nations and Kentucky Regular forces under General Martin. We have the combat equivalent of a division here under my command, and perhaps another division under the Technos. I am not sure what your strength is, Miley, but I can only assume it about the same." Ryan paused as Miley nodded. "The NUS will probably send in two or three divisions. The Germans will send in about the same. We can expect the Irish to field one or two divisions. The French will send no more than two. The Polish Army is slightly smaller than the German one, and they have more units involved fighting the Serbs than the Germans do, so they will probably provide only one division." The faces of the assembled factions looked grim as Ryan listed the forces they would have to defeat to survive.

Ryan consulted his notes and continued. "Japan will only send one brigade. They are worried that if they move too many of their forces here China may attack. With the bulk of Japanese forces still in the Pacific theater, China will only send what Japan does. They really don't like each other, which works to our advantage."

"So by my calculations, they will have more than a six to one advantage in technologically advanced divisions," Miley said.

"That is about right, because your people will not fight with modern weapons," Ryan said.

"Perfect!" Miley exclaimed. "They will not have the advantage, we will." She turned to Paine and said, "I asked you here because you have information we can use." Miley asked him, "How did you defeat the Neo Luddite forces you faced when you came to New York two years ago?"

"We had superior firepower but your people kept coming at us like madmen and women. I had to improvise a weapon to take out a lot of them at one time or we would have all died in the street." Paine replied.

"Exactly," Miley exclaimed. She looked at the blank faces of the assembled leaders and laughed, "God, you people are so dense! Don't you see, if we take away their technology, they will be helpless." She turned back to Paine and pressed him for an answer. "What would you have been able to do if your hypervelocity weapons failed, or if your improvised weapon plan had not worked?"

"We all had back-up weapons, but most of us don't carry much ammo for them. It's too heavy and our hypervelocity weapons are much better..." Paine paused and looked at Miley with a newfound respect. "You want to dampen the energy they need to make the weapons work and fight a low-tech battle, don't you?"

"It will have to be orchestrated perfectly. We will need to get their army, whatever size, into the proper place in the battle zone and then spring the trap. If we do this right, we will have a good chance at surviving the first assault. You do realize that after they find out what we can do, they will re-train their armies to fight the way we do and come at us with overwhelming force." Miley looked at the befuddled Keenan, who could not grasp the concept of getting rid of technology on the battlefield. "This is where you come in."

"What did I do?" Keenan asked. "I don't like the idea of killing our technology and if you do this, it will make my people ineffective."

"I know that." Miley patted Keenan's hand. "Your people will have to came to my lands and learn how to fight the enemy face-to-face instead of at a distance. We need every able-bodied person in this fight." She looked around the table again and said, "But that's not all we need. We need to keep them from coming back at us."

Ashley had been listening quietly during the conversation, but now spoke. "I think I see what Miley is proposing." She looked at Keenan and said, "It won't be enough to stop technology here. Your people will need to come up with a doomsday device, something that will destroy all technology on the planet and keep it destroyed for a long time."

Keenan stood up and began to walk toward the door, but was stopped by Miley, who quickly limped over to block his escape.

"Look at me," she said. "I do not want to stop you from living the way you want to, I just want us all to be able to live in our own way." She took Keenan by his arm and gently pulled him back to the table. "We need each other to survive! Please sit back down and at least listen."

Keenan allowed himself to be led back to his chair and slumped in it, his head in his hands. "How can I destroy everything I believe in?" he sobbed.

Ashley said, "I can see what Miley is asking us to do." She looked at Miley, who made a 'go ahead' motion with her hand.

"A hundred years ago, nuclear weapons were the most destructive force on Earth. The old United States of America and the Union of Soviet Socialist Republics faced off against each other in what was known as the Cold War. They fought a lot of undeclared proxy wars around the world, but they never directly fought each other." Ashley paused for effect and continued, "That's because if one launched a strike against the other, it could lead to nuclear war. Both sides would be completely destroyed, along with the human race. We saw what the plague did to the world; we are still trying to recover from it. I think the nations of the world who want us gone would think twice about attacking if they realized they would be back in the Stone Age if they did."

Ashley glanced at Miley and said, "I mean, without advanced technology and access to space. I meant no offense."

"No offense was taken," Miley smiled. "I agree. We have to threaten our foes with something so horrific to them that they will think twice about starting another war. We have to show them what not having technology will do to them." She looked at Keenan, "Remember what it was like to have your devices disconnected, not working? You had a hard time walking here with only one communications device, and you almost lost it when that one was shut off and you had no contact with the Techno world. And you feel terrible right now, don't you?"

Keenan nodded. "I am completely lost, but I am getting used to it."

Miley continued, "They will be just as confused and won't be able to be very effective. That is when we must strike and strike hard. We have to fight this battle to demonstrate what will happen if they come at us again." Once more, she touched Keenan's hand, "And you have to build us our doomsday device, and soon."

Keenan looked around the table and saw resolve in the faces of everyone there. "I think it can be done. We already have developed the dampening devices to protect us from Corvis nanoprobes, and we've built our own medical nanoprobes." Keenan saw the look of concern on Ashley's face and said, "My people are used to having perfect health and designed their own versions, ones that do not transmit their location to anyone or anything. We want to protect our privacy as much as you do."

Ashley looked relieved as Keenan continued, "But who will control the switch? I can't believe that one of my people could be entrusted with the power to shut down his or her way of life. I know I couldn't do it myself."

Miley made a suggestion. "How about giving control to one of my people?"

"No!" Keenan looked at her in complete surprise. "That would be like giving a steak to a dog and telling it to keep it safe for the rest of the pack. Your people hate technology and would destroy it if they could."

Miley bristled and replied, "Not all of my people hate technology; they just hate the ones who use it to hurt others!"

Ashley tapped her notebook on the table. When she finally got everyone's attention, she began. "There is no reason to argue about something that does not exist. We don't know if a world-wide dampener is possible, so let's proceed with the issue at hand. There will be an attack on SUNY, probably in the next few weeks, although General Flagehty assures me that it will be at least two months. That means we have to have a solid plan in place, and our people trained, by the end of March. That doesn't give us much time."

"We have access to the public libraries, and have been looking at history books that have been gathering dust in basements for years," Miley said. "They will provide us with good information on ancient warfare. We also have access to many of the displays and antique weapons located in the museums. We should be able to find things that we can use against the invading forces. My people also have gotten recent experience fighting against a superior force and have begun to develop ways to combat the technological advantages."

She grinned at both Paine and Ryan, who had shocked looks on their faces. "We didn't know what honest people you were until recently. One must prepare for the next battle, not the last war." She turned to Ryan and said, "My leaders will be happy to share those plans with you, General Flagehty, so you can incorporate them into your training."

Ryan responded, "Thanks. I'll inform you when we can begin. I may have a few things we can use as well."

Paine spoke next. "I grew up without modern weapons; we had old-style weapons for years, going up against gangs and the drug cartel. Marcus grew up fighting with whatever was handy, so he has a skill set most people do not know about, until it's too late."

Carole added, "Don't forget Katrina. She survived on the streets for years without using weapons at all." She looked around the table, "I'm aware she is enhanced, as most of you are, but her skills can be learned. She is very good at hand-to-hand combat."

"Miley, when can we begin our program?" Ashley asked.

"Today seems like a good day to start, but before we do, I have to establish some ground rules." She pointed at Keenan. "Your people can't use their technology in our lands until the attack, and then they can do whatever they need to defend themselves, before the dampener is activated."

Miley turned to Ryan next. "The same goes for your soldiers, General." Miley looked at Ashley, and then shifted her gaze to Paine. "You have a temporary stay of execution, until the end of the upcoming battle. If you come into our territory, you may still be attacked. I can't promise that all of my people will obey me. But I, for one, will not try to kill you until the fight is over, and will order my people to do the same."

"Once again, agreement at the table," Ashley said. "We have a lot of work to do."

As soon as they walked out of the shielded room, Keenan activated his communicator. "Walter, I have another little project for you. Could you please meet me in my office in one hour?"

Chapter 48 – Promises

It took a few days to set up the meeting, but Ryan, Marcus and Paine were finally standing with the head of Miley's fighters just south of Times Square, in Techno territory. It took Walter Biddle a few hours to figure out how to boost the dampening field to cover a much wider area. Marcus was not allowed outside Techno lands since the new dampeners were in place and operational around Neo Luddite territory. They were so powerful, his nanoprobes would be instantly inactivated and he would die. Biddle was still working on a super-dampener that would blanket the entire area occupied by the Neo Luddites.

Brad, the head of Miley's loosely organized defense force, spit on the ground in front of Marcus and Paine. "I will not kill you now. My leader has told us you have a stay of execution, and I will honor that. But do not think for one minute that I like you two."

Paine's hand stopped Marcus from responding with a blow to Brad's face. "I understand. We have a bigger enemy to worry about than two soldiers who did their duty."

"Your duty?" Brad was trying to keep control of his emotions and having a hard time. "Your duty to kill as many of us as you could with your modern weapons? You killed my friends with your trick, the lifter on its side. I almost lost my life in that blast of fire." He held up his arm to show the burn scar that ran up to his armpit. "Look what it did to my arm! And I was one of the lucky ones. Many of my friends died an agonizing death because of you." He closed his eyes as he flashed back to that day.

"My duty, as it was your duty to come after me." Paine took a step closer to Brad. "You and your people would have torn us to pieces if you had gotten your hands on us. You almost succeeded in stopping us with the attack from the buildings; dropping the desks and computer consoles on us was a stroke of genius. You surprised us, I can tell you that." Paine continued, "I did what I was told to do, and so did you. And the reason we are standing together here today is that we have a duty to protect our country now. We have to put aside our differences and our past and work together."

"I know, but the pain and suffering of my people is hard to forget." Brad clenched his hands and looked at his feet. "Be aware that I don't always have this much control. And my friends may not be able to stop themselves, so you need to watch your back." Brad pointed at Marcus, "You, too."

Marcus looked Brad in the eye and said, "Don't even think about it. I've been killed once already. Dying is the easy part. It's coming back that's hard." Brad looked at Marcus quizzically; Marcus just returned the spit on the ground.

"We need to talk about capabilities." Ryan interrupted the three warriors who were staring at each other in anger. "Brad, what can you tell us about your forces?"

"My guys usually come running when we have a threat. Word is spread through our communications network," Brad said. When the others just looked at him, he said, "We use pigeons, messenger dogs, and child couriers to carry our written messages. Immediate warnings are usually sent through whistles or drum beats."

"Can you show us how it works?" Ryan asked.

"Yeah, but you'll have to come into Neo Luddite lands to see." Brad looked at Paine. "And I warn you, you need to watch out."

Paine sighed. "I've taken risks my entire life. New York is more important than my safety." He turned to Marcus. "You have to stay here. We'll be right back, I promise," he said.

Marcus opened his mouth to speak, then shut it as Paine looked at him, determined to go through with the plan.

"OK, I will wait right here," Marcus said.

Paine and Ryan both handed Marcus their hypervelocity side arms and carbines. Paine took off his ear bug and removed the communicator from his breast pocket and gave them to Marcus. Ryan put all his electronic equipment in his rucksack and put it on the ground. Both of them checked to make sure no technology was going into the Neo Luddite lands and then set out.

As Paine walked away with Brad and Ryan, Marcus ran to the nearest building and sprinted up the stairs to the roof. He unslung his carbine and settled down on the flat rooftop. He quickly found the trio walking toward the boundary two blocks away. The cross hairs stayed on Brad the entire time.

Once they entered Neo Luddite lands, Ryan reached out and stopped Paine from moving deeper into the territory. "Show us how it works," he said to Brad.

Brad put two fingers in his mouth and emitted a shrill whistle. The workers who were tearing up the roads ran toward the sound, carrying their digging poles like spears. Within thirty seconds, Paine and Ryan were surrounded by sixteen men and women, all pointing their hand-held weapons at them.

Both Ryan and Paine reacted by putting their hands in the air. Marcus was just about to fire when Carole ran up to the group, trailed by a much slower Elle. She pushed her way into the circle and stood in front of her brother. Carole put her hands on her slim hips and glared at Brad.

"I heard the alarm. Just what is this?" Carole demanded.

"I was only showing these soldiers how we do things here in our land," Brad replied. "So let me finish my demonstration. This is none of your concern."

"Brad, do you know who these men are?" Carole asked.

"Of course I do. I was supposed to meet with them. They came on their own," Brad smiled an evil smile and glared at Paine. "Therefore, anything that happens just happens."

Elle entered the circle, breathing heavily. She put her arm in Paine's, holding him loosely in case he needed to defend himself. "Would you mind too much if we leave now?" she gasped out.

"I've seen you; you were with him the day he killed so many of my people," Brad said. "If you want to stay, I won't mind at all,"

Ryan lowered his hands. "Brad, we had an agreement. You've shown us how the communications work; now let's get back to discussing how to save our country."

"I am sorry; I want blood." Brad drew his knife.

Paine had that tingly feeling on the back of his neck, but he knew it was not because of Brad. He flashed, "Warning shot" in patrol sign and was rewarded with the crack of a hypervelocity round passing over their heads.

"Marcus has sixty-nine more rounds in his weapon right now. He will not miss." Paine pointed to Brad and said, "You will be first on his target list. Can you just let us go?"

Brad gritted his teeth. "Then we all die."

Paine made a decision. "Wait!" He turned to Ryan and said, "General, I will surrender myself to the Neo Luddite leader as soon as SUNY is safe from this attack. I will take whatever punishment the leader gives me." He turned back to Brad. "You have my word as an officer and fellow soldier."

"You will willingly allow us to kill you?" Brad asked.

"You just got my word. I promise to surrender and face whatever happens." Paine stepped toward Brad, who was still holding the knife in his hand. "We need to save SUNY, so we must set aside our issues for now. Either believe me when I tell you I will turn myself over to you and keep twenty fighters alive for the coming battle, or stab me now and never know if we won or lost."

Marcus was taking up the slack on the trigger when Brad put the knife back in its sheath. He let out his breath but did not take the cross hairs off of Brad.

Brad looked at Paine with a mixture of hate and respect. He waved his hand and the weapons of the crowd lowered. "No one will hurt you." He looked at his fighters and repeated, "No one." He stared at Paine and said, "We will win, and I will see you die. Then I will be happy."

"We both have to survive the battle first, but if I make it through the coming fight, I will do as I said." Paine took Elle's hand and pushed his way out of the circle of Neo Luddite fighters. Ryan followed Carole as she walked behind her brother back toward Techno territory.

As Paine led Elle out of Neo Luddite territory, Elle's mind was racing. She was going to tell Paine she was pregnant, but he had just confirmed his own death sentence. Ryan caught up with them and started talking to Paine as if nothing had happened, something about training the soldiers under their command. Paine was so focused on what was being discussed he didn't notice as Elle gently disengaged her hand from his and fell back to walk beside Carole.

"What in the world do I do now?" she asked Carole. "I can't hide this forever." Elle patted her belly, hidden by the winter coat.

"I can't tell you what to do. You have to decide for yourself. But above all, think about the child." Carole surged ahead, trying to catch up with Ryan. She said something to him and the two of them turned and walked toward her apartment, leaving Paine by himself.

Chapter 49 – Baby Talk

"Paine, please wait." Elle walked faster as Paine turned and stopped in the road. They were just outside of Neo Luddite territory and the group of fighters who followed them to the boundary dispersed and were returning to their work.

"What is it, Elle?" Paine asked.

Elle put her arms around Paine and stood silently for a moment. Then she opened her coat, took his hand and placed it on her swollen abdomen.

"You're pregnant?" Elle nodded to Paine. "How, I mean why? What happened? We only had that one night. I thought you had your birth control or I would have never…"

Elle stopped him with a finger to his lips. "Do you want the child or not? I need to know now so I can abort it if you don't want it." Elle was fighting back tears.

"Of course I want the baby. I can't believe it right now, that's all." Paine mentally calculated a timeline in his head. "I guess the child will be due in July. That will give us plenty of time to get ready."

"Paine, you may not be here!" Elle wailed. "I hate you! You just promised to die after the battle is over. Can you leave your child behind, fatherless? Or do we decide to end this now, and get on with our lives, whatever we have left."

"Elle, we have both been under a death sentence our entire lives. I always try to think positively, but find that more difficult with each day." Paine shook his head as the realization of what happened hit him. "I almost died today! I almost got you killed, too. We could both die tomorrow."

Paine gripped her arms. "But we are alive now, here. And the child inside you is alive, too. He or she deserves the chance to grow up. If I'm gone, the baby will have more parents than it will ever want. My mother, Ryan, Marcus, Katrina, Carole, you; the kid will be spoiled rotten." He smiled at Elle.

"But fatherless." Elle had tears running down her face. "I know what it's like to be without a father and mother, and so will our child. If you die, I die with you. In fact, I want to die."

Paine looked into her tear-filled eyes. "Promise me you will not abort the child."

Elle reached up and touched Paine's face. "I promise the child will be born. After that, I'll go with you. I love you, and I will not stand by and watch you die alone." Elle was crying. "I suppose I understand Miley's desire to kill you, she wants revenge, just like I do."

Paine looked at Elle and said, "I know, you want to pay back Corvis for killing your folks."

"It's more than that, Paine. My mother was also pregnant. Her birth control didn't work, either, and she and I got pregnant at about the same time." Elle continued, "I killed the wife of the CEO in Paris, and one of the grandsons in Plzen." Elle closed her eyes and re-lived the moments. "I stopped in Dallas on my way here from Europe and killed one more Corvis, and at least two of his guards, I am not sure who. The press has kept a lid on that shooting. I don't know why. I want two more lives to even the score."

"What do you mean by two more lives," Paine asked.

"When I started this crusade, I was going to kill one member of the Corvis family for each of us; Father, Mother, her baby, my baby and myself. I was going to blow myself up at Corvis headquarters once I had avenged the family. I want to die."

"No, Elle, you don't. You could have died with your parents, but here you are. Where there is life, there's hope!" Paine said.

Elle was sobbing as she tried to speak. "Then I saw you again, and now I want to live. I love you, but I also hate you. I want us to raise our child together but you are going to let yourself be killed."

"When I gave the order to kill the guard, I did what I had to do to accomplish the mission," Paine said.

"I was there when you gave the order to eliminate the guard, so shouldn't I bear some of the responsibility?" Elle asked.

"Elle, even though you were there, you had nothing to do with the decision to take out Walter. That was my choice, and it's my choice to accept the punishment." Paine had a determined look on his face as he continued, "I have to do this to at least try to save our country and my family," Paine hugged Elle hard as he choked out, "you and our child."

He stood there, his arms wrapped around Elle and then he continued, "Without Neo Luddite help, SUNY will fall. The United Nations has issued death sentences for my entire unit, for my mother and for Ryan. If we fail, we will all be executed. We decided to fight that way if we die we die fighting for freedom." He pushed Elle back and looked into her eyes. "And if promising to surrender to Miley means getting Neo Luddite help, so be it. Then we will win."

"You said I was your family," Elle said.

Paine took her in his arms again and held her tightly. "I never said it, but I've loved you from the moment you threw up on me during the flight into New York." Both of them laughed through their tears at the memory. "I want to be with you all the time."

Elle pushed away and looked up at Paine. "If that is a proposal, the answer is yes."

"Then we need to plan a wedding." Paine hugged her close to his chest. "I am just an old-fashioned guy, I guess. I suppose we should go tell my mother."

The ceremony was short, with Marcus, Katrina, Ryan and Carole as witnesses. As President of SUNY, Ashley granted herself the authority to perform the wedding ceremony and officiated at the service. She then sent the newlyweds off on a very short honeymoon. Training was going to begin in two days.

Chapter 50 - United Nations Force

Andre Chevalier of France, Secretary General of the United Nations, called the Security Council to order once again. John Gutenberg, Sean Fergusson, Oshara Tdacki, Lin Chow Tsing, John Wilson Smythe, Juri Navolska, Gerhard Schmidt, and Andre Laval were in attendance. It was one day after the deadline for the ultimatum and still no response had been received from SUNY.

Andre opened the meeting. "The government of SUNY has not agreed to our demands. We were right. Therefore, we have no choice but to conduct military operations against them. We have already received permission from the General Assembly to use force to go and remove them from New York."

Chevalier sat at his screen and the resolution appeared. "Let's look at what each of you have proposed to provide in terms of forces."

He read from the screen, "The NUS has agreed to offer two divisions, one being the 82d Airborne that the self-proclaimed General Flagehty deserted from during the last battle for New York. I am assuming they want revenge. Our German friends are sending three divisions; one of Alpine troops, the other two being infantry divisions. Sean Fergusson indicated that the Irish will send two regular divisions and a volunteer division from their colony in North America. My own countrymen have indicated we will offer four full-strength divisions of infantry. Poland will send their best division. Japan and China, stating difficulties in their own territories, will deploy only one brigade each." Chevalier turned to Juri and asked, "And what of Ukraine? I see no troop list for your support."

Juri leaned back in his chair. "As I stated earlier, I will go along with the plan to attack, but do not want to put my people in harm's way."

"Come on, Juri. Even these guys are sending a brigade." Sean Fergusson pointed at the Japanese and Chinese members. "In for a penny, in for a pound."

"I do not understand the reference, but assume you want me to commit more than my moral support." Juri sighed. "Very well, I will send those forces that were a part of the United Nations Military. They are waiting redeployment from German lands, so they can be attached to one of the German divisions. My newly promoted Lieutenant Colonel Kompaniyets is used to dealing with foreign armies and will lead a battalion of Ukrainians into this conflict."

"So, our total force will consist of a little less than thirteen divisions. I would assume that all of them will be armed with state-of-the art weapons?" Chevalier got nods from all the members. "My only concern is with communications. Not all of our leaders speak English, so how will we be able to pass orders down and control the battlefield?"

"The NUS and Irish share a common language, and most, if not all, the German soldiers speak enough English to be conversant." Fergusson said. "The Japanese and Chinese also have English as a second language, so they should be all right. The Ukrainians assigned to the United Nations are under Kompaniyets; he speaks very good English. It seems only the French don't have many English speakers."

"We French are secure in our own culture," Chevalier bristled. "We do not choose to speak in a lesser language."

Oshara Tdacki laughed out loud. "Your arrogance is beyond belief. My people have documents that are thousands of years old yet my children can read them perfectly today, and I am sure that my friend Tsing can say the same about his family in China." He almost sneered as he continued. "Your people could not even write, much less speak the same way then. You were probably grunting monosyllables and living in caves while Oriental culture flourished. And yet we have all decided that a common language is best for commerce and diplomacy." He stopped and looked at Chevalier. "I mean, almost all. You have no excuse except for conceit."

Juri raised his hand to stop the retort from Chevalier. "Gentlemen, let us not quarrel over something so trivial, when our mission is to destroy a mutual enemy. We will be able to find a way around this problem, perhaps by finding English-speaking French officers to act as liaison within the headquarters."

Chevalier spoke again. "It would be better if French-speaking officers from the other forces were sent to the headquarters. As the provider of the most forces to this operation, I assumed the French would assume overall command of the operation."

Multiple conversations broke out around the table. Chevalier had to bang on the table to regain control. "It only makes sense! My people are going to assume the brunt of the fighting, so we should lead."

"If this is your way of securing French supremacy in the United Nations after the war is over, I refuse to allow it. My forces are no longer available to you," Tsing said.

Tdacki said nothing. He stood up and slowly gathered his communications devices and notebook and walked out the door.

Smythe looked around the table at the set faces of the ambassadors. "As someone who is not involved in the fight, I can see this coalition is doomed for failure. I can offer you Australian communications units for the headquarters. I believe we have enough French speakers."

Tsing spoke again, "You mean you have Vietnamese refugees who still kept the French language alive in Southeast Asia." Vietnam, Cambodia and Laos were once again under control of the Chinese, and there was a low-level insurgency occurring in those lands. China kept a large military force in Vietnam and had conducted a purge of Vietnamese intellectuals and dissidents in the past ten years. Many of the refugees from these purges sailed for Australia, which had lifted its ban on immigration after the plague ended.

"I am talking about Australian citizens," Smythe said. "Besides, your people won't be a part of the forces anyway, so why should you care?"

Tsing stood up and followed the example of Tdacki. As the door closed behind him, Smythe said, "Now that that is over, does anyone else want to leave?" No one spoke. "I believe the floor is yours again, Mister Secretary."

"We need to set a timetable for the invasion. The French contingent will be ready for deployment by April first. What about the rest of your forces?" Chevalier looked around the table.

"I think we need to do planning and training at least at the command level before going to battle. I would propose a two-month timeline," Gustafson said. "I would also believe a demonstration that may make the SUNY people rise up against the government and keep us from having to invade. Perhaps we can starve them into submission?"

The discussion went on for another hour. Chevalier finally sat back in his chair and conducted a recap of the decisions. "Our forces will attack no later than the first week of June. The units will assemble in New Ireland and launch the attack from the North. The terrain favors our attack from there, and the Neo Luddites control that part of SUNY, so opposition should be light. Once we have secured a base of operations in the North, we will continue the attack into Manhattan, culminating in the destruction of the SUNY Techno and regular forces that should be in the lower part of the country. Air Forces from the NUS will interdict any movement of SUNY forces trying to escape the island. Meanwhile, a blockade of all traffic into and out of SUNY will begin at once. The blockade will keep any more supplies from entering SUNY territory." Chevalier looked around the room. "Are we all agreed?"

Everyone at the table nodded.

Chapter 51 – Blockade

"And so it begins!" Ashley said as the United Nations General Assembly voted overwhelmingly to initiate an immediate blockade of all traffic in and out of SUNY territory. China and Japan abstained from the vote, declaring their neutrality in the upcoming war. Of course, the SUNY ambassador cast the single no vote, just before being placed under house arrest by the French Government.

Ashley was looking at her screen. SUNY shuttles and other aircraft were being impounded in space ports worldwide; their crews were placed in custody. The SUNY ambassador to the United Nations was placed under house arrest in Paris.

Ryan reported to Ashley's office as soon as he got the news.

"Madame President, we have seven shuttles remaining at Kennedy. Most of our fleet is now in the hands of the UN, but we do have word from China that the four shuttles seized in Hong Kong will be returned to us after cessation of hostilities."

"How are we doing on power cells and weapons?" Ashley asked.

"Our army has enough carbines and rifles to outfit two divisions of troops. The Technos have about three thousand of the old-style hypervelocity weapons from the Times Square Massacre; they managed to retrofit them to accept the improved power cells we use today. No one knows where the other two thousand went. They also have personal weapons, all state-of-the art. That means the Technos can field about a brigade." Ryan looked at his notes and continued. "The Neo Luddites have a loose military organization. They can put twenty-thousand fighters in the field, but their combat ratio is about one-tenth that of a modern division. We will even the odds if," he stopped himself and then continued, "I mean when the new dampening devices run as planned. We just need to work out the logistics and the training piece for Neo Luddite units."

"How long do we have before the ground attack begins?" Ashley was hoping for a long estimate, but knew that hope was not a method.

"My staff estimates that the NUS could attack at any time." He held up his hand when Ashley gasped. "We don't think NUS will act alone. They probably can only provide three divisions, which would mean a one-to-one ratio. No commander would agree to fight facing those odds. They will be fighting us on our home ground and in an urban environment. With modern technology on both sides, they will need at least a six to one advantage. We have to keep our intelligence people working on identifying the total UN troop strength to decide when they will be able to attack."

"Is the UN going to try to block our communications? I want to be able to hear what is going on in the rest of the world, to see how other nations will react to the fighting." Ashley said.

"It doesn't look like they will try. They still have to talk to each other, and without a central communication's system, the different units will not be able to coordinate their efforts," Ryan said. "I think it's more likely that we will block their communications as well as our own if the Technos come up with the super-dampener we asked them to build. Then we'll have to rely on the Neo Luddite's communications network." Ryan looked back at his computer screen to review his notes.

"How will we deal with the blockade? The UN has threatened to shoot down any aircraft and sink any ships coming in and out of our lands." Ashley was concerned. "We need to think about rationing, starting now. They may sit and try to starve us out."

"Thank God for the Neo Luddites on this one. Miley sent me a complete inventory of all food stored in her part of the country." Ryan pulled out a leather-bound book and turned to a page he had marked earlier. "By her estimates, with everyone receiving about two thousand calories a day, we should have enough to last us until the crops come in this fall. People in the city are resourceful; they will be able to stretch that out longer if need be."

"I picked up a recipe for rat stew that was pretty darn good when I first got to New York," Ashley smiled a wry smile. "And you'd be surprised what you can do with a little salt, hot sauce and a hand full of bugs." As Ryan grimaced, Ashley laughed and said, "I had a child to feed."

"I never really had to worry much about food; the NUS Army always got enough to eat." He patted his stomach and said, "All this desk work has put extra weight on me. I need to get back into fighting trim, so fewer calories may be just the thing." Ryan laughed.

"I was meaning to talk to you about that," Ashley replied. She was eyeing his body and began to blush.

There was an awkward silence for a moment as they both looked at each other.

Ashley broke the silence first, blurting out, "All right, let's look at our training." Ashley asked, "How is it going?"

"Better than I expected." Ryan replied.

Chapter 52 – Training

Paine slid his right hand farther up the metal rod he was holding. It improved the balance of the weapon in his hand. He thrust the tip of the rod through the sandbag hanging from the rafters of the ceiling, then pulled it out and swung the butt of the rod in an arc into the side of the bag. It split open from the force and sand spilled out onto the floor.

Similar thrusts and jabs were being conducted all around the room.

Brad blew his whistle. He yelled to the scout platoon, "All right, bring it up."

Paine took out a bandana and wiped the sweat from his forehead as he leaned on the steel rod that had once been used for digging up asphalt from the street.

"Not too shabby. You guys learn quickly. Does anybody have any questions." Paine asked.

Sergeant Kligemann raised his hand. "Why do we need to do this stuff? I got me a pistol that will do the job at close range."

Paine looked at Brad, who grudgingly nodded. "Lukas, how many rounds do you have for your pistol?" Paine asked.

"Fourteen," he replied.

"And what happens after the rounds are gone? Are you going to be able to do as much damage using your pistol as a club, or do you want to be able to do this?" Paine pointed at the tattered bag he on which he had been training. "We will need your pistol, but we also need you to be a dangerous weapon yourself."

"Anybody else have any thoughts?" Brad asked. No one took the bait. "Fine, then put the spears back in the racks and get your knives. I am going to show you how to take out a man's kidney." He drew his knife and looked at Paine. "Who wants to go first?"

Marcus stepped between them and ran his thumb along the edge of his own knife. It was an old design he'd found in the museum, something called a Bowie. He liked the weight and balance of the long blade, and the double edge halfway from the tip gave him the ability to slash in either direction. "I think you and I could show them how it's done. I've done a little knife fighting myself." He remembered the night he killed his master and escaped from slavery in The Young Nation. Marcus crouched and began to wave the knife through the air in an intricate pattern.

Brad, recognizing an expert, chose not to try anything. He stood to the side and described what Marcus was doing as he cut the sandbag to ribbons. Everyone watched with interest and then went through the drills Marcus had demonstrated.

"The knife is for close quarters, like in a hallway or on the stairs. The spears are more for open spaces. If you find the need for more long-range fighting, then we shift to arrows and darts." Brad pulled a bow from the rack and strung it. It was a recurved design that had been taken from an old sporting goods store many years ago. The bowstring had been replaced several times, but it still functioned perfectly.

Brad fitted an arrow onto the string and pulled it back to his cheek. He let fly and the arrow penetrated the sandbag, passing through and burying itself into the wall. "Kligemann, shoot the bag with that pistol of yours."

Lukas smoothly pulled out his pistol. It was an automatic, ten millimeters, with a silencer. He loved the pistol and hated to waste a bullet, but he put one round center mass into the sandbag. The bag barely moved, and the bullet was trapped.

"OK, I get your point." Kligemann said.

"Practice, people; you will need to be able to train your soldiers how to fight this way soon," Brad said.

The next day, Paine had the scouts go in pairs to the Techno units and the soldiers of the SUNY army to teach their newfound skills.

General Flagehty directed that all units would practice close-combat techniques at least two hours a day and keep their low-tech weapons close at hand. He sent out word that anyone who turned ammunition or empty shell casings in to the SUNY armed forces would be rewarded with extra food rations. The stockpile of bullets increased, but there just wasn't a lot of old ammunition left in New York.

Chapter 53 - Josh's Orders

When the communicator buzzed, Josh was thankful for the interruption. He was as bored as he'd ever been. At least when he was on the capsule, he had something that interrupted the boredom once in a while. He had been inactive for more than three months, with nothing to do except wait.

"Martin." He answered.

"Josh, it's so good to hear your voice. I have a mission for you." Steven Corvis' voice came out of the speaker.

"I am ready to do anything," Josh replied.

"The combined forces of the United Nations are going to launch an attack SUNY on June 6th. I have the transcripts of the discussion on when they plan to launch the assault, and the French and NUS generals insisted upon that date." Steven paused. "They said it was significant."

"You need to work on your military history more often. June sixth was the day the Allied Forces stormed the beaches at Normandy, against the German Third Reich." Josh mused. "I am surprised the Germans allowed that day to be chosen."

"If you would like, I can send you the transcripts of the meeting. No wonder it go so heated!" Steven chuckled.

"Enough of the history lesson, what is it you want me to do?" Josh asked.

"Somehow, I need you to get word to the SUNY government of the plans. I need the UN to look foolish once more. The French are getting too powerful and may be able to pull this off. That will ruin my plans for a world government again." Steven did not trust Chevalier. He was afraid Chevalier would make a power grab, just like Josh did.

"Once you get word to them, I want you to get into the attacking forces." Corvis said. "I need you to take out the SUNY government once the battle is almost over. You see, I can't have them survive because they have information that may damage my reputation."

Josh thought about how he would rid the world of his ex-wife and son. "I can do that, with pleasure. I need help to find them, and to set up the UN during the attack. And I have just the man for the job. Could you use your assets to locate Bobby Lee," Josh asked, "He is a Command Sergeant Major in the NUS armed forces."

Steven put Josh on hold and punched in a few commands on his console. It only took a few seconds to locate a Master Sergeant Bobby Lee, 101st Airborne Division, Fort Campbell, Kentucky. Steven pushed the speaker button and asked, "There is a master sergeant named Lee in Kentucky. Is that him?" Lee's picture appeared on Josh's screen.

"Yeah, that's him. Patch him through. Text only."

The screen in Steven's office showed the texting.

Martin "What happened, I thought you were a sergeant major?"

Lee "Got busted one rank after being sent back to NUS from UN. Now working in operations."

Martin "Perfect, need you to get hold of plans and come to SUNY."

Lee "Can be there in three days. Blockade will make passage difficult, but not impossible."

Martin "Your cover - deserted with plans. Deliver plans to Paine, join unit he is in, then wait for further instructions."

Lee "WILCO."

Steven cut the secure communications link to Lee, and the screen returned to Josh's room. "Looks like you've got a good man there."

Josh just nodded, then disconnected.

Chapter 54 – Deserter

Bobby Lee took off the NUS uniform and changed into civilian clothes. He had a microchip subcutaneously embedded in his right arm that had contained of his personnel data. He had downloaded the operational plans for the invasion of SUNY on it, leaving out all the annexes for support due to the limited space on the chip. It should be enough to help the SUNY Army prepare for the initial assault. After that, they were on their own.

Lee had been in the office late Friday night and had copied the plans just before putting them back into the secure storage facility. No one questioned him; he was always working late, even on Fridays when most of the NCOs were at happy hour down at the club. The division's operations officer barely looked up when Master Sergeant Lee checked out.

Lee left the office and signed out for home. He got into his personal lifter and flew out to a ranch near Pennyrile Lake. As he neared his rented cabin, he slowed the vehicle to a hover and took out a syringe from his cargo pocket. It contained the nanoprobes he'd removed from his body early that morning at the aid station. He squirted the nanoprobes into the mouse he'd caught in the live trap outside his office and then set the autopilot. He opened the door to the lifter and stepped out.

The platform Lee had stolen from the rigging shed worked perfectly. He stepped off in front of his house as the lifter sped toward Lake Barkley. The nanoprobes would stop working as soon as the lifter smashed into the middle of the lake. Lee doubted that anyone would be trying to recover the body; the invasion was less than a week away. He stripped the cover off the old car that he'd lovingly restored, threw the lift platform in the back seat and started it up. He settled down and put the compact disk player on. He had more than enough country music to take him through the eighteen hour drive to New York.

Lee stopped the car and stretched. He rolled his shoulders and did a few deep knee bends to get his blood flowing and then opened the trunk of the car. He stripped off his clothing and put on the wet suit he'd stored there. He carefully checked the rebreather to make sure it was fully functional. He knew he wouldn't require it for its rated four hours, but he wanted to be sure it worked if he needed it.

Lee had intentionally stayed in normal traffic and passed by the blockade zone. He was fifty miles north of SUNY territory when he walked to the bank of the river and slipped into the water. He let the current take him down river toward Manhattan at about two miles an hour. He would go under water when he had three miles to go.

As he neared SUNY territory, he had to submerge three times to escape detection by patrol craft. They were looking for contraband being sent down river by SUNY sympathizers in Up State New York. Lee saw several large boxes being pulled from the river. The searchers were not looking for one man, so he remained undetected. His GPS told him he was near the dividing line between Neo Luddite and Techno territory when he surfaced and climbed the wall to a grassy area that once had been a park. He stripped off the rebreather and then froze as a voice came from behind him.

"Put your hands where I can see them." A Neo Luddite farmer, tending his garden, was standing twenty feet away with a drawn bow, its arrow pointing at Lee.

"I am here to help. I have plans for the invasion in my possession and need to get them to the authorities as soon as possible." Lee spread his hands wide.

Lee saw a figure walk up behind the farmer and stab him in the back. The arrow, released by the dead hand, sped straight into Lee's shoulder. As the figure approached him he passed out from the pain.

Josh ran an electronic device over the unconscious Lee, then pushed the arrow through his shoulder and put a quick heal patch on the wound. He took out a syringe and injected the contents into Lee's arm.

Lee woke up dressed in the dead man's clothes. He was lying on a cot, in front of a fire in a darkened room. He sat up and rubbed his hands, soaking up the warmth of the fire. He suddenly noticed the man sitting across the room from him. Lee quickly stood up and assumed the position of attention.

"General Martin, Master Sergeant Bobby Lee, reporting as ordered." Josh said nothing. "How did you find me? I took all my nanoprobes out and sent them to the bottom of Lake Barkley."

"GPS works both ways, Bobby. I have been tracking you since you entered New York territory. Did you get the information I asked for?" Josh asked.

"Of course, Sir, it's on my personal chip." Lee extended his arm. "It can be retrieved by any standard reader."

"Good, then you'd better leave now." Josh knew what the plans were, he'd read them a few minutes before Lee woke up. He stood up to go.

"But how did you fix me up so fast? Isn't this Neo Luddite Territory? Don't they have a ban on technology?" Lee asked.

"Sergeant, you ask too many questions. I've told you all that you need to know." Josh turned away. As he walked out the door, he said, "Your instructions are on the table. Don't leave anything behind and get out of Neo Luddite lands as soon as possible."

"Yes, sir," Lee said to the closed door. Josh had always treated him just like he did his own sons, only maybe a little worse. Ever since his mother died on the raid to Florida, Lee had looked up to Josh as a father figure. Josh had helped him learn the skills he needed to survive on the battlefield and had promoted him ahead of others even Lee himself considered more qualified. He always wondered why, but had never gotten up enough nerve to ask. Lee was sad when Josh's death had been reported, but more surprised when he got a message from him asking him to do things to help him get back at Paine and Marcus.

At first, Lee refused until Josh texted him the details of his mother's death. Gabby had been the squad leader of both Paine and Marcus and was killed on a raid to clear out squatters. Josh told him that they deserted her and that had led to her death. That made Lee want to kill both Paine and Marcus, but he was told not to by Josh. "All in good time," was what the text had said.

With Marcus dead and SUNY in trouble with the United Nations, Lee could now concentrate on one target; Paine. The thought of being in proximity to Paine again made his blood boil. Lee took control of his emotions and picked up the instructions Josh had left him.

Chapter 55 – Plans

Bobby Lee walked up to the State House and stopped as the guard in front of building raised his weapon. "I have an important message for the president. It concerns the coming attack." Lee held his arms over his head and dropped to a sitting position.

Two more guards came out of the building and stood on either side of him. A Techno with a wand came running up and held it on front of Lee. The pad the Techno was looking at lit up and pages began to scroll on the screen. "I have it," he told the guards, who then grabbed Lee under the arms and half-carried him into the building. He was placed in a small room, with bars on the windows. Lee checked the door; it was locked from the outside. He settled down to wait.

Forty-five minutes later, the electronic-locking mechanism actuated, and the door swung open. Paine walked in with a garment bag in his hand.

"First Sergeant, it's good to see you!" Paine said.

Lee kept his face calm as his heart was burning with the desire to kill Paine. "I trust that you downloaded the plans for the attack?"

"We have them and don't have much time to prepare. I would be grateful if you would rejoin A Company as the first sergeant again." Paine handed Lee the bag.

Lee pulled open the Velcro fasteners to reveal the SUNY uniform with a first sergeant insignia on the breast strap. "I thought I was your Sergeant Major?"

Paine smiled and said, "You were a good one, but Marcus is back in the position. I had to get him out of Plzen before he could be finished off, so we staged his death, much like General Martin staged my death back in Kentucky. Marcus has been here in SUNY since before the massacre, working for my mother. Now he's back in the unit with me."

Paine saw the troubled look in Lee's eyes and misunderstood it. "Bobby, Marcus is good at what he does, and you are a great first sergeant for A Company. You yourself said that your replacement wasn't ready to take on the company. Now you can go back to your old job." Paine looked at him in the eyes and said, "We need you, especially if what you brought us is true."

"All right, I'll take it. They had me working in an office and I was going stir crazy. At least I'll be back in the field where I belong." Lee was glad he was going to be close, but not too close, to Marcus and Paine. The temptation to kill them might be more than he could resist. He was told to wait until he got the word to execute them from General Martin.

"Get changed, then, and I'll have someone escort you back to your old unit." Paine walked out, leaving the door unlocked. Lee could see one of his troopers from A Company standing outside the door as it closed. The private gave him a wave of welcome.

Once Paine left Lee, he walked upstairs to the meeting room. Ryan was pouring over the plans that Lee had smuggled to them.

"Come on in, Paine, and take a look at this." Ryan called up a map on the tabletop and began to draw on it with a red stylus. "The NUS divisions will be airlifted into Kennedy, just like the plan I used to get here last year. It calls for a strike on the facilities and the air defenses, then a platform drop in three waves." Ryan looked at the map. "How could they be so stupid? They must know I wrote that plan."

"Something about this does not seem right," Paine said. "I think maybe we'd better keep an eye on Sergeant Lee."

"Look at this part of the plan. It has the Irish coming down river in fast assault craft. That would just get them killed." Ryan shook his head. "We could put chains across the river just below the surface and rip the bottoms out of their boats. And as much as I'm aware, they don't have enough boats to lift a battalion, much less a brigade."

"Lee worked on the plans, so why don't you and Marcus talk to him about what we've seen here? Maybe if you ask him to tell you the plans from memory, it will confirm that they're legitimate." Ryan was still shaking his head as Paine walked out.

J. B. Durbin

Chapter 56 – The Revelation

The unit was out training when Paine and Marcus walked into A Company's area and stood in front of the charge-of-quarters clerk who was intently examining a document. She looked up from her desk and jumped to her feet when she recognized the battalion commander. "Building, attention!" she shouted.

Paine replied, "At ease, sergeant. I will be in the area all day. Would you be so kind as to find the First Sergeant? We need to talk to him."

"Yes, sir," she said as she relaxed slightly. "Would you like to wait in his office?" She led them to Lee's desk.

Lee entered the office in less than a minute, wearing his brand-new uniform. Paine indicated that he sit behind the desk while he and Marcus took seats in front of him.

"I want you to go over the plan you were working on for the invasion with me. It seems like the chip had bad sectors on it and all the pages did not come through." Paine took out his tablet and consulted it. "It says here that the 82nd is going to drop, and then the text is garbled. Could you help me fill it in?"

"Certainly, Colonel Martin; the 82nd and 101st are supposed to come in low-level and drop into Central Park, utilizing the same delivery system General Flagehty tested. The weapons of the Neo Luddites will be no match for the firepower two modern divisions will bring to the fight." Paine looked at Marcus, who sat stone-faced in his chair.

"And the Irish are still coming in by fast boats?" Paine asked.

"Fast boats, no, they are coming overland from the North. They plan on using old technology to scare the citizens into submission. I saw pictures of armored vehicles, you know, the ones that were made obsolete by hyper velocity weapons. The plan is to take over Neo Luddite territory, then build up their forces there for a final assault on Manhattan." The look on his commander's face made Lee realize he'd been suckered by General Martin. "What plan are you looking at?" Lee asked.

"The one you brought us and said was genuine," Marcus growled.

Lee got up from his desk and pointed the sidearm he had taken from beneath the desk at Marcus and Paine. "Put the tablet down, Paine. And don't reach for that pistol, Marcus."

He spoke in a loud voice, "If you are listening, I need to be picked up outside my company headquarters in ten minutes."

"Who are you talking to?" Paine asked.

Lee did not answer. "Stand up slowly and walk into the day room." He waved the pistol toward the door.

The clerk jumped to her feet again as the men walked out into the hallway. Her eyes opened wide when she saw the pistol in her first sergeant's hand but she didn't stand a chance as the bullet ripped into her body and she slumped back into her chair.

Lee put his pistol against the center of Marcus' back and pulled the trigger. The small-caliber slug passed through Marcus' body and buried itself into the wall opposite Paine. Marcus dropped to the floor; Lee kept the pistol pointed at Paine as he reached down and felt Marcus' neck for a pulse. There was none. He looked down at the Marcus and said, "For my mother."

"Put your hands up, you are under arrest," Lee told Paine.

"Why are you doing this?" Paine asked.

"The General sent me to get you. I have been following you every step of the way, waiting for my chance to make you finally pay for the murder of my mother." Lee pushed the clerk onto the floor and motioned that Paine should sit in the bloody chair. "You forced my hand. Put these on," he said as he tossed a pair of plasticuffs to Paine.

Paine caught the cuffs and put them over his wrists. They immediately adhered to his hands and immobilized Paine. "Why are you doing this?" Paine asked again.

"The General said you were evil, and you proved it with the GUNFOR massacre. I made sure the camera Sergeant Kligemann had was one that worked. The General told me you were going to kill those people, I didn't believe it until I saw it with my own eyes. He told me to come here so I could take you captive and turn you over to the UN for execution." The pistol never wavered.

"General Jung found out about the mission as it was being launched," Paine said. "How could he have known this was going to happen? Someone else who has the technology to change vid recordings tampered with them. The footage you saw was not real.

You, Kompaniyets and Jung all saw it at the same time. If you can remember who you got the camera from, then it could tell us who wanted to change what actually happened."

"It doesn't matter who gave it to me." Lee remembered the Corvis technician who handed him the recorder. He was found dead in his hotel room later that night. "I just want you dead, but the general said not yet."

"General Jung was shot during the trial, they said he killed himself." Paine insisted.

"I did not say it was General Jung. You are just one of many he wants to see suffer, the way he did. I have a long list of people I am going to see. The General wants your entire family to die." Lee smiled, thinking about how sweet revenge could be.

"You keep mentioning the general." Paine said, "To whom are you referring?"

"General Martin. He also told me that Gabby, and he had been intimate once, after your mother ran away, and that I was his biological son."

Paine looked at him in shock. "We are half-brothers?" Paine asked.

"I would not call you my brother!" Lee yelled as he extended the gun close to Paine's face. "How can we be brothers when you killed my mother?"

The nanoprobes in Marcus' body began their work as soon as the bullet hit him. The wound was already sealed, blood loss was minimized and Marcus was fully conscious within ten seconds. He stayed on the ground listening to the conversation, then silently rose to his feet and stood behind Lee. Paine moved his hands as if flexing them against the plasticuffs, telling Marcus, "Wait," in patrol sign.

"What did father tell you about your mother's death?" Paine asked.

"He said you and Marcus left her, you left her to die." Lee gritted his teeth. "I wanted to kill you both then, but father said I should wait until the moment was right. He said I could take my revenge on Marcus, and you know what? It was good to watch him die. For you, however, we have a different fate. There were worse things than dying, like being locked away for a long time, awaiting death that may come at any moment. UN justice works, but it works slowly. Father told me. You will be held in a small prison cell, pending appeal, which you will lose. Then there will be a second appeal, and you will lose again, all the while wishing you could escape. Then one day the appeals will run out, and they will take you out and shoot you like the dog that you are." He paused and raised the pistol. "And I want to be there when that happens."

"What if I told you that the general ordered me to leave Gabby, your mother, where she was because he needed her plasma weapon for the assault?" Paine said.

"I would not believe it," Lee retorted.

Marcus grabbed Lee in a bear hug and almost crushed his rib cage as he threw him to the ground and pinned him there with his weight.

"Paine is right; I was there with him when we got the orders. General Martin ordered us to leave your mother behind. Paine was trying to save her, but we were told leave her and to move on to the objective." Marcus easily kept Lee immobile as Paine tried to free his hands from the cuffs.

"No!" Lee wailed as he struggled in Marcus' grip. He managed to get the pistol hand free for a moment and fired one shot at Paine before Marcus broke his neck.

Marcus got off Lee's still body and moved to Paine.

The bullet had just grazed Paine's right arm. Marcus pulled a quick heal patch from his first aid kit and put it on the oozing wound.

Paine looked at Lee Lee's broken body and cursed his father. Marcus cut off the plasticuffs and checked on the clerk. The clerk and Lee were both still breathing as Marcus and Paine carried them outside to the lifter and took off for the aid station.

Steven Corvis had lost contact with Bobby Lee as soon as he went into the company office. It was as if the nanoprobes had been removed from his body. The transcript only said that he was told to meet with his commander, and then transmission ended.

"Paine!" Corvis hissed through clenched teeth, and then slammed his hand down on the desktop console, shattering the screen.

Chapter 57 – Lee's Plans

The meditube hummed as it worked on Bobby Lee's spine. Technicians hovered outside, and a neurosurgeon typed in commands to fix the damage Marcus had done. It was to no avail.

"Sorry, Colonel Martin," the doctor said, "We didn't get him in the tube soon enough. I am afraid the damage is permanent."

Paine looked at the body on the gurney, hooked to a respirator. Lee could not move his head, but his eyes followed Paine as he stepped up to the bed.

"Bobby, can you hear me?" Paine asked.

Lee blinked once.

"I am not sure if you care or not, but your clerk will live. I thought you might want to know." Lee's eyes closed. Paine continued after Lee reopened his eyes. "Do the math in your head, Bobby. General Martin said you were his son, and that he had an affair with Gabby after my mother left us. That would make you fifteen years old. How could you believe him?"

Lee blinked twice.

"Yes, it's true; he's been lying to you all this time, trying to get you to do his bidding. And look what it got you." Paine held up a piece of paper for Lee to see. "The machine just ran a DNA sample from both of us. There is no chance of us being related."

Lee's head was quivering as he tried to scream at Paine, but nothing worked.

The doctor gently pulled Paine away from the paralyzed man. "I need you to look at this." He guided Paine to the meditube and showed him the readout. "There were nanoprobes in his body, ones that should have prevented the damage to his spine from being this severe, but they were specialized, like nothing I have ever seen. The dampening fields around our facility keep any Corvis manufactured probes from transmitting information to their servers. The Technos have seen to that. But these probes seem to be designed only for transmission purposes. They couldn't repair his broken neck."

"It was lucky for me I took Marcus along, in more ways than one. He has a portable dampener that probably kept the communications from getting through to Corvis." Paine shook his head. "Now we'll never get the true plans of the enemy, until they attack."

Marcus had been listening to the conversation. He chimed in, "At least we found out a few things, like the airborne assault on Central Park and the plan to use tanks against the Neo Luddites. Let's go brief General Flagehty on what we've got."

Lee was furiously blinking his eyes as Paine and Marcus walked out.

Alejandra Francesca Colon Cruz, who was a volunteer nurse's aide, walked in and wiped the tears away from Lee's eyes. She looked into them and was captivated by how deep green those eyes were. She stared at Lee for a moment. Just before she turned away, Lee slowly blinked three times fast, three times slowly, and then three times quickly again. The aide, who was more than she appeared, recognized the message: SOS. She sat down next to Lee, picked up a pad of paper and a stylus and simply said, "Go ahead." The Neo Luddite deep-cover spy slowly wrote down what Lee had to say.

J. B. Durbin

Chapter 58 - Walter Biddle

It had been a challenge to develop a dampening device small enough to be swallowed by a human and protect it from the digestive system, but that had only taken Walter Biddle a day to complete. He then went to work on a second project commissioned by President Miller, a portable dampening device with a five-hundred-foot radius. Child's play, he finished that design while on the phone with Carley Squires, the president's chief of staff; fabricated the parts; assembled it and delivered it to the president's office that same day. He was then asked to develop a random-speech generator for the scarred man with no heart. He considered that task beneath his status but did it as a favor for Keenan.

Walter's next project was no challenge at all; He updated the plans for President Miller's portable device and had seventy built. They were placed around the borders of Neo Luddite land to keep technology from operating there. Walter couldn't understand why anyone would want to keep technology out, but he did what he was told.

His last challenge was to build a device big enough to stop all electronic devices within a thirty-mile radius. That should have been harder, but without having to miniaturize everything, four large generators were built and installed around the perimeter of Neo Luddite territory within three days. No technology would work while inside the field created by these devices.

Walter was now extremely bored. He was stuck testing the new guidance system and obstacle-warning device he had invented for the unmanned repair vehicles Ashley was sending into the subway system. Ashley hoped to get the transportation system operational again, and clear out the subways just in case they were needed as shelters in the upcoming war.

Biddle was simultaneously playing a game while watching one of the cars making repairs to the ceiling of a tunnel through his video display. An alarm sounded as the car suddenly stopped. Biddle switched cameras to the front of the car and found he was looking at a young girl of perhaps twenty standing right in the center of the track, with her arms crossed.

Walter was annoyed. He actuated the speaker and yelled, "What are you doing there. Get off the tracks and let me get back to work!"

The girl simply stared at the red light of the camera, and then turned, bent over and lifted her skirt to show Biddle her backside. She turned back around and smoothed her skirt. "This is Neo Luddite territory; your machine is not welcome here." She crossed her arms once more.

Walter was shocked by her brashness and even more by the display of her shapely derriere. He sputtered, "This is a New York project, one approved by the government. I don't understand why you will not move out of the way."

"You need to check with your superiors, because I am not letting any machine cross into our territory." The girl sat down on the tracks and pulled her backpack close to her. She reached inside, took out a skein of yarn and continued to work on a half-finished sweater.

Walter watched in fascination as the girl's hands and fingers moved quickly and the sweater began to grow row by row. Mesmerized, he watched her work for at least five minutes without moving a muscle. Then he shook himself and cut the video feed. He called his superior. "We have a problem; there is a girl who says she is a Neo Luddite on the tracks. I can't do any more work unless we get her to move out of the way."

The shift supervisor told Walter to hold the vehicle in place and he would get back to him in a few minutes. Walter shut down the engines with a flip of a switch. He went back to his game but found he couldn't concentrate. When his avatar exploded, and the screen flashed red, he knew he was severely distracted. The vision of the girl lifting her skirt flashed through his head.

Walter turned the camera back on. The girl noticed the red light shining from the front of the car and said, "What, you're not going to run me over?" When Walter did not reply, she continued. "All you Technos are all alike, trying to jam your technology down everyone's throat. Why can't you just see that not all people want that stuff you call progress. Just look what your precious technology did to New York." She held up her fingers and began to put them down one at a time as she stated the problems. "One, you guys built the plague that nearly wiped out the entire Earth.

J. B. Durbin

Two, you developed another plague that threatened all us New Yorkers with certain death. Three, you blew up a large part of New York with your giant bomb." Only her middle finger remained as she shook it at him and said, "Technology is not progress; it's a march to destruction."

The communications panel in front of Walter lit up, and his supervisors face appeared. "Walter, if you weren't such a good programmer, I would fire you. Were you daydreaming again or playing a game?"

Walter blushed and did not respond as his boss continued. "The girl is right; you are in Neo Luddite territory. You are to back the car out of the tunnel and go to this intersection." A map appeared on the split screen, "Continue repairs from here." A red dot showed up on the map of the subway system. "Have you got that, Biddle?" his supervisor asked.

Walter looked at the display, then back at the girl and said, "I got it." He started the engines up again, and the girl got to her feet and stood in the way once more.

"I am not going to run you down; I am going to leave," Walter insisted.

"What do you mean?" She mockingly imitated his voice, "I am not going to run you down."

"You're sitting in a room somewhere, not driving this monstrosity," she gestured at the subway car, "or enjoying a beautiful day outside." She laughed out loud, and then said, "Listen to me talking about enjoying the outside world. I'm forced to sit in a dark tunnel because of geeks like you." She turned and began to walk away from the machine.

Something stirred in Walter, he could not describe it. His heart began to race as his mouth ran away with him. "Maybe we should meet outside somewhere!" he blurted it out and regretted his words.

"Maybe we should," the girl mused. "For all I know, you could be an ugly troll, waiting to ensnare a beautiful girl like me in a trap!" She laughed again, and it sent a thrill through Walter's heart.

"Actually, I am twenty three, five foot nine and one hundred forty pounds. I don't wear glasses, I have all my teeth and I have fairly long brown hair. My last trip to the meditube showed I was in excellent health. So there!" Walter had never talked to a girl like that in his life, not even through a camera, and it felt strange.

She laughed again. "I tell you what; you meet me at the edge of Neo Luddite territory, say in Times Square at high noon tomorrow. Then I can show you what my life is like." She looked into the camera and stepped closer. "You have to leave every piece of technology at home if you want to come and see me. I mean it. If you bring so much as a battery-powered watch with you, you could be ejected from our territory."

Walter gulped as he thought of being without his connection to the world. "How will I recognize you?"

"I will be wearing this sweater," the girl held up the partially completed knitting she had been working on during their conversation. "How will I recognize you?" she asked.

"I will be the one looking like a lost puppy," Walter said.

The girl laughed again. "OK, it's a date. My name is April."

"And I am Walter," he said as he backed the train away. He watched as April waved goodbye.

The next day, he went to the aid station and modified the program on the meditube, climbed in and shut the door. Then Walter called in sick. Leaving everything in his apartment, he walked out the door and headed for his rendezvous. Walter had never called in sick before, and when his supervisor tried to contact him, he got an out-of-office reply.

J. B. Durbin

Chapter 59 – April

Walter felt absolutely naked as he stood at the edge of Neo Luddite territory. He tugged at the jacket he'd found in the bottom of his closet. Walter so seldom left his rooms; he never needed to dress warmly. He had everything he needed to do his job right at his fingertips, and if he needed to go to another work station, he would just walk down the hallway to a different office. He hadn't been out of his building more than five times in his life.

The late spring wind was caressing him as he walked down the canyons of New York toward Times Square, but he liked the way it felt on his face. The warm sun was shining down between the high-rise buildings. He never knew how it felt; he'd only looked at it through glass windows.

As he walked into Times Square, the ground changed beneath his feet. He looked down and saw green blades of grass instead of concrete. He stopped and got down on one knee. He reached down and touched the grass. He was still kneeling when he heard a voice behind him.

"You were right; you do look like a lost puppy." He heard that beautiful laugh again and looked up to see the girl from the subway standing there. "How do you like my sweater?" April twirled around, barefoot in the grass, as her skirt flared out to show her bare legs.

Walter forgot he wasn't connected to the outside world. He was lost in a new world, full of wonder and life. "I like it fine."

April knelt beside Walter and ran her hand over the grass. "We took out all the asphalt and concrete that was here, and we planted grass that is just starting to grow. Grass is so much better for your feet than hard concrete." She held up a blade of grass. "It smells good, too." She stuck it in Walter's face.

Walter could smell the grass, but he could also smell the girl as she reached out her hands toward him. Her body smelled fresh and clean. He thought that she might stink, due to the unsanitary conditions he'd presumed would exist in her world, but her scent was captivating. He was intoxicated as he was inundated with sensations.

"Easy there, Walter." April caught his arm as Walter almost fell into her. "Are you OK?"

A thrill run through his body as her hand touched him. Walter leaned forward and took in another deep breath of air filled with April's aroma. He wanted to live in that moment forever. He looked into her eyes and said, "I've never been better. I finally know what it feels like to be alive."

"Then you are ready to leave your old life. I have heard of this happening before, but never saw it myself. You came here on your own; no one forced you to come. You sampled the good life, and found you like it, perhaps even loved it at first taste." She bowed he head and said in a soft voice. "You have been reborn." April slid her hand down his arm and entwined her fingers in Walter's. She looked into his pale eyes. "Do you want to go home?" she asked.

Walter replied, "I am home."

Walter Biddle was one very happy man. He gave up his former life to live in Neo Luddite territory and now enjoyed a peaceful tech-free existence with his girlfriend, April, tending animals on the small farm they'd been given in Central Park. He had never realized what a great world there was out there until he and April happened literally ran into each other on the subway. He made quite a show of carrying her over the threshold on their first day in their new home. It was the fifth day of June.

The Corvis operative in SUNY had finally discovered who the architect of the dampening field was. He went to Techno headquarters and asked for Walter Biddle. When he learned Biddle had disappeared, he asked Corvis for instructions.

Steven did not trust Josh with that mission, he was needed for other things. He located his contacts in the Cartel to help find Walter Biddle.

The drug addled man who had been tasked with tailing Walter tried to type in the address of the house in the park but the communication's device he had been given did not work. He was beginning to come off of his high and shaking from withdrawal. He put the device back into his pocket and walked out of Neo Luddite territory, toward the corner where his dealer friend was waiting with more snarf. He would send the message as soon as he got his fix.

Chapter 60 – Combined Headquarters

"Our blockade does not seem to be affecting them that much." The German intelligence officer flashed the satellite imagery of Manhattan and the northern part of SUNY under the control of the Neo Luddites. "Estimates are that the food production last year was more than sufficient to sustain the entire population, and that even more territory has been reclaimed for planting this year's crop." He turned to the assembled generals and their staffs and said, "And we don't know what their stored food supplies are like."

"No matter," General Fochet, the supreme commander, said. "We have a good plan to take the Neo Luddite lands first, thereby cutting off food supplies to the rest of the country." Fochet drew on the map that was simultaneously shown on the other commander's tablet. "Major General Murphy, leading the Irish Guards, you will smash through the Neo Luddite defenses and move to a blocking position along the Harlem River. Thanks to the riots following the plague, most of the Bronx was burned to the ground, and the Neo Luddites have cleared the lands for farming. Your tanks will have no problems moving through, and you should encounter no resistance of any consequence."

Major General Patrick Murphy scratched his reddish brown hair and looked thoughtfully at the projection of the plan. "Tis a good plan, mon General, unless the Luddite folk allows the real fighters to come in with hypervelocity weapons. Then my tanks, strong as they are, will be nothing more than death traps for the crews."

Tanks had not been used by any of the major powers since 2024 when hypervelocity weapons allowed a simple infantryman the capability to shoot carbine rounds through the heaviest armor. To make a tank heavy enough to withstand an attack by a rocket-launcher team required billions of dollars and a ten-man crew. Since the governments were more interested in feeding the people than spending money on worthless equipment, they bought hyper weapons instead. The hypervelocity rocket launcher cost a little more than a million dollars and could be fired by one man. Tanks became ineffective.

But the Irish, once they expanded into North America, found that the Quebecer's who survived the famine caused by the plague were a pesky lot. They needed something to keep them in line, and the tank seemed like a good choice. The French Canadians resisted Irish encroachments on their lands, but had no way to fight them. Before the Canadian government collapsed it had outlawed and confiscated all personal weapons. With no major weapon systems, especially hypervelocity weapons, to worry about, the police forces in New Ireland pulled the tanks out of mothballs and used them for crowd control.

General Murphy commandeered the fifteen working tanks and nationalized the police force to form an armored company capable of striking fear into the hearts of the Neo Luddites. It was attached to his lead division, the Irish Guards.

General Fochet dismissed Murphy's concerns with a wave of his hand. "They will not be allowed in and the tanks will do what we want them to do. Strike fear into the hearts of the peasants. And if they do come in, what will you lose?" He again waved his hand in the air, "A few men and some old tanks. If it works, good for us. If not, we lose little; c'est la guerre."

Murphy's nostrils flared as he thought about his men dying. "Maybe death means nothing to a French general, but it means a lot to me!"

Lieutenant General Maxwell, commander of the NUS 18th Airborne Corps, reached over and patted Murphy's hand. "Calm down, Patrick. We need you to secure the Bronx so we can get our airborne divisions into the fight. We will be much closer to the Technos and regular SUNY troops than you will and will take a lot of casualties if you don't secure our Northern flank. I really don't want to fight surrounded."

Maxwell turned to Fochet. "Your plan to put the 82d and 101st Airborne Divisions into Central Park reminds me of a failure on the part of the Allies in the second half of the Great War," he said. "During Operation Market Garden, the airborne units were going to lay down a carpet of troops that the British armored Divisions would roll over, crossing the Rhine River and ending the war with Germany. The only problem was a couple of heavily armed

German divisions managed to hold off the entire might of the Allied Armies because they were bottlenecked, with only one road to move on."

Fochet asked, "What is your point, General Taylor?"

"Once we hit the ground, the Neo Luddites, who are fighting on their home turf, will have the tactical advantage." Taylor looked at the raw numbers of Neo Luddite fighters the staff had estimated would be involved in the coming battle. "We may a technological advantage, but they have an estimated twenty-thousand troops. What happens to us if they decide that living simply is less important than utilizing technology? What if they arm themselves with modern weapons? We will only outnumber them about two to one, which means we lose."

Fochet almost exploded. "They will not do it! My staff assures me they would rather die than use technology!"

Maxwell sat back and said, "I don't like the plan, but my president placed us under your command. We will do our best."

General Gerhard Schroeder also spoke. "My dear General Fochet, you have the German division attacking on a small front to the east of Central Park, into the most dangerous ground. The city south of 100th Street is heavily built up. Most of the buildings are still intact and it will require my men to fight building to building. We know from experience that street fighting eats up units. We could lose many of our combat forces in a short time without much success."

Fochet again spoke heatedly. "And the French divisions will be on the other side, enduring much the same thing." He pointed at the aerial views of the terrain. "Once we get past these buildings, we will be in cleared ground. I am putting my own forces in the most dangerous of positions and will personally lead them into battle. We will outnumber the poules mouillées by six to one. And we will, in your vernacular, kick some butt."

Maxwell, who's French was pretty good, muttered, "Sissies with hyper weapons can also kick butt."

Fochet, who did not hear the aside, continued. "The plan is sound and will work! The Irish will open the attack and secure our northern boundary. They will frighten the Neo Luddites and force them out of their homes and farms. The NUS Airborne will land in Central Park and hold the flanks just inside the cleared land.

German units will then pass through the Irish and attack along the East River, making contact with the NUS forces and moving to clear the way to 57th Street. France will have the honor of the right flank, and attack along the Hudson River. The Irish Divisions will then follow in support and keep our rear area clear. Once we reach our objectives on 57th Street, we will coordinate the continued attack all the way down to the end of the island."

Chapter 61 - D-Day

Miley woke to the sound of someone pounding on her door. She looked at the old wall clock hanging on her bedroom wall and wondered why anyone would be trying to see her this early in the morning. It was still dark, so Miley believed the clock had to be fairly accurate. The big hand was on three, and so was the little hand.

She waved to her guards to let the visitor enter.

Alejandra Cruz came in with a long document. "Miley, I think you need to see this now, before it's too late."

"Before what is too late?" Miley asked.

"The attack, it comes today at dawn. I have spent the last 48 hours writing down the plan, one letter at a time, from the bedside of a paralyzed man." Alejandro held out the document.

Miley glanced through the first few pages and told one her guards, "Get me Carole Bean, now!"

The message went out by drum and Carole was roused from her sleep by rough hands minutes after the summons. She rubbed her eyes and quickly pulled on her jeans and an old sweatshirt and followed the running messenger down the unlit streets to Miley's headquarters. There was a lot of activity. Carole noticed candle light and torches being lit all over the Neo Luddite enclave near Techno territory. The guards waved her inside.

Miley was dressed for combat. She had her hunting bow already strung and across her back, a full quiver of arrows at her hip. A large knife hung from the right side of her belt as she walked from her sleeping chamber. She handed Carole the plans Alejandra had copied down and told Carole, "The battle has begun. Get these to your mother as soon as possible. Tell her to come with all haste; the ban on Techno weapons has been lifted."

Carole turned and ran off into the night. It was a long way to Techno territory. Even though speed was essential to success, she would have to make it all the way, so she paced herself.

Keenan was easier to get to than Ashley, and Carole knew that the communications Keenan had would get the message out quicker than she could run. The invisible barrier around Keenan's headquarters lit the area up with searchlights, and a mechanical voice commanded that she halt and hold her position. Carole skidded to a stop. She knew enough about the defenses to understand if she moved any closer, the automatic weapons would fire. They didn't think; they just responded to perceived threats.

"Sit down on the ground," a mechanical voice rang out, to be replaced by Keenan's voice. "Sorry, Carole, the automatics are on. What is it?"

"Sound the alarm. The attack is beginning today. We have two hours before it starts and I need you to get this to my mother now!" She held up the hand written document.

Keenan dimmed the lights and appeared at the door. "Bring it here, girl and hurry!" As Carole entered the building, he grabbed the document from her hand and ran to the scanner in his office, with Carole close behind. He fed the document into the scanner and watched until it finished sending the orders to Ashley's headquarters.

Keenan looked at the computer readout of the document. His program automatically read and analyzed the intent of the plan. Keenan scrolled through the two page analysis and issued orders to his division commander. He watched as the display began to light up with unit symbols as the Techno division split into thirty-six separate company-sized units and began to move on different routes into Neo Luddite territory. He looked at the status of the jammer system for Neo Luddite lands and issued orders to shut it down.

Ashley roughly pushed Ryan's shoulder. She had entered his sleeping chamber in the tactical operations center without knocking. He reached for the small-caliber pistol he kept on the desk next to his bed, but Ashley already had it in her hand. She knew he would react first and see who or what he shot second.

"General, it's time. As your president, I order you to execute plan X-ray," Ashley formally announced.

Ryan arose to his feet, saluted smartly and replied, "Yes Ma'am."

UN Real Paine

Chapter 62 – Zero Hour

The first three tanks roared to life. They had not been upgraded to hydrogen power by the Canadian government; it was deemed more cost effective to overhaul the JP4 fueled engines. Black smoke belched out of the back of the old Leopard A6M tank as it pulled out of the revetment and started down the road to the Bronx. The forty-year-old tank still had awesome firepower; a 120 millimeter gun, a coaxially mounted 7.62 millimeter machine gun, and retrofitted for two hypervelocity machine guns remotely controlled and mounted to the top of the turret.

The four-man crew watched intently for any ground activity as the lead tank passed into Neo Luddite territory.

The scout prayed that the Technos had turned off the dampening field as she lined up the crosshairs on the center of the behemoth moving toward her.

The tank was stuck by a hypervelocity rocket as soon as it crossed the border. The crew died instantly as the tank turret flew off and splashed into a nearby creek.

Irish Army legend has it that General Murphy's expletive could be heard in Londonderry.

"Stop the damned tanks and get the infantry to the front!" He ordered his guards forward. He turned to his aide and said, "So much for scaring the peasants with tanks. And our French leader was wrong about hyper weapons in Neo Luddite lands."

The three soldiers from the scout platoon's heavy weapons squad began to run to the next position. The plasma riflemen and the rest of the scouts covered their retreat. Paine had placed the scouts in Neo Luddite Territory the day before, acting on the preliminary information Bobby Lee had revealed before pulling the gun on Paine and Marcus. Miley had agreed to Paine's request because they both assumed, correctly, that if modern weapons were used in Neo Luddite Territory, the Irish would pull their tanks out of the battle.

No more weapons of any kind were fired at the slowly advancing infantry soldiers. They began to get nervous as most of the lead elements had seen the destruction of the lead tank and were searching for any sign of response from forces with technologically advanced weapons. They were told in their briefings that they would not have to fight modern weapons until the final assault.

The lead company was spread out in open formation, leapfrogging forward with one platoon providing cover while the other moved in a classic overwatch formation. All sensors were on full-detection mode, following the energy signatures of the rapidly retreating scout platoon. No other energy signals were detected.

As the first platoon entered a wheat field, it looked as if they were wading hip deep in the stalks. Suddenly, the point man of the first company went down, and the remainder of the platoon dropped to the ground. Follow on soldiers could not see what had happened, but they could hear the screams of the lead platoon members. They opened fire to cover their fallen comrades. Hyper velocity bullets took the tops of the wheat plants off. They were shooting at ghosts.

General Murphy was following the progress of the lead company through the helmet camera of the commander. As the commander swiveled his head to give the general a good look at the battlefield, a projectile struck the lens of the camera, causing Murphy to jerk back.

"What the hell was that?" He yelled at his communications operator.

"I will try to slow it down, sir," the tech replied, and ran the video again in freeze frame.

Murphy stared intently at the display and saw a long projectile enter the field of view. His communications tech froze the frame as he said, "What is that?"

The steel tipped arrow was caught in flight. "Play it through to the end, at the slowest speed," Murphy said. He watched the point until the lens shattered. "Get another camera online, now!" he yelled at the tech. He switched the frequency to all bands and issued new orders. "All units, this is Emerald Six. Be on the lookout for slow-moving projectile weapons. Shoot anyone who is visible. You are now in a free-fire zone."

The Irish Guards were moving slowly, on line, firing at anything that moved. As the executive officer of the lead company walked up to the first platoon, he panned the area with his camera.

General Murphy's initial view was of his company commander lying face up, his eyes wide open and a black, feathered shaft sticking out his head. As the XO moved forward, he came upon the lead platoon.

When the platoon reacted to the point man's downward movement, they fell onto carefully placed caltrops - metal devices the Neo Luddites had made consisting of four projecting spikes arranged so that when three of the spikes are on the ground, the fourth is always pointed upward. As the platoon dropped to the ground, they skewered themselves on the projecting spikes hidden in the wheat field. Most of them were trying to get the barbed spikes out of various parts of their bodies. Two had died when the caltrops stabbed into vital organs and they bled out.

The point man had fallen into a pit and was dead, impaled by the steel rods sticking up from the bottom and sides of the pit.

"All units, hold in place," General Murphy yelled over the network. "Plasma riflemen are to move to the front. I want any vegetation burned to the ground before we move forward."

The advance stopped for five minutes until the heavy weapons squads moved into the front lines. As the plasma riflemen began firing hot bursts into the fields, the unit began moving forward again. Orders were given to close ranks and keep the weapons squads protected. Soon, smoke was drifting over the battlefield, providing concealment for the Neo Luddites.

"Switch to thermals," Murphy ordered. The flames from the plasma bursts whited out the heads-up displays of the advancing soldiers, but they were able to pick out a few targets and began inflicting casualties on the Neo Luddite fighters retreating from the advancing Irish Guards. The Neo Luddites were unable to stop them.

The movement of the Irish into the Bronx was going more slowly than the plan's timetable. General Murphy called General Fochet with an update. "General, we are advancing, but it will be another hour before we are in position to support the airborne assault."

Fochet was fuming as he berated the frustrated Murphy. "The timetable is set. General Murphy, you need to push through and get to the support positions or you will be responsible for the deaths of many of the NUS soldiers." Murphy resisted the impulse to slam the headset down and issued orders to his lead units to pick up the pace. He cut the communications and said to himself, "Just wait until it's your turn, you French skitter arse."

Chapter 63 – Josh's Mission

Josh could hear the sound of weapons fire in the distance and was waiting for the call from Corvis. He answered on the first buzz.

"That was nice," Steven's voice purred over the secure line. "I really need you to be whole for this mission."

Josh frowned as he said, "What is it?"

"I want you to go to this location." A map appeared on the communicator's screen. "Draw it on a piece of paper, because you will be out of touch with me for a few hours. The Technos have developed a dampening device for the Neo Luddite Territory and I need to find out how it works." Steven paused and said, "When you have the map drawn, I have more instructions for you."

Josh took his time sketching the map.

Steven impatiently asked, "Aren't you finished yet?" just as Josh finished the drawing.

"I'm done, so now what?" Josh replied.

"You will find this man at the location on the map." The screen changed once again, and a picture of Walter Biddle appeared on the screen. "I want you to take him to the following address," a street and building number appeared on the screen. "Hold him there until I can get my people to pick him up."

"Got it," Josh said, "When do I go?"

"Shave the beard off first; you need to look like a soldier to blend in with the attacking forces. Then go to Columbus Circle and hide in one of the buildings until the time is right," Steven directed.

"And when will that be?" Josh asked.

"You will know. Fail me and you will die. Corvis, out." The connection was severed.

General Maxwell was in the lead NUS aircraft, standing up on the outline of the number one platform. He was always the first one out of the plane. This was his fifteenth platform exit, and he liked the experience of free-fall and the excitement of the jump. His communication device buzzed in his ear, and he heard the coalition commanding general's voice come over the air.

"Maxwell, can you still make the assault without Irish support?" Fochet asked.

The light turned green and Maxwell just had enough time to say, "Too late to stop the drop now, General," as the platform was ejected from the plane.

"Now, now, now," The Techno yelled into the microphone.

The southernmost of the four jammers was switched back on, cutting all power sources within a ten-mile radius. That included a ten-mile high dome of air space.

General Maxwell's platform, one of the first to land, worked to perfection. He stepped off and looked in front of him as the rest of the first wave was dropping from the sky. He watched in horror as platforms began slamming into the ground at more than one hundred miles an hour.

The lead aircraft was losing altitude, but the engines came back to life just as it crossed out of the dampening field. The pilots managed to get enough control to pull up and miss the buildings to the south. Maxwell tried to contact the follow-on planes, but his communications were dead.

"Abort the mission. Immediately turn ninety degrees and do not enter the drop zone," the pilot of the first aircraft screamed into his mouthpiece. Six of the planes were able to turn. Two were not so lucky.

Plane number two had already dropped half of its troopers before the power went out. Less than a third of them got to the ground before the platforms ceased to work. As it regained power, the plane was unable to clear the buildings. It clipped one wing, and both pilots had to fight to regain control, but miraculously managed to keep the plane flying. Trailing smoke, they flew the crippled plane back to base.

Plane number three could not release its platforms. Flying directly behind the other two because of the narrowness of the drop zone, it was caught in the full effect of the dampening field. As it passed over General Maxwell's head in an unpowered glide, the troopers were trapped in their cells, waiting to be ejected. Four hundred soldiers and six crew members died as the plane crashed into the buildings on the south end of Central Park.

Of the twelve hundred men in the first three planes, three hundred and twenty two were on the ground and ready to fight. They were about to be joined by one more.

Josh had moved into a position on the first floor of one of the deserted buildings opposite Columbus Circle. He could see the incoming airborne assault, so he had a front-row seat for the deaths of the troopers whose platforms were disabled. Josh was leaving cover when the second plane clipped a building. He had to sprint across the street into Central Park. He ducked under a bridge as part of the building collapsed behind him. The shock wave generated when the third plane crashed almost knocked him off his feet, but he kept moving into Central Park.

As Josh ran deeper into the gardens, looking for soldiers who had survived the drop, he came across several mangled bodies before he was confronted by a young captain who yelled at him to stop. As Josh continued to advance, the captain took out his sidearm and pulled the trigger. The weapon did not work; the firing mechanism ceased to work when the dampener was activated. Josh's automatic pistol worked flawlessly, and the captain fell with a hole in his head.

Josh stripped the clothes off the dead officer and dressed himself. He left the body naked in the grass and, after consulting his hand-drawn map, moved slowly toward the center of the park.

J. B. Durbin

Chapter 64 – Irish Mistake

"Sir, we have accounted for at least two hundred of the enemy and are making headway. We should be at our blocking positions in thirty minutes." The lead battalion commander's report was no comfort to General Murphy, who could not raise General Maxwell on the command net. He switched to General Fochet on the command frequency and asked for a status report.

"We have begun our movement, as have the Germans," Fochet reported. "I lost contact with Maxwell as soon as he jumped."

Murphy swung his head around to the south and activated his helmet camera for Fochet. "There is a lot of smoke in the drop-zone area. It does not look good for us, General."

"Murphy, I order you to speed up your advance. My divisions and the Germans will be passing through your positions in one hour," Fochet said. "We need the north bank of the river secured so we can cross. We need to move quickly to help the airborne units."

"We are going as fast as we can. Resistance is light, but still heavier than expected." Murphy wished he could be standing next to his commander, so he could choke the life out of him.

"Approaching more farms," The lead battalion commander said as the unit came up on a concentration of buildings. The scene played out in Murphy's heads-up display.

Miley had ordered that the area be evacuated the day before, so no Neo Luddites were at the farm. The scout who volunteered knew she was going to be exposed, but volunteered to do the mission, anyway. A hundred or more rounds from her assault carbine sprayed the lead platoon with accurate fire. Six guardsmen went down, and the rest opened fire on the small shed from which the fire came, blowing the wall to pieces. The scout disintegrated in a hail of hypervelocity bullets.

"Burn it to the ground," Murphy heard his battalion commander say.

The assembled plasma gunners from the battalion who had been clearing the way through the grain fields for the rest of the soldiers spread out and trained their weapons on the barns. The battalion commander raised his arm and dropped it when everyone was ready. They all fired at once.

A giant fireball appeared in the sky as the plasma rifles ignited the eight buildings, all packed to the rafters with fertilizer. The shock wave from the resulting explosion could be felt by the rear echelon of the German and French divisions. The lead battalion ceased to exist.

General Murphy picked himself up off the ground. He was close enough to the front lines to be knocked off his feet by the shock wave. He shook his head to clear and heard his aide say, "Jeeesus." The aide made the sign of the cross as he lay there.

"Get up, Pat," Murphy snapped at the stunned captain, "and send out a message to all troops. Stay where you are and do not shoot at anything that doesn't shoot at you first." Murphy looked at his heads-up display at the mounting casualty reports. He called Fochet, "General, we've had it. I've lost twenty percent of my force and don't know what else to expect. I can't order my men to continue. It is up to you and the Germans to do this now."

"Coward." Fochet screamed over the command net. "You are relieved of your command."

"You can't relieve me, only my president can do that." Murphy replied. "But you are certainly welcome to pass through my units and take the lead."

"We French and Germans will take the city. We will prevail!" Fochet cut the communication's link.

Murphy's aide, who was privy to the conversation, said, "I think our dear commander is a half a bubble off true, if you get my meaning."

"He'll find out soon enough, Pat." Murphy answered. "God bless his troops, they'll need it."

General Fochet gave specific instructions to his troops. "This is order number 2108. Do not fire unless fired upon. Do not set fire to any buildings. Maintain contact with the units to your left and right as we enter the main areas of Neo Luddite habitation. Any civilians are to be considered combatants unless and until they surrender. Prisoners will be taken to the rear areas and kept under guard." Fochet paused for effect and then shouted into the communication's device, "Vive la France!"

The French divisions passed through the Irish lines an hour after the halt. They surged forward; they had learned from learned from the Irish Army's experiences. Fochet had his drones out front, identifying targets and directing his forces to maneuver to flank or surround pockets of enemy resistance. His lead division was making good headway against the Neo Luddites, using the drones for reconnaissance.

The Techno controlling the field got word of the death of the scout at the farm and turned on the remaining three dampening devices. The Neo Luddite territory was now technology free, nothing with a power source worked inside the field. Suddenly, the drones began to drop out of the sky, one by one, until all of them were out of commission.

"Get the drones back!" Fochet ordered his lead technician.

"Sir, I don't understand what happened. They were all working perfectly a few minutes ago," the tech replied.

"Send in a pair of lifters. Make sure they stay low. There are modern weapons out there." Fochet directed. "Have the second one shadow the first, but stay back."

The lead lifter pilot, flying nap of the earth, slowly approached the area where the drones failed. As he got to the coordinates, his engines stopped, and the lifter dropped like a stone to the ground. The skids absorbed most of the impact as they collapsed under the lifter. The crew chief was badly injured when he was thrown from the open doorway, and the copilot was unconscious in his seat. The pilot tried to call the second lifter for support, but his communications did not work. His back was broken; he could not feel his legs.

The second lifter pilot saw the lead bird plummet to the ground. There was no indication of enemy fire, so he stopped his forward movement and set his aircraft down.

"Butch, go see what the hell happened," he told his crew chief.

The crew chief jumped for the lifter, drew his sidearm and ran toward the downed shuttle. "Nothing to report yet, there's no sign of any enemy activity." He got no response from his commander. He stopped, turned around and tried his communications again.

The pilot waved and pointed at his headset, indicating no transmission was received. Butch took two steps back toward the lifter and heard, "get it. Why won't the message get through?"

Butch answered, "It works now. There must be a signal-blocker here."

Butch walked backward toward the fallen lifter, eyes on the pilot, counting out loud over the radio as he went. The pilot held up his hand to signal stop when Butch's transmission was cut off.

The pilot turned to his co-pilot and said, "See if you can help Butch get those guys out. I will report this to headquarters."

As the injured crew was carried to the waiting aircraft, the pilot described what had happened to his commander.

General Fochet listened to his technical advisor explain why the drones went down. "So our communications and our weapons may not work in the field. If we move forward, we will be going in blind and defenseless."

"Merde! I refuse to let this stop us! Get all the division commanders on a conference call, now!" Fochet demanded.

It took a few minutes to get everyone into the network.

"This is General Fochet, your commander. I need you to understand the situation. Our communications will be severed if we go in to relieve the NUS paratroopers, and we will not have the use of our modern weapons. But go in we must! We have a six-to-one advantage in soldiers, and we must accomplish our mission. I therefore order you all to fix bayonets and close with and kill anyone that you encounter who offers any resistance."

Fritz Hertlen, the overall German commander, asked, "What do you propose we do when the enemy attacks?"

"Do what soldiers did in the old days. Form a phalanx and fight them face-to-face. I surmise this is what the enemy wants. They will invite us to battle them in close quarters." Fochet's mind was racing as he made alternate plans in his head.

"I will have lifters and fighters stationed outside this field that is killing our technology." Fochet looked at the situation map and watched as the area affected by the dampening fields was displayed on the overlay. "They will be able to shoot long-range missiles at the enemy, and even if they can't be guided, they can still inflict damage to our opponents. The destruction of their soldiers will cause the formations to fall apart, and we can kill them all."

Fochet paused, staring intently into the camera. "Follow the plan as we discussed. Your objectives stay the same. We will be out of touch for a while, but I will meet you commanders at the rendezvous point in exactly twenty-four hours. We will prevail! Fochet, out!"

Chapter 65 - Sneak Attack

Marcus could not stand being out of the main fight, but the dampening field was turned on and he had to be out of its range. If he didn't stay out of Neo Luddite territory, his nanoprobes would stop functioning and he would die. Paine directed him to take half of A Company, now equipped with rocket launchers and carbines, and deploy the unit in two-man teams along the east bank of the Hudson River. Chris Curtis took the other half of A Company to the west bank of the East River.

The scouts, those who had safely returned from the front lines, remained under Paine's control. They were equipped with all the low-tech firearms they could locate. Ammunition had been hard to find, but thanks to the food for bullets campaign they had a formidable force armed with rifles and handguns and at least one hundred rounds per weapon.

Paine's instructions to Marcus and Chris were clear. "Once the main battle begins, shoot down any aircraft come within range. That will limit the ability of the attacking force to gather intelligence or fire on us from long-range. You need to be where you can support each other because the first to fire will be targeted by any remaining aircraft. Shoot and scoot, or you won't ever shoot again. Good luck, gentlemen."

Chris deployed his teams through the subway tunnels south of Grand Central. He sent them on different subway lines so if anyone was discovered and stopped, at least some of his teams would get through. They all made it to their designated positions.

Because the Neo Luddites had filled many of the subway tunnels with debris from the buildings they had dismantled over the years, Marcus had to use a different deployment method. He had the two-person teams commandeer small water craft and space themselves at least a hundred meters apart along the east bank of the river. They were prepared to cross on his command.

Katrina strapped the rocket launcher and all the rounds she could carry onto her back and wrapped her arms around Marcus' waist as he checked the time. "On my mark, go!" Marcus commanded.

Katrina, who hated the water, was holding on for dear life as the Jet Ski Marcus had found roared out of its hiding place. Thirty-two other small craft departed the shoreline at the same time, each carrying two soldiers loaded down with rockets. In the three minutes it took to cross the river, five of the watercraft were destroyed by a UN jet fighter on station above the city, and one of the teams was strafed and killed as they tried to climb the wall on the opposite shore. The remaining teams melted into the buildings lining the New Jersey bank and moved into position.

The pilot of the Rafale 6000 fighter called for more support as he reported, "Tango three three, I have deserters leaving the island. At least twenty-five were killed."

The call came back, "Roger. Keep on your station, watch for the lead elements of the French division. Fire on any enemy formations that come to engage them," the air traffic controller said. "And stay out of the dampener field or you will crash."

The fighter began to circle, with his heads up display showing the advancing French divisions. Five more fighters and twelve heavily armed lifters flew into the airspace over Jersey City.

Marcus threw Katrina, loaded down with ten rockets, up onto the dock. She landed lightly on her feet and then reached down to help as Marcus quickly climbed up carrying the launcher. "Teams, report in," Marcus directed. As the rocket teams answered, he plotted their positions on the map.

"Hold your fire until I give the word and then shoot at the designated targets." Marcus planned for each fighter to be hit by two rockets and assigned one rocket for each lifter. The hypervelocity rounds should be able to get to the loitering planes quickly enough to ensure a hit, but the fighters had the most dangerous weapons systems and merited the extra rounds. Marcus and one other rocket man, located in the center of the deployed teams, were the back-up crews. Their mission was to take out the any of the aircraft that survived the first attack.

Marcus settled down and waited for the battle to begin in earnest.

Chapter 66 – March or Die

The French divisions moved across the Harlem River and headed due west. As the lead element reached the river bank, the division wheeled, so that they were facing south. The other four divisions followed and the entire force moved on line. Pockets of Neo Luddite resistance were quickly cleared out through the use of modern weapons as the attacking soldiers were not yet in the dampened zone. Fochet began to lose contact with his lead units as they moved forward into the zone. They had their instructions. As soon as the weapons stopped working; soldiers closed ranks and fixed bayonets. Soon, the entire force was moving in close formation toward the rapidly retreating Neo Luddite forces.

Fochet, in a command and control lifter orbiting just outside the dampening zone, saw his troops facing light resistance. The Neo Luddites were not doing what he thought they would do, which was to stand and fight. Suddenly, buildings began to collapse in the path of the advancing army. Neo Luddite engineers were dropping buildings that had been prepared to be dismantled earlier in the year. Miley ordered the demolition to stop once the ultimatum had been received, but had her people continue to prepare the buildings. Now was the time.

Fochet could see that his forces were being guided, but he had no way of contacting and warning them. He cursed and helplessly watched events unfold.

The rubble made the streets impassable, causing flanking units to be channeled into another unit's line of advance. Commanders either stopped their advance or mixed their units together as there was no communications to tell them what to do.

The Neo Luddites knew exactly what was happening. Scouts sent messages via pigeons and dogs to Miley's command post. Miley plotted the advance of the French on a sand table her staff was constantly updating. She watched as another report came in and the markers for the lead elements were moved closer to the kill zone. Miley issued her orders.

Drums began to beat in the distance as the commander of the lead French battalion entered a plowed field. The mud began to stick to his boots and his soldiers struggled to maintain their formation. He slowed the march and continued to move the unit deeper into the mire. The follow-on battalions began to bump into each other as the forward units slowed down. Soon enough, twenty-thousand French troops were packed into a huge muddy field.

Miley limped as quickly as she could to the assembled Neo Luddite troops. "Now is our time!" she shouted and raised her arm skyward. When she dropped her arm, five thousand Neo Luddite archers began to unleash a flurry of arrows into the packed Frenchmen.

The front ranks were the hardest hit, with hundreds of casualties. The rear ranks, not seeing what was going on, continued their advance packing the field even tighter. Wounded soldiers not killed in the initial onslaught were trampled to death or drowned in the mud as their comrades were pushed forward.

Fochet was able to see into Neo Luddite territory from his command lifter. He watched in horror as the attack began and screamed into the microphone, "All air units launch your attacks now!"

The fighters and lifters, which had been shadowing the French advance, launched 48 rockets at the massed Neo Luddites. As the missiles were being launched by the coalition aircraft, Marcus initiated his own attack.

Two things happened almost simultaneously. The rockets of the coalition aircraft slammed into the Neo Luddite formations, but the dampening field kept the warheads from exploding. The UN rockets entered the formation from a high angle and caused casualties, but not as many as Fochet thought they would. Sixty-three Neo Luddites were swept away by the barrage.

Marcus saw the launch and ordered his unit to fire. The two-man teams launched their barrage at the hovering lifters and scored direct hits on all twelve. Four of the six fighters were destroyed instantly, one managed to survive a direct hit and limped off, trailing wreckage until the pilot ejected and the plane disintegrated. The sixth fighter was missed by both rockets fired at it. The pilot jinked hard to the left in an effort to escape Marcus' rocket, launched a few seconds after the first two missed, and flew into the dampener zone. She lost power. Her glide path took the jet into the

French lines. As her ship bored into the ground, it came apart. The fuel ignited, and the flames took out half a battalion with her.

Miley threw down her bow and picked up a spear. She hobbled forward yelling, "Attack!"

The Neo Luddite formation, barefooted so the mud would not impede their advance, ran forward across the freshly plowed fields and slammed into the chaotic French lines. Men and women died as the soldiers from both sides fought for their lives. The footing of the French was not good, and they were tired from slogging through the muck. The physical mayhem being wrought by close-combat weapons also took a toll, and French soldiers began to turn from the slaughter, trying to escape the advancing Neo Luddite phalanxes. Because they could not run due to the closely packed ranks, many of them threw their weapons down and walked into the Neo Luddite lines with their hands held up in surrender. Follow-on companies of Neo Luddite troops marched them off of the battlefield under guard.

The French were in full retreat, weapons abandoned, bodies scattered across the field. "That is enough for one day," Miley said, sickened by the death of so many, but glad to be alive. Miley had her guards blow their horns to signal a stop to the advance. Her personal medic was applying a bandage to her leg just above the knee. A French soldier had stabbed her with her bayonet just before being cut down by Miley's guards.

"Send a message to Brad that the plan works," Miley said as she brushed away the medic, telling him, "Go see to the more seriously wounded, leave me alone." Two pigeons fluttered into the sky.

General Fochet, hoping for a victory, watched in horror as his units fled the battlefield. He handed his headset to his aide, opened the aircraft door and stepped out.

J. B. Durbin

Chapter 67 – Eastern Front

Ryan had issued wind-up watches, taken from stores and borrowed from civilians across New York, to all the Technos and SUNY soldiers who had hypervelocity weapons. The watches had been synchronized two days before in a mass formation of SUNY and Techno forces, and commanders established times when all watches would be wound to make sure they were still working and on the correct time. Ryan looked down at the timepiece on his arm and marveled at its beauty. It was a Rolex.

Ryan held the soldiers out of the dampener zone until he got word of Miley's success and then launched two attacks.

Ashley, leading one of the brigades of SUNY forces, moved them into the dampening zone and began to advance toward the German forces. The Germans were making headway against Brad's force on the eastern side of the front lines. Brad was not as fortunate as Miley, in that one of the fighters providing cover had managed to survive the rocket attacks and was sending unguided missiles into his formations. Brad was losing soldiers, and the Germans were not as tightly packed as the French had been. It was going to be difficult for the Neo Luddites to win as the Germans slowly reduced the size of the defending force.

Ashley deployed her men and women into a defensive line two blocks from Brad's forces. The buildings were already down, so the Germans would have to come through her to get to Central Park. Ashley sent Carole with two scouts to the front lines to find Brad.

Paine's lead scout, Imani Jamal, was one of the personal bodyguards assigned to protect Carole. She still carried her antique firearm, a center-fire pistol with a long silencer attached to the barrel. Her partner still thought it was a piece of shit but knew from experience it was really effective in close combat and it had saved both of them more than once. Imani had loaded all the spent casings she could find and had thirteen rounds for the battle. She hoped that wasn't a bad omen.

Imani slung her now useless carbine over her shoulder, carrying her pistol in her left hand and a machete in her right hand.

The Neo Luddite who trained her was so impressed with her expertise that he gave her the machete as a present.

As they searched for Brad, they came upon a dangerous venue.

Brad was standing in a clearing looking into the distance. He had already committed half of his guard force to the battle which was not going well. He turned and waved the rest of his guard forward to attack a German squad that was cutting down Neo Luddite fighters.

Brad did not see the two German soldiers who had slipped through the lines and were advancing upon him undetected. The noise was deafening, with screams of dying soldiers from both sides filling the air. Imani reacted by running forward and shooting the two Germans in the back with her silenced pistol. Brad, sensing an attack from behind, spun around and impaled Imani with his spear. He pulled it out and raised it over his head for a killing stroke.

Carole ran up and stopped Brad from finishing off the scout. "Stop," she screamed, "she just saved your life."

Carole knelt down and slapped a quick heal patch on the scout's shoulder. She picked up the pistol, handed it back to Imani and helped her to her feet.

"I am sorry. I just reacted," Brad apologized.

"I should have announced myself, I guess." Imani joked, "Serves me right, I always shoot first and ask questions later." Lightheaded, she looked at the dead Germans and said, "Pretty good shooting, if I don't say so myself." She put her hand on the quick heal patch and said, "It's doing its work. I should be OK in a few minutes." Then Imani passed out from the pain.

Brad caught her as she slumped into his arms. As he laid her down, he asked Carole, "What are my orders?"

"Check your watch. Ashley said 1415 hours, for ten seconds. That does not give your people much time." Carole looked at her watch, which indicated it was two o'clock.

Brad picked up the scout's pistol and tucked it into his belt. He called for his drummer and issued her instruction. She began to beat out the signal for retreat as the trumpeters and other drummers in nearby units picked up the command and spread it throughout the Neo Luddite formations. Then Brad picked up Imani, put her over his shoulder in a fireman's carry and began to move toward Ashley's position.

The Neo Luddite soldiers broke contact and began to run away from the battlefield. They sprinted for two blocks and joined up with Ashley's forces.

A cheer went up from the German ranks. The soldiers, still muddy from the fight in the fields, had a hard time chasing the retreating Neo Luddite force. Commanders struggled to keep their units together, so they would not be scattered and easy targets for the bowmen or a reinforcing phalanx of Neo Luddite troops. A temporary halt was sounded, and the Germans got back into formation and advanced upon the new defensive line, bayonet tipped rifles pointing straight ahead.

Lieutenant Colonel Kompaniyets, not satisfied with the supporting role initially assigned to his Ukrainian battalion, had insisted on being attached to the lead German Division. His soldiers were positioned on the far left flank, nearest the East River, instead of being assigned as the rear guard. They had the most difficult ground to walk through and Kompaniyets was pleased with the way his men kept in formation despite the worsening conditions. The Ukrainians had inflicted many casualties on the Neo Luddite forces. At one point, Kompaniyets had to slow their advance to allow the German battalion on their right to get back on line with them.

Keeping an eye on the time, Ashley watched as the Germans slowly marched toward her position. As the second hand swept around and it got closer to 1415 hours, she lifted her carbine to her shoulder, sighted in on the line of soldiers to her front and held the trigger down.

The Techno in change of the dampener field shut off all four machines as the second hand hit the 12.

Five hundred hypervelocity weapons of the SUNY force unleashed hell as thousands of darts traveling more than eight-thousand-feet per second poured into the attacking German forces. The stream stopped after ten seconds when the Techno restored power to the dampening field.

The Germans managed to return fire for a few seconds, inflicting casualties on Ashley's formation, but the carnage was nowhere near the destruction wrought on the massed forces in front of the combined Techno and SUNY unit. The hypervelocity rounds were followed by a rain of arrows and darts from the now counter-attacking Neo Luddites. It was too much for the Germans to take. They broke and ran, leaving their dead.

Juri Kompaniyets surveyed the carnage wrought by the fuselage of hyper weapons. He looked at his formation, brave soldiers closing ranks over their dead and wounded comrades but still moving forward with bayoneted rifles at the ready. Juri held his hand up to stop them as the unit on his flank turned and ran. The fuselage of arrows continued and was beginning to fall among his troops. He ordered his soldiers to sling their weapons and face the other way. The arrows stopped when the Ukrainian troops turned and began to march off the battlefield. While other battalions ran, his proud soldiers marched, in straight lines, out of the fray. They left no wounded soldiers on the battlefield.

Brad ordered the drums to beat once more and the rain of arrows stopped. Both Ashley and Brad sent medics out to care for the wounded of both armies.

Chapter 68 – Airborne Reunion

Ryan's unit of Technos, SUNY and Neo Luddite forces swept into the middle of Central Park, forcing the remaining 82nd Airborne soldiers to retreat. Josh was also retreating with them as they were heading into the area where his target was located.

Josh was making his way through a maze of garden plots. He froze when he heard, "Halt, who goes there?"

He looked down and read the nametag on the uniform and took a significant risk when he answered, "Captain Johns, 82nd." If any of the troopers facing him served under the now-deceased captain, Josh was in for a fight. He only had five rounds left in his pistol and counted twelve troopers surrounding him.

"Advance to be recognized," the soldier ordered.

Josh walked, open-handed into the circle of airborne soldiers. They had fixed bayonets to their carbines and would make short work of Josh after he ran out of ammunition. His hands dropped as he barked out, "Report, trooper," in his most commanding voice.

"Corporal Morrison, with a party of eleven," the young soldier said. "Sir, am I glad to see you. Just what the heck is going on?"

"There is a dampening field covering the area we are in keeping our weapons from functioning. My mission is to find the source. It came straight from the top. I need you men to follow me and keep your eyes open for anything that looks strange." Josh checked his hand-drawn map and determined he was about a mile from Biddle's house. "We need to step it up; our guys are getting massacred out there. Follow me." Josh directed the soldiers into a wedge formation and led the way.

The confused soldiers were glad that they'd found an officer who acted like he knew what was going on, and followed him, ready to fight if necessary.

Civilians, mostly children and old women hiding in the farm houses, were sending a constant stream of information out through the carrier pigeon service. The Neo Luddite information center transferred the notes to dogs that were then sent to trail Paine and his command group. The latest message gave the 18th Airborne Corps' command post location.

Ryan was near the head of the company-sized column moving toward what was reported as the attacking forces headquarters. His total force was nine-hundred fighters strong. The units were mixed so that each squad consisted of three two-person teams; Technos armed with the soon-to-be operational advanced carbines; Paine's soldiers, carrying hypervelocity equipment in addition to every chemical powered weapon imaginable; and Neo Luddites with a multitude of archaic armaments. They were ready to respond to any threat.

The latest message indicated that the airborne troopers were fighting in small, but highly organized units against heavy odds. They were holding their own and inflicting casualties on the attacking SUNY forces. Ryan thought of a way to end the killing. He checked his watch; it was five minutes after two. He raised his hand, and the unit stopped.

Ryan holstered his personal weapon, an ancient Colt forty-five pistol. He walked into the open area near the NUS commander's location and removed the carbine from his shoulder as he called out, "General Maxwell, I am asking for your surrender. Please come out now."

"I will not surrender as long as I have the means to fight, you understand that, Flagehty." General Maxwell appeared at the entrance to the barn containing his CP. His command group appeared behind him, bayonets fixed and spreading out to meet the enemy force.

"I remember you taught me that." Ryan said. "You also taught me that to let your men die for no reason was unacceptable. In less than ten minutes, all of our weapons will be operational. We outnumber you three to one, and after our weapons take out more of your men and women, it will be more like ten to one. My people have orders to shoot any trooper who does not lay down their arms within five seconds of your call. I can't make them do that, but you can," Ryan said. "I need you to make an all-hands call to save your soldiers. They will be taken prisoner, then marched to the Irish positions and turned over to UN control. You have my word."

"Why would I take the word of a deserter and a traitor?" Maxwell asked.

"To save my men, I would." Ryan walked closer. "I trust you will make the right decision, because if I am wrong, we both die."

He handed his carbine to General Maxwell and looked down at his watch. "You can shoot me in five minutes, or you can save what is left of the division. It's your choice." Ryan stood with his feet apart and hands behind his back. "One way is life, the other is death." He lifted his left arm and looked at his watch. "You now have three minutes."

General Maxwell stood staring at his former subordinate. He shook his head in resignation and handed Ryan back his carbine.

Maxwell called out, "Sergeant Jimenez, come out here, with your communications gear." His communications sergeant came out of the barn. Maxwell took the handset, pushed the talk button and waited. Ryan looked at the watch again and held up his right hand, fist clenched. He extended one finger at a time as the seconds counter down.

"All troopers - put your weapons down and your hands in the air, now! This is General Maxwell. Stay where you are until contacted." He yelled into the handset.

A few shots rang out in Central Park, and then there was silence once more. Suddenly a barrage of sound drifted in from the east.

"If you lied to me," Maxwell began.

"That is my second force, dealing with the Germans. President Miller and the Technos had to support the Neo Luddite forces in the East." Ryan listened as the roar of the weapons cut off after ten seconds. The sound echoed in the distance. "I had no choice there; they have us outnumbered five to one. We did what we needed to do, both of us." Ryan was visibly shaken as he thought about the death this day had brought to SUNY. "At least I saved lives."

Ryan turned to his Neo Luddite communications team and said, "Tell our people to collect the weapons from the prisoners, and give them safe passage to the front lines."

General Maxwell handed over his sidearm, gathered what was left of his staff and started walking northward. He had only taken a few steps when he stopped and turned. He saluted Ryan, who drew himself up to the position of attention and returned the salute. Then Maxwell began the long walk to the Bronx River.

Chapter 69 – Biddle's Capture

"Walter, there is a man outside with a gun," April was looking out the window from behind the lace curtains.

Walter looked up from his book and sighed. He was afraid his new life would not last, but for only six days? They just couldn't leave him alone.

"Techno, Neo Luddite or NUS?" he asked.

"NUS from the looks of the uniform, and he has twelve others with him," April replied.

"Get into the cellar and hide. I have to deal with this on my own." Walter gave April a kiss and then pushed her toward the trap door leading to the cellar. She was softly crying as Walter closed her in and pulled the rug over it to conceal the opening.

Walter walked out onto the porch and asked, "Is there anything I can do for you people?"

"You can come with me," Josh replied. He pulled a rope from the fence and tied Walter's hands in front of him and held onto the rope. As he was finishing, the troopers all stopped in their tracks and laid their weapons on the ground. Josh did not have a helmet on, so he did not hear General Maxwell's orders.

"What are you men doing?" Josh asked.

"We just got a stand-down order from General Maxwell," Corporal Morrison replied. "We all are to wait until further orders."

"I am ordering you to come with me!" Josh exploded.

"Sorry, captain, but the general's orders will be followed." Morrison sat down on the ground. His fellow soldiers did the same.

Josh thought once again about the limited ammunition he had and decided it wasn't worth it. He had Biddle, and he needed to get him to the pickup point. He would be able to move faster and more stealthily without the rest of the force making noise and attracting attention.

"I have my own mission, and my orders come from a higher authority than the general." He took off into the maze of fields, with Biddle in tow.

Paine and the remaining scouts moved through the NUS lines without incident. They told the surrendering soldiers to begin moving due north until they reached the UN front lines. That slowed them down.

Paine arrived at Walter's house ten minutes after Josh's departure. He walked up to the sitting troopers.

"Did any of you go inside?" Paine asked.

Corporal Morrison shook his head, "No, we did just what the general said. We haven't moved since the call came over the net. Our captain left though, and he took the man who lived here with him."

"What did the captain look like?" Paine asked.

"Older than most of our captains, but pretty sure of himself and he looked like he'd been around a battlefield before. He had a hand-drawn map that he kept looking at and it brought us to this place. He said he had orders, so he took off in that direction." Morrison pointed south.

Just then, April came out of the house. "Where is Walter?" she asked as she looked around the yard at the seated soldiers.

"We were asking them the same thing." Paine made a quick decision. He turned to April and asked, "Could you get me clothes Walter might have had on in the last two days?"

April ran into the house and returned with a shirt and a pair of socks. "Laundry only gets done once a week around here. I hope this helps," she said. She handed over the clothes and then began to cry as she said, "Please find Walter."

Paine had the message go out; he needed all the dog handlers in the force to meet him at the edge of the Central Park.

Fifteen minutes later, sixty dogs and handlers were assembled in front of the old Essex House. Paine stood on the bench of a horse-drawn carriage and yelled for everyone's attention. "I need all the dogs to smell these." He handed the nearest handler the clothes Walter had worn. "Spread out and check every lead. We need to find Walter Biddle. If you see him, chances are he will not be alone. Approach with caution, but do not, under any circumstances, hurt Biddle. The other man should be considered armed and dangerous. Shoot to kill."

Paine stepped down and handed a message to the pigeon handler. "Get this to my mother, ASAP." The note read, "Josh is in New York, has Biddle."

Three minutes later, one of the dogs began to bay. The chase was on.

Chapter 70 - Birth and Rebirth

Elle was frightened for Paine. She could hear the fighting going on in the distance and feel the shock wave of the explosion that stopped the Irish assault. Carole had left her in her apartment with a communication's device, but that had stopped working. Shortly after her communications failed, the ground shook with the impact of the cargo plane hitting the buildings near Carole's apartment. Elle stayed as long as she could, but flames were approaching and she had to get out. She pulled on a raincoat and put a scarf on her head. Even though it was June, she didn't want to catch cold. Her baby was the most important thing to her right now.

Eight and a half months pregnant, Elle had a hard time getting to the Neo Luddite boundary. It was after two o'clock when she finally had communications restored. She tried to call Paine, but could not get through. She left a message for him to call as soon as he could. Her next call was to Ashley, again no response. She was about to give up when a call finally came to her.

"Carole?" the voice said.

"No, this is Elle. Who is this?" Elle said.

"It's Walter Biddle. I am just inside Techno Territory and need a ride. Can you help me?" Walter was pleading for help.

"Sure Walter." Elle had heard Paine talking about a brilliant Techno programmer named Biddle. She knew he was an important person. "Where are you?" she asked.

"I am at Bryant Park, near the Public Library. Please come soon, I need to get to my old offices quickly," Walter said.

"I just need to get a vehicle, so hold tight." Elle switched off.

Josh released the hold he had on Walter's thumb, which was aching fiercely from the pressure that had been applied. "You did good, Walter. Now let's hope she comes alone." Josh checked the carbine he'd picked up from a dead trooper and saw the charge light was green. He had several extra packs of darts and a spare power pack.

"Let's get ready to greet our ride," Josh said as he chambered a dart and checked the sights.

Elle walked slowly down the street, looking for an operational vehicle. She finally found a delivery lifter parked outside a cafe and climbed in with difficulty. The baby was weighing her down. She started it and moved toward Bryant Park.

As she approached the park, the communicator buzzed again. "Elle, this is Carole. Are you all right? I went by my place and you were gone."

"I am doing OK; I am just going to pick up Walter Biddle. He called me from Bryant Park. I am almost there," Elle replied.

"Stop the car and turn around; Walter is being held prisoner by someone," Carole screamed into the microphone.

Elle had just come to a stop. "Too late," she said as she tucked the communicator into her waistband under her swollen belly. Elle raised her hands in surrender as Josh pointed the carbine at the windscreen. "Oh my God, it's General Martin. I will leave the line open for as long as I can. Just don't talk!"

Josh stepped up to the lifter, dragging Walter behind him.

Carole listened helplessly as Josh got into the lifter. She put her own communicator on mute and told everyone nearby to be quiet, then grabbed a second communicator from a nearby soldier and called Paine. She got no answer, so she called her mother.

Ashley answered.

"Mother, I am afraid Elle and Walter are both prisoners of my father. I am going to patch you into the conversation." Carole paired the phones. "Elle has her communicator on, but it's not on mute. Please do not say anything." She turned on the second phone so Ashley could hear.

Josh was in the vehicle by now. He said, "I need you to fly southward. And don't fly too fast. I do not want to attract any attention."

Elle looked straight ahead, out the windshield. The scarf hid her hair, and the raincoat concealed her condition. She prayed Josh would not recognize her; he had only seen her once - in his office, when Elle had asked for his help in finding her parents. He also thought she had been on the shuttle carrying her parents, the one he'd destroyed by crashing a satellite into it during its flight. Elle kept her head down as she flew the lifter up into the HOV lane and headed south. She was angry with herself for not carrying the

247

pistol that Paine had left for her because it hurt her swollen belly. She very much wanted to kill Josh, to avenge her parent's deaths.

Josh was scanning left and right as Elle merged into traffic. It was very light as the majority of able-bodied men and women were at the front lines. Most of the traffic was military, flying supplies forward and bringing wounded back from the front lines. That gave Josh an idea.

"Put us down next to the nearest aid station," Josh directed.

Elle searched for the red cross signifying an aid station and finally found one. Three lifters were at the emergency room doors, and two more were hovering in a holding pattern waiting for the landing pad to be cleared.

"Find a place to park this that's out of the way." Josh commanded.

Elle circled the aid station, hoping to buy some time so that SUNY forces could come to her rescue.

Impatiently, Josh gestured to an opening between the buildings and said, "Put it down in the alley to the left," he said pointing with this carbine.

Elle maneuvered the lifter into the narrow alleyway. Once they landed, Elle cut the power. Josh reached over the seat and grabbed her by the collar, pulling her into the cargo area and throwing her on the floor. Her breath left her when she hit the hard deck and she saw stars as Josh roped her hands together.

The force of the fall to the hard floor of the lifter shattered the communication's device. Ashley lost the signal.

Once Walter and Elle were securely tied, Josh climbed up and slid into the driver's seat. He pulled the vehicle forward until the cargo doors were wedged shut between a dumpster and the wall of the alley. Josh took the remote starter with him as he climbed out the passenger side window.

Josh took off the NUS uniform shirt and threw it into the dumpster. Then he took out his knife out and sliced open his right arm. After he bandaged it with his tee shirt, he walked bared chested toward the emergency room doors.

As he entered the building, Elle winced in pain. Walter noticed and asked, "Are you alright?"

"My water just broke, and the baby is coming fast. You have to help me." Elle gasped as another spasm shook her body. She held her hands to her abdomen as she said, "That bastard may have killed us both."

Walter was a bit faint as he looked at Elle. Then he steeled himself and became businesslike in his manner. "All right, let's do this thing. I need to see how the baby is doing if you don't mind."

Another contraction hit Elle hard. She gritted her teeth and said through the pain, "Just do something!"

"You have to untie my hands, if you can." Walter held out his wrists to Elle.

It only took Elle a few seconds to loosen the knots. She gritted her teeth and said, "Now will you please do something!"

Walter remembered his first experience with labor. April's prized possession was her milk cow, and it had given birth the night Walter arrived at the farm. April made him come to the barn to help her deliver the calf. He was used to the fluids and the contractions, but not the moaning Elle was emitting. She did not want to scream, but finally let loose a horrific shriek that made Walter flinch, and the baby came out. Walter remembered that the umbilical cord needed to be cut, but he had no knife. He looked at the now dazed Elle and gathered himself. He bent down and bit through the cord and then tied it off.

Walter pulled off his shirt and wrapped the baby in it. He handed the crying baby to Elle.

"It's a boy," he said.

Josh stumbled up to the emergency room doors and pushed the door open with his good hand. He looked around for an available technician. The duty nurse looked at him and asked, "How bad is it?"

Josh pulled the bandage back to expose a ten-inch wound in his arm, down to the bone.

"I caught a bayonet. The other guy didn't make it." Josh said with a grin.

"Funny man; that is a sick sense of humor you have there." The nurse waved him toward the tube on the right. "Get into tube number three, but there is a line."

Ashley called Paine after she lost contact with Elle.

Paine's crews ran toward Techno Territory. As soon as they got far enough from the dampener zone, his communicator buzzed. It was his mother. Paine answered as he watched the dogs milling around, they'd lost the trail in front of the public library.

"Josh has Walter and Elle. I heard him tell her to land near an aid station, before the phone went dead," Ashley said. "Focus your searches on these addresses." A stream of data listing the hospitals in the Techno area scrolled across Paine's screen.

The battlefield was not completely cleared of the surrendering attackers yet; not many of Ashley's soldiers were available to conduct the search. Paine split the list into sections and directed the three search teams at his disposal to fly to Battery Park and head northward as quickly as possible, checking all the hospitals between there and Bryant Park. She didn't know where Josh was, but she wanted to find him before he got Walter out of SUNY, or before he hurt Elle and the unborn child.

Paine commandeered a vehicle and flew it fast as it would go to the Freedom Tower area. Then he began a careful search around each one of the hospitals listed on his GPS. There were ten. He saw a lifter in the alley at the sixth hospital he checked and set his own vehicle down behind it. He emerged from the door with his carbine ready.

Paine looked though the rear windshield and saw Walter, his face bloody, leaning against the cargo door. Fearing the worst, Paine climbed into the passenger seat through the open window and looked in the back. Elle was there, holding a baby.

"It's a boy," Walter mumbled.

Paine nodded to Elle and hot-wired the vehicle, pulling it forward so the doors could be opened. He looked down at his son and reached for him, but Elle pulled away.

"Go get that bastard father of yours!" she screamed. "He went inside."

Paine tossed his pistol to Walter, who awkwardly caught it with both hands. He yelled at Walter as he left, "Protect my wife and child." Paine headed for the hospital entrance.

Josh had gotten into the meditube seconds before Paine entered the building. As Paine checked the faces of those waiting to be helped, the tube was removing the nanoprobes Steven Corvis had put into Josh. Techno manufactured nanoprobes worked to heal the gash on his arm. The machine cycled Josh's blood through the system four times to make sure all the Corvis nanoprobes were scrubbed from his body, and then, cycle complete, opened the door.

Paine turned and rushed out of the building to the lifter after realizing he'd counted on Walter Biddle to protect his wife and newborn son.

As Paine left Josh emerged from the meditube. He picked up the vial of blood laced with nanoprobes, his carbine and the remote starter. Josh grabbed a fresh shirt from the pile next to the meditubes and headed for the stairway.

Paine ran back to the lifter and saw Elle nursing the baby. He was overwhelmed by emotion. Walter stood by, wiping blood from his face and hands, pistol forgotten on the floor of the lifter.

"You have a fine son there, Paine." Walter said. "Thanks to you, maybe someday I can have a son just like him."

Josh looked down from the rooftop with the remote starter in his hand. He could see two men standing by the lifter; one of them was Walter Biddle. All he needed to do was push the button and the lifter would surge forward, possibly killing them both.

Josh thought about it for a second and then dropped the starter. He could see more military lifters approaching the building and decided it wasn't the right time. He had an appointment he needed to keep. Josh took a running leap to the adjacent roof, made it across, and began moving closer to the pickup point. He wanted to see what was waiting for him there. He climbed down a fire escape to street level and began walking to the Freedom Tower.

Chapter 71 – Freedom From Corvis

Josh answered the communicator on the first ring.

Steven Corvis looked out at Josh from the small video screen. "I trust you have my package with you?" he asked.

"Of course; just send your people to the 100th floor, south side of Freedom Tower." Josh looked out the window at the swarming UN and coalition aircraft flying over the harbor, out of rocket range. "The UN has a blockade in place. Are you sure they can get here?" He asked.

"You leave that to me, my friend." Steven signed off.

Josh placed his carbine on the floor and waited; holding the hooded figure at the window. He saw a heavy cargo lifter approaching from the south, over Ellis Island. No UN aircraft ventured near the lifter. It flew unimpeded, close to the surface of the water, toward the Freedom Tower. Josh took out a laser pointer and flashed the recognition code Corvis had sent to him to the pilot. He pulled his captive to the back of the room.

The lifter changed direction, flying straight up and then into the side of the building with enough force to shatter the reinforced plasteel window. The lifter was inside the building. Three men with assault weapons jumped out of the left-side door and waved Josh into the waiting vehicle. Josh practically threw the hooded man into the lifter as it pulled out of the side of the building and headed out to sea.

The three guards held their weapons muzzle down as the lifter cleared the SUNY airspace.

Josh's communicator buzzed once more.

"Are you safely in the lifter?" Steven asked.

"Yes, I am. Now what do you want me to do?" Josh asked.

"I want you to die." Steven Corvis pressed the button that controlled Josh's nanoprobes. They began to wreak havoc on the nervous system of their host and convulsions began almost immediately.

The maintenance man Josh had injected with the nanoprobes the machine had taken from his body died as Josh calmly shot the three guards, once each in the face, and jumped into the crew compartment, eliminating the copilot. He pushed the pistol against the temple of the pilot as the aircraft dropped to sea level, heading away from the blockading UN planes and dropping below the radar.

The ship's communicator indicated an incoming call. Josh put it on speaker and Steven's voice came on. "Dump the body somewhere off the coast, the farther out the better."

"I think I will do that," Josh said. "I have unfinished business with my family to take care of and unfinished business with you. I will be seeing you, Steven."

Steven heard a shot and then lost contact with the lifter.

Chapter 72– The Doomsday Device

The search for Josh continued as Paine flew Walter and Elle to the Techno headquarters building in the Lower East Side. It was located on the top floor of the old Bellevue Hospital. When the lifter landed on the roof, Walter stepped out and walked down the stairs to the top floor rooms. Since the lower floors still contained a working hospital, Elle, and the baby were taken to the neonatal unit to be checked out.

Walter shook his head as he walked through banks of servers and computer station. He'd spent most of his life there, but it seemed foreign to him. "I can't do this; I gave all this up for a real life."

Keenan was sitting at his console when Walter stepped into the office. He got up and reached his hand out to Walter, leading him to the screen.

"Walter, we need you to help us keep this from happening again," Keenan showed Walter the pictures of the battlefield littered with SUNY and French dead. "Our best minds have been working on the doomsday project and we haven't figure out how to make it work. We must get your input. Please help us."

"I made a promise to April." Walter said.

"And I release you from that promise." Walter turned as Carole and April walked into the room.

"And if you do not help protect us, and I mean not just you and me but all of us here in SUNY, then I release you from the other promise, too," April said. "Do this one thing or I will not marry you."

Walter looked at the only person he'd truly loved in his life; he felt like all that he had sacrificed was for nothing.

"Walter, not only do we want you to try to solve our problems, but we want you to control it. You are the only one who has lived in both worlds. You understand what ending technology will do to both of the groups you care for. Could you really destroy this?" Keenan waved at all the computer banks lining the walls of the top floor. "Or do you want April to live in slavery, or worse, be killed so that someone else can control SUNY?"

"What happens if I die?" Walter asked.

"Send the execute code to six other people, people you trust. Make sure that each of the six only gets part of the code. They should all be aware of their counterparts and know what to do if the nation is in danger. It will take two people, acting together, to activate the machine. If you make sure that one is a Techno and one is a Neo Luddite, it will have to be mutual to make it happen." Keenan said.

"It may take me all day to do this." Walter said.

"Take your time, my boy. Take your time." Keenan waved all the other techs out of the room and closed the door.

Ashley arrived at the headquarters and rushed to see her son.

"We've searched everywhere and cannot find your father. He's still out there somewhere." Ashley said. "That means that none us of is truly safe."

"Maybe he's dead. Corvis hates him and it looks like Josh failed to accomplish his mission." Paine pointed at the glass wall.

Ashley could see Walter Biddle as he sat motionless in front of a computer console.

Keenan stepped out of the room and the glass wall became opaque, obscuring the view from the outside.

"It's in Walter's hands, now." Keenan said.

Paine took his mother's arm and led her to the stairway. "Come on, Mother, I want you to meet your grandson."

Walter looked over the data that the programmers had downloaded to his console and was immediately immersed in the problem. He scratched his head, and then his face lit up as he recognized the solution. He began writing code, his fingers flying across the keyboard. He sat back and thought about what he'd developed. Walter now had the power to destroy every electronic device on Earth. He broke out in a cold sweat as he contemplated what that would mean for mankind and then encrypted the activation code.

Two days later, Walter summoned the impatiently waiting Technos and Ashley.

"It's done." Walter wiped his eyes with his hand. "The codes are out to people I trust, they know who their counterparts are, and they also understand what circumstances must exist for them to activate the program."

"I am surprised it took you so long, Walter," Keenan said.

"Oh, the device took me ten minutes to figure out. Who I would trust with all this power took me two days." Walter stood up. "Now I want to go home, again."

"I'll get you a lifter," Ashley said.

Walter shut down the console and said, "I think I'll pass. It's such a nice day, I think we'll walk." April joined him and they went home together.

Chapter 73 – Calculated Risk

The seven SUNY shuttles were moved in absolute secrecy to undisclosed locations throughout the nation. A state of war still existed, the UN blockade was still in effect, and no aircraft were getting in or out of SUNY airspace. Each of the shuttles was loaded with small satellites, and all of them had a guidance program loaded into their on-board computers. They also were equipped with portable dampeners, like the one used by Ashley to protect her privacy while working in her headquarters.

The best gamers in the Techno world were given instructions. They were to fly the shuttles remotely through the air defenses of the United Nations, and once in orbit, they were to turn the guidance programs on and sever their connections.

Because the shuttles were unmanned, they could be launched vertically using one of the plasma engines designed to lift the farming platforms into space. Special plasteel supports were welded to the interior of the shuttles to strengthen the structural integrity of the spacecraft. Any human pilot trying to fly one of the ships would have been crushed by the resulting G-forces, but the gamers were flying the craft remotely. The leading space launch scientist on the Techno staff estimated that escape velocity would be reached in a matter of seconds.

The word went out via communicator and drum beat to get under cover as the launch clock ticked away the countdown. At zero seconds, all seven shuttles blasted into space. The shock wave from them breaking the sound barrier knocked down anyone foolish enough to be outside. A few unprotected people lost their hearing that day, but no one was seriously hurt.

UN fighter planes gave chase, but could not intercept the speeding shuttles. Once in orbit, the gamers turned over control to the autopilots and shut down their consoles. Seven non-descript devices were launched from each of the shuttles and began to orbit the Earth.

Chapter 74 – Armistice

A summons of sorts had been issued. President Miller of the Sovereign United New York had formally requested that all members of the UN Security Council be present for a conference call hosted by her.

Andre Chevalier of France, Secretary General of the United Nations, called the Security Council to order. They waited impatiently for the call from President Ashley Miller. Accusations flew as the council members tried to determine who to blame.

John Gutenberg was furious. "Two aircraft lost, seven hundred of our best soldiers killed and for what? SUNY is still in existence! We had a chance to win this fight, but you French had to be in control." He blew on his moustache as he paced the floor and said, "If NUS commanders had been in charge of this operation, it would have gone differently, I can tell you that."

Chevalier sneered, "You would have anticipated the actions of the SUNY forces? I very much doubt that! The outcome probably would have been even worse!"

Sean Fergusson had been reviewing new information released by the news network that they may have been duped by doctored videos of the 28 December Massacre. Advanced copies of the retraction story were already making their way around the internet. He interjected, "If the Germans hadn't been so hell bent on revenge for something my sources are now saying was fabricated, we would not be in this position now."

"No one is going to lay all the blame for this war on the Germans!" Gerhard Schmidt cried out, slamming his hands down on the table. "Everyone wants to blame the Germans when something goes wrong. We are all at fault here, so stop trying to put the blame on us!"

Oshara Tdacki from Japan and Lin Chow Tsing, from China, looked at one another from across the table. Tdacki spoke for them both.

"If you recall, both my neighbor here," he nodded at Tsing, "and I declared that our nations would stay neutral in the coming fight."

John Wilson Smythe, puffing on his pipe, blew smoke at the part of the table where the Orientals were sitting. "You voted with us all to take action. You only pulled out your military support when you thought it was not to your advantage to send troops. I agree with Gerhard, everyone is to blame. We all had a part in it. Don't think you are not going to share it with the rest of us."

"Ukraine should share no blame," Juri Navolska stated. "I went along purely for reason of trade and to keep peace. You forced my hand."

Expletives in seven languages exploded around the table as the other delegates harangued Juri for such a bald-faced lie.

The din was interrupted by the chime announcing an incoming call. Chevalier put the call through to everyone's tabletop console as President Ashley Miller's stern face appeared on their screens.

"SUNY is still at a state of war with the United Nations and will be until you revoke the ultimatum you so unjustly delivered to us last January. The battles we have won on the ground were won through a combination of modern and ancient technology, a feat which you are all well aware. We have no hope that SUNY could achieve the same results on the battlefield again; as I am sure your commanders are busy working on solutions to the tactics we developed. As a poor nation, we have no choice but to find another way." Ashley said.

"The battles on land and in the air have been won by us, as have the battles in the laboratories. We developed a dampener device that rendered your advantage in technology useless, and that ensured out victory in this one battle, but certainly not in the war you are waging against us. The balance of power has now changed." She paused and checked her notes before continuing.

"If you remember your history, nuclear weapons managed to maintain an uneasy but lasting peace in the world during what was called the Cold War. At any time, the combined nuclear might of the old United States and the former Soviet Union could have been unleashed and destroyed civilization as it was back then. The fear of that happening, the fear of mutually assured destruction, kept the world from destroying itself," she said.

As Ashley paused for effect, Chevalier gasped out, "Surely she is not threatening us with nuclear blackmail!"

Ashley continued, "Twenty hours ago, you may have noticed the launch of seven shuttles from the Sovereign United New York. The seven shuttles each contained seven satellites. All forty nine of them are in orbit above the Earth. The orbits are secret, not even I know them, and they are controlled by pre-programmed computers. Make no mistake; we will activate them if SUNY is threatened." Ashley looked directly into the pickup and said slowly, "If you force us to activate them, they will completely destroy every productive enterprise on the planet that depends on technology, all communications, and all computer systems."

A collective gasp came from the Security Council members.

Ashley held up a piece of paper. "You all will receive this. It's our ultimatum; very short and to the point. I will read you what it says now." She looked down at the paper. "The United Nations and its member states will immediately cease all military operations effective today, by 2100 hours Greenwich Time. You will stop all attempts to take over the Sovereign United New York. Any new attempt to do so will result in the activation of the doomsday devices. All of your forces will return to their own lands. All prisoners, in both SUNY and United Nations hands, will be returned to their respective countries. No attempts will be made to seek retribution or restitution from any country involved in the war. The embargo on SUNY will be lifted immediately and all assets of SUNY will be returned to the rightful owners."

Ashley looked up from the paper and said, "The last one may be hard for you to accept as a group." She stopped once again, looked down at the paper for a moment and then stared straight into the pickup for the video feed. "SUNY will have a permanent seat on the Security Council, with the commensurate veto powers." Ashley looked sternly at the camera.

"If you do not accept our terms, you can expect a rain of ruin from space, unlike anything that the Earth has ever experienced before. All the colonies and enterprises in the solar system will be unable to come to earth for supplies, and space craft, including most satellites and many of the orbital farms, that are within five hundred kilometers of Earth will be rendered inoperable. You have one month from today to decide." Ashley cut the feed.

Chapter 75 – Brad

Brad walked through the streets of New York, watching as revelers paraded and danced with the news that the United Nations had ended their attacks on SUNY. He hated the idea that people were on their devices, talking to their friends who might be miles away instead of meeting those they cared for face-to-face. To him, it all seemed disrespectful and impersonal.

Brad entered the Government Building and presented the guard at the front desk with an archaic parchment. "This is to be delivered to Colonel Martin as soon as possible," he said. Brad turned away and went on his second visit; he had another debt he wanted to repay.

The sergeant at the desk, on duty as the charge of quarters, told the Brad to wait until he could find Imani. He called her on the communicator and told Brad, "Have a seat. She should be here in a few minutes." He indicated a row of chairs just outside the office.

Brad stood up as Imani Jamal walked into the barracks. He barely recognized her. She looked nothing like the warrior who had saved his life in the battle on the eastern Front. Imani was in civilian clothes, her hair was tied back in a ponytail and she was wearing makeup. Brad thought she was the most beautiful woman he'd ever seen.

Imani saw it was Brad and walked to him and held out her hand. "Good to see you made it through, too," she said.

"I wanted to tell you again how sorry I am. I just reacted." Brad apologized.

"I know how it's. We all make decisions in the heat of battle based on our training and desire for self-preservation." Imani smiled, which made Brad's heart beat a little faster.

Awkwardly, he said, "I brought you a present; actually, I am returning something you lost." He reached behind his back and pulled out Imani's pistol and handed it to her, butt first. "I think there is one still in the chamber, so be careful."

"Man, I thought I lost it forever." She took the pistol, released the magazine and ejected the round, catching it with her right hand.

She set the pistol gently on the nearest chair and gave Brad a big hug. She pulled back slightly and said, "Thank you very much," and then gave him a big kiss.

Brad was flustered by the suddenness of it all and said, "I owe you my life, and I don't think I can ever repay you." He took a deep breath and blurted out, "How about dinner? Are you hungry?"

Imani laughed and said, "Sure, if you don't mind mess hall food. I'm buying, though." She took his hand and led him into the dining room. "That way, you'll always be in my debt."

Chapter 76 – Life after Death

Ashley was conducting a meeting with her staff. Paine, Chris Curtis and Marcus were standing in the background. Carley Squires, General Flagehty, Keenan Revis, and Carole were seated at the table. Carole was not taking notes at this meeting as it concerned Paine and Miley Pickers.

Ashley held up the parchment Paine had given to her. "This is a summons from Miley directing Paine to come to Radio City Music Hall today for execution of his sentence. It says that Paine promised to turn himself in once the war was over."

Paine looked around the table at the concerned faces of his friends and family. "I promised Brad that I would do just that if we survived the war. General Flagehty was there, he heard what I said."

Ashley looked at Ryan, who simply nodded his head.

Marcus spoke first. "Paine, you are an idiot! How could you promise something like that to Brad! I can't let you go through with this."

"I made a promise. I gave my word." Paine said.

"What if I fill you up with nanoprobes like I have? I survived being shot by Bobby Lee; surely you can survive whatever they have in mind." Marcus said.

"It won't work," Carole interrupted. "The Neo Luddites will want to have the body. They usually don't do this, but I have seen them tear people limb from limb," she choked out the next sentence. "Paine wouldn't survive even with the nanoprobes."

Marcus sat musing over this piece of information, still trying to figure out how to save his best friend from himself.

Ryan spoke next. "What if we ask them to banish Paine from SUNY? Will that satisfy them?"

Ashley shook her head. "No, they will just say, 'it is our way', and refuse." Tears filled her eyes as she said, "I have sent you into battle on many occasions, and feared for your safety. But I never thought I would have to send you to your death. As your mother, I would say no. But I have to think about the future of our world, and of the nation, just like you did, son."

"I know, mother. My decision was sound at the time; it kept us all together and allowed us to win this fight. I have to stick by it. I either do this or any hope of keeping SUNY together will die, and we won't be able to protect ourselves from the next attack from the UN." Paine lowered his head and continued, "We know there will be another attempt, and you all have to be ready for it, including the Neo Luddites."

Ashley looked around the table. "No one is to interfere with Paine's decision. That means you, Marcus." Marcus started to speak, but Ashley held up her hand and said, "That is final!" She gave her only surviving son a hug and fled the room, crying.

Paine left the government building and got into the waiting lifter. Elle was there with the baby. Paine reached over and took the boy from Elle and cradled him in his arms. He looked down into the blue eyes of his son, and silent tears ran down his cheeks. Paine knew he would never see him walk, never hear his first words, never watch him grow up and one day have children of his own, Paine's grandchildren.

Elle took the baby back. "Paine, I love you but I hate you. You are leaving us alone."

"I have to do this, I told you before. But you are alive, so is the baby. I will live on in you two." He touched her cheek. Elle had no more tears left. "Did you decide on a name yet?"

She looked down at their son and said, "His name is William Paine Martin, after my father and you." Elle opened the door and got out of the lifter.

Marcus got into the passenger's seat that Elle vacated and sat silently as Paine drove toward Neo Luddite territory.

Brad was waiting as Paine and Marcus finished the long walk to the meeting place. As agreed, they joined Brad outside Radio City Music Hall. Miley and her council were standing on the stage, surrounded by thousands of Neo Luddites. Paine and Marcus walked into the cavernous hall; the crowd silently opened a path for them as they walked to the platform.

"Thank you for shutting down the damping field so Marcus could be here," Paine said as he came up the stairs to the waiting Miley. "As promised, I have come to surrender myself for justice.

The fighting is over, and it's time to heal old wounds and reunite New York once again."

Miley struggled to her feet, still hurting from the wound to her leg.

"Paine, you are an honorable man. But as I told you and your mother, this is our way." Miley reached for the knife at her side.

"Wait" a cry came from the crowd. Chris Curtis and Trisha Jones walked up onto the stage. Hand in hand, they stood between Paine and Miley. Trisha spoke, "We were both there, and we deserve to die, too."

Miley started to speak when another voice cried out. "I was there, too. I deserve to die with Paine." The crowd parted as Elle walked through it to stand by her husband. She put her arm around him.

The thirteen surviving members of Paine's scout platoon slowly climbed the stairs of the platform and stood behind their leader. Imani Jamal stepped to the front and said, "I was the one who pulled the trigger." She heard Brad gasp at that revelation. "If anyone deserves to die, it should be me."

Miley turned to her guards. "Clear the stage, but do not hurt anyone." Elle, Marcus and the platoon members did not resist as they were escorted from the stage. Miley turned to the crowd and said, "Noble gestures do not set aside the judgment of our courts. Do not harm these self-confessed murderers. As their leader, Paine must bear the ultimate responsibility of the actions of his people."

She drew her knife and held it up.

Marcus tried to come back on the stage, rough hands held him back and a roar came out from the crowd.

"Marcus, no!" Paine said as he waved him back. "We agreed; you are here to take my body home to my mother. That is all."

Marcus stopped struggling. He slumped in the hands that held him.

Miley advanced on Paine. He stood, waiting for the blow.

She extended her arm with the knife pointing at the ceiling, and not taking her eyes from Paine's, cried out, "My people, all in favor of life, say Aye."

The hall was silent.

"All in favor of death," the knife quivered in her hand, "Say Aye."

Brad fingered the scars on his arm, and then looked at the tear-stained face of Imani and clamped his mouth shut, tightly.

Paine closed his eyes as a deafening silence again filled the room.

Miley waited until Paine opened his eyes and looked around. "They have given me the choice, it is our way." Miley said. "By not voting, they consider you already dead." The knife dropped from her hand and stuck point first in the floor, "As do I."

Miley turned away. The people on the platform also turned their backs on Paine.

As Paine moved to the stairs, the crowd parted, and all the people in the building turned their backs in silence. Elle took his hand as they all walked out into the sunshine.

Legacy of Paine – Book three of the Paine Saga.

Sovereign United New York is safe, for now. But Josh Martin is still on the loose, and the Corvis Foundation still has the power to reach out and hurt anyone they think of as a threat. Ashley Miller is intent upon rebuilding the United Nations building in a way the members could not imagine. Elle is continuing her mission of revenge, and old hatreds begin to resurface as the world repeats the sins of the past. The world is not a safe place as the saga continues.

Made in the USA
Middletown, DE
06 July 2016